THE
TAKEOVER

Oli White

www.YouTube.com/OliWhiteTV
www.Twitter.com/OliWhiteTV
www.Instagram.com/OliWhiteTV

Terry Ronald

www.terryronald.com
www.Twitter.com/TerryRonald

GENERATION NEXT
THE SEQUEL

THE TAKEOVER

OLI WHITE

With Terry Ronald

HODDER

First published in Great Britain in 2017 by Hodder & Stoughton
An Hachette UK company

First published in paperback in 2017

2

A CIP catalogue record for this title is available from the British Library

Paperback ISBN 9781473634442

Typeset in Sabon by Palimpsest Book Production Limited,
Falkirk, Stirlingshire

Printed and bound in Great Britain by Clays Ltd, St Ives plc

Hodder & Stoughton policy is to use papers that are natural, renewable
and recyclable products and made from wood grown in sustainable forests.
The logging and manufacturing processes are expected to conform to the
environmental regulations of the country of origin.

Hodder & Stoughton Ltd
Carmelite House
50 Victoria Embankment
London EC4Y 0DZ

www.hodder.co.uk

THE END

It was over. Finished. The final exam papers had been handed in and school was finally done and dusted. The classrooms were deserted, the computers were shut down, the rugby posts had been taken down from the playing field and the folders, notebooks and textbooks that had been all-important to us for the last few years had disappeared into drawers or wheelie bins or, I'm pretty sure, in a few cases, ceremonial fires. Of course, if you've already experienced that end-of-final-exam euphoria, you'll know what I'm talking about; if you haven't, then you've got something seriously amazing to look forward to. Trust me.

And guess what? On that final day of school, my friends and I wanted to celebrate big time – well, you would, wouldn't you? We were all already eighteen, but now, for the first time, we actually felt like adults, and as far as I was concerned, there was a hell of a lot to look forward to.

Crashing through the front door of my house with what my dad later described as the world's smuggest grin, I shouted a quick hi to the parents and took the stairs two at a time, eager to get out of my uniform for the very last time.

'So long, St Joe's,' I sang, yanking at my tie and pulling it over my head. 'It was nice knowing you and all that crap.'

I was just about to kiss said tie goodbye and drop it into the waste-paper bin when some freakish sentimental vibe washed over me, leaving me momentarily confused. There I stood, frowning at the tie – which really had seen better days – before letting out a deep sigh and then folding it, almost lovingly, and putting it gently back into the drawer where it had always lived. I mean, school hadn't been all that bad, had it? Who knows – I might even miss it after a few weeks.

Yeah, right!

After a shower, a blast of Right Guard, and an impromptu dance in my pants to a bit of Conor Maynard, I stood at my window for a quiet moment, looking out across the street at the rows of houses, and then into the sky, imagining what amazing things might be waiting out there for me from that day on. So many possibilities, but just as many questions: how long would I stay living at home, for instance? What did the future hold for me and Ella, my girlfriend? What was next for GenNext, the social media platform that my friends and I had literally started from scratch? Sure, it had taken off in a way none of us could have even dreamed about the previous summer, but was that amazing upward trajectory going to continue? Would our beloved GenNext keep on burning bright?

I didn't have the answer to any of them but there was a little voice in my head – quiet but firm – reminding me of something I already knew. *You've got to get this right, Jack.*

It all starts now and you can't screw it up. Not any of it. And, thinking back to a few of the events of last summer, when I'd made a couple of decisions that weren't the best or the brightest: *Not this time.*

I dressed and headed downstairs, ready to give Dad a hand with the mammoth barbecue he was busy preparing. OK, I suppose it was the least I could do, as the long-planned event in our back garden was actually being held in honour of my friends and me: the same friends who'd so been looking forward to that afternoon, to that day, when it was finally all over and done with. School was out . . . and it was time to party.

Within an hour, the last few stubborn clouds of the morning had lifted. The garden was buzzing with noisy chat and laughter and I was surrounded by almost all of the GenNext crew: my best mate Austin with his girlfriend Jess, his mum and his little brother Miles also in attendance; Sai and his uncle AJ, and Ava, who was debuting a brand-new tattoo – an intricate dragonfly design on the nape of her neck in deep greens and reds, which complemented her freshly dyed bright-red hair perfectly.

'What's up, people?' I shouted as we all congregated by the pear tree. 'Summer has officially begun and I've got a feeling it's going to be—'

'Yeah, save the speeches for later, J-boy,' Austin cut across me. 'Just shut up and get me something to drink.'

'Me too,' Ava laughed. 'Let's get this shindig started before I pass out in the heat.'

Some people have absolutely no sense of occasion, you know?

Last to arrive was the fifth member of GenNext, my girl-friend Ella, who threw her arms around my neck and kissed me, causing Ava and Sai to simultaneously stick their fingers in their mouths and fake-barf.

'Hey, Jack Penman!' she said, grabbing a drink from the table as she swept past it.

'Hey, Ella Foster. May I say how particularly amazing you're looking this afternoon?' I said, pulling her back towards me. Even though we'd been dating for almost a year, the mere sight of Ella's smile still made me feel fantastic.

'You certainly may,' she laughed, kissing me again.

Cue more fake barfing and cries of 'Get a room!' from our so-called friends.

Jess narrowed her eyes and gave Austin a sharp poke in the ribs as he stared downward, immersed in his phone. 'Austin! How come you're not as affectionate as Jack? Look how lovely he is to Ella.'

It was becoming a regular thing for Jess, comparing her relationship with Austin with mine and Ella's. It always made for uncomfortable viewing.

'I so *am* lovely,' Austin protested, an embarrassed look creeping across his face while I blushed like a beetroot. He looked round at the rest of us for help. 'Aren't I lovely?'

'I think you're lovely, Austin,' Sai said, laughing.

Jess seemed unconvinced and placed her hands over Austin's eyes, glancing knowingly at Ava and Ella. 'Watch this, girls. Austin, what colour dress am I wearing?'

'Er . . . it's pink,' Austin said with certainty, and everyone lost it as Jess removed her hands, revealing her white T-shirt and denim skirt combo.

'See what I mean?' she said. 'Now if I'd been wearing a MacBook Pro with Retina Display, he'd have nailed the bloody description.'

Everyone cracked up again and I slowly shook my head, feeling kind of bad for Austin.

'Jess, come on,' Austin said. He smiled winningly. 'I think you look gorgeous no matter what you're wearing.'

'Whatever.' The pissed-off expression on Jess's face wasn't going anywhere. 'And on that note, I'm going to put some more suncream on,' she said, and stalked off towards the house.

Austin shrugged as she disappeared, looking a tad world-weary it must be said. I sent up a silent prayer of thanks that I was dating Ella, who was the total opposite of high-maintenance.

Austin's mum and Miles were on the other side of the garden chatting to AJ and my parents, so Jess's exit meant the five GenNext members were alone together for the first time that day. It wasn't long before we were grinning at one another like idiots. I guessed we were all thinking the same thing.

'Can you believe we did it?' Ava said, putting her arm around Sai's shoulder and hugging him close. 'We actually got through school. It's all behind us.'

'God, didn't you feel like it would never end?' Ella said. 'I did, I can tell you. Those last few weeks and all that cramming was torturous.'

'I know,' Ava agreed. 'I had to promise myself a reward at the end of it all as an incentive. That's why I dyed my hair red the second I got in from school after my last exam.'

'*That* was your reward?' I said, with a sly grin. 'Couldn't you have just had a Magnum Double Caramel instead?'

'Don't listen to my smartass boyfriend,' Ella jumped in. 'You're beautiful, Ava, and your hair is sensational, as is the new ink.'

'Thank you, Ella Foster. That is why you are and always will be my bae,' Ava said, punching my arm.

'Anyway, it's not all over yet,' Sai – ever the worrier – said ominously. 'We've still got results to go. I'm quite worried about my Psychology, actually.'

'We're all quite worried about your psychology, Sai,' Austin said. 'Have been for some time.'

Of all of us, Sai was the biggest study-geek and more likely to ace every exam than anyone. That said, Austin seemed pretty confident too, assuring me that he was going to kick my ass in the Computer Science exam.

'You know I've always been the brains of this outfit, Penman,' he said, gently goading me.

'Yeah, well, I'm more than happy with being the looks, Slade,' I said. 'Look, whatever our results are, guys – and I'm sure they're going to be everything we want them to be – we've got so much to look forward to with GenNext. There's just so much potential. So much we can achieve now school's out of the way.'

'I really hope so,' Ava said nervously. 'It's all been a bit slow-moving recently.'

Ella grabbed my hand and squeezed it hard. 'Jack's right, Ava. Look, we've pretty much had the brakes on GenNext what with all the exams, but from now on I'm sure there's going to be a ton of great stuff on the horizon. We'll make it happen.'

'More than you even know,' AJ said, joining us under the shade of the pear tree. 'Much more.'

Good old AJ. I wondered if he was merely being optimistic or if he had something up the sleeve of his cream linen jacket. To be honest, if it hadn't been for Sai's brilliant uncle and his team at Metronome, I'm not sure we'd have kept GenNext from sinking without a trace during the exams. As our manager, he'd properly looked after us, practically running the entire operation while we were beavering away with our revision. The five of us had to pull together the best content we could whenever we could: the occasional vlog or local celebrity interview, plus some re-edits and unseen bonus bits from stuff we'd put up before. It was still quality content, of course it was, but not as great as I knew we could make it if we'd had more free time. The thing was, we'd all decided to be smart and take our foot off the pedal while A levels were looming. We knew it wasn't going to be forever, and luckily our viewers seemed to be of the loyal variety and didn't seem to notice the slight lull. In fact, we were still gathering more subscribers by the day.

Now that exams were over it was time for a reboot, and from that day on, we, the team, were poised and ready to get back to some serious business. We'd collectively made the momentous decision to take a year out from job-hunting, uni or anything else to concentrate solely on GenNext. Yes, even Ava, who we all knew was bound for a top university. At our GenNext New Year's Eve fancy dress party last year she'd semi-drunkenly announced her intention to defer further education and take a gap year, leaving us all speechless.

'Hey! Oxford University has been there for a few hundred

years,' she said. 'I'm pretty sure it can wait another one or two for me, don't you reckon? GenNext needs me.'

OK, so she was swaying a bit at the time, but we'd all stood in awe of her dedication to the cause, staring at the bow and arrow she was brandishing and wondering why she'd decided to come to the party as Robin Hood. In fact, it was only when her outfit lit up with a concealed battery pack at the stroke of midnight that we realised she was supposed to be Katniss Everdeen from *The Hunger Games*.

For a while I thought Ava might have just been spouting off in the moment, but as time went on she seemed pretty confident that taking a gap year was the right way to go, scary though it was. We all did. That was why AJ's little tease about there being 'more than you even know' on the horizon pricked up my ears. I was intrigued.

Dad bellowed over from the barbecue, sweating from the heat and waving his burger flipper like it was a Jedi light sabre. 'Sausages and burgers are done, folks. It's all from the organic butcher in town; no supermarket rubbish. My dear wife has managed to purchase every sauce and relish known to humankind, so go nuts.'

'I heard that,' Mum said, emerging through the patio door. She looked happy and relaxed, I noted. Her funky new pixie-crop hairstyle really suited her; it made her look younger. 'You just keep your eye on the grill and let me worry about the rest, love.' She popped the cork from a bottle of fizz while Austin's mum hovered with glasses.

'Now, it's not champagne. Just the last few bottles of Prosecco left over from my end-of-chemo celebration a couple of months back.'

An impromptu cheer filled the air, small but heartfelt, and Dad put his arm tight around Mum's waist as she poured.

'It's a nice one, mind you; not too dry,' Mum went on, clearly embarrassed by the fuss. 'Just something to toast the end of an era.'

'Yes, people, the end of exams and the end of school!' I shouted. 'Freedom!'

'Actually, I think we should be toasting the start of a new era today, Mrs Penman,' AJ said, stepping forward.

'Well yes, that too, of course,' Mum said, shoving a foaming glass in his direction.

I'd known AJ long enough that I could read him like a Kindle, especially when he was about to impart some juicy piece of news. His mouth turned up, just on one side, and his eyes widened like a kid watching a magic trick. It was the very look he had at that moment while he sipped his drink.

'Is there something we should know, AJ?' I said.

He shrugged and smirked. 'There might be; you'll have to wait. Let's eat first.'

Dad doled out the burgers and sausages and everyone started queuing up for a glass of fizz, including Jess, who'd emerged from the house freshly suncreamed, and Miles, who clearly thought he could sneak a glass while his mum wasn't looking. While everyone was distracted Ella pulled me aside, behind the tree where we were out of sight, putting her arms around me and nuzzling my neck.

'It's so good to be here like this,' she said. 'Just having zero pressure for the first time in months. God, I feel like I've hardly seen you.'

'I feel the same,' I said, 'but I think we'll more than make up for it now. You'll be sick of the sight of me after a couple of weeks of GenNext.'

'Never,' she laughed. 'Seriously, though, do you think Ava's OK? She seems a bit shaky about the whole thing all of a sudden. Do you think she's regretting not going straight to uni?'

To be honest, I thought it would be a good thing for Ava to throw herself straight back into GenNext. After breaking up with her girlfriend Suki over the course of the exams, she needed the distraction. It was an amicable enough split and they were still friendly, but the break-up had hit Ava harder than she ever let on – we could all see it.

'I think she'll be fine,' I said. 'We all will. It's just such a big thing, isn't it, all this? Such a massive change. I mean, I was putting my school uniform away today and I actually felt really sad.'

'Steady on, Jack Penman,' Ella said, furrowing her brow. 'It's the end of school, not the bloody *Notebook*.'

By the time we were back in the thick of the party, the next-door neighbours and their three badly behaved kids had joined us in the garden, so it was mayhem. Dad could hardly keep up with the demand for his much-heralded organic burgers and sausages, with plates being jammed under his nose every five seconds, while Mum juggled her multitude of condiments and relishes and Austin's mum doled out piles of unwanted salad.

Meanwhile, Sai was shirtless and telling anyone who'd listen how much he was enjoying being young, free and single. This, apparently, was mainly due to the fact that after six months of Tiger Claw kung fu lessons at the Guan Yu Academy of Martial Arts, he'd really buffed up and was getting plenty of female attention.

'So that's why you've started taking your T-shirt off at the merest hint of sunshine?' Ella said. 'You want to show off your muscles.'

'No, I just get hot, that's all,' Sai said. 'I can't help it if women are drawn to an athletic physique, can I?'

'Yeah, but you're still short,' Austin said. 'And let's not forget that the last girl you went out with dumped you mid-date when she found you looking for Pokémon outside the women's toilet of the restaurant.'

A few feet away, Ava was trying to prise information out of AJ. 'Come on, spill the beans. You're being very cagey about something. What's going on?'

I grabbed AJ's free arm. 'Yeah, what Ava said. What's all this about toasting the start of a new era?'

I was speaking too loudly, and by this time everyone in the garden was staring at AJ, holding their glasses aloft and ready to drink to something else. He really had no choice but to come clean.

'Well, I wanted to save this news till later, but—'

'Yeah, whatever,' Austin said. 'Just tell us!'

'Total Festival,' he said firmly. 'One of the biggest and best music and arts festivals in America . . . in the world.'

'What about it? Apart from the fact that it's supposed to be amazing?' I said.

'Even I've heard of that one,' I heard Mum mutter to Dad.

'Well, would you like to do it?' AJ said.

'"Do it" how?' Ava said.

'It's not set in stone, but the idea being tossed around is something along the lines of a complete GenNext takeover of the Total Youth stage.'

'The *what* stage?' Ella said, screwing up her face in disbelief.

'Total Youth. It's the third biggest of all the festival performance spaces, and one of the highlights of last year by all accounts,' AJ said.

'And what would a GenNext takeover mean exactly?' I said, my excitement mounting.

'All sorts,' AJ said. 'Introducing the acts, interviewing them before and after their performances, and on top of that live-streaming the whole thing through the GenNext channel. Well, that's what I'm pushing for if it comes off.'

'Are you frickin' kidding?' Austin said, his mouth falling open to the size of a small cave.

'I am not kidding,' AJ said. He was loving all this, I could tell.

'So we'd get to, like, curate our own festival stage . . . at Total. Is that what you're saying?' Ella said.

'In conjunction with the festival organisers, yes, that's exactly what I'm saying. Any questions?'

Aside from Meghan Trainor drifting out of the Sonos on the patio, there was silence for a moment while we all took this piece of news in. The Total Festival was immense. Huge. It was fast becoming known worldwide as *the* summer event to be at if you were a lover of music, great spectacle, and life in general. And what? GenNext were going to be presenting their very own stage there! It was too much to take in, what with the end of school and everything . . .

Eventually Sai broke the silence. 'That's held somewhere up north, isn't it? Just outside Leicester.'

Everyone looked blankly at him for a second.

'No, dear nephew, it's in California,' AJ said calmly, and we all cracked up laughing.

Within a few seconds the laughter had turned to cheering, cries of 'GET IN!' and general pandemonium. Dad made a sterling effort to distribute a few more of his organic sausages, but everyone was too busy jumping up and down and screaming to fill their faces.

I turned to a satisfied-looking AJ, raising my voice over the noise of the others. 'It's a bit close to the knuckle isn't it, AJ? I thought these things were planned a year in advance.'

'You're right, Jack,' he said. 'The team originally hosting the Total Youth stage had to pull out at the last minute. The festival organisers weren't happy about it, but . . .'

'Their loss is our gain?' I said, noticing that everyone had stopped leaping about like idiots and was now paying attention.

'Exactly,' AJ nodded. 'The organisers want the Total Youth stage to be about young people communicating with an audience their own age, with younger acts and DJs and a fresh, raw approach to the presentation. They think GenNext is the perfect fit. We'd have a lot of work to do, but it's an amazing opportunity. Do you think we're up to it?'

My mind was racing like Bradley Wiggins round a velodrome. We *were* the perfect fit, and this could be the thing to propel GenNext back into the stratosphere. Sure, I'd always known we'd find something decent to mark our relaunch, but even I couldn't have dreamed up this project.

'We're up to it, right, guys?' I said, raising my glass.

There was a rousing cry in the affirmative, followed by the now customary group huddle. In a few short minutes we'd gone from celebrating the last day of school and wondering what the hell was going to happen next to being handed the most fantastic opportunity; something that could splash GenNext across the map internationally. I had a really good feeling about what was about to happen . . .

THE TASK

Things aren't always as easy as you think they're going to be, are they? Far from it. The next couple of weeks were a whirlwind that swept me up and carried me along, my feet barely touching the ground. Down at our freshly spruced-up and whitewashed HQ – Austin's mum's converted basement – the GenNext team beavered away like crazy: designing, discussing and planning into the late hours. We'd suddenly gone from being students, snowed under with essays and revision, to full-time working adults with a huge task ahead of us. A task that we were all up for despite having little to no idea of its magnitude. I mean, in my head it all felt reasonably straightforward: there was a stage and we were going to put artists on it, but there was so much more to it than I imagined. There were the festival organisers and various artists' management to liaise with, merchandise to design and produce, potential sponsors to be sourced, contracts, insurance, equipment, travel . . . Jeez! The list seemed endless and most of it was completely new territory. Thankfully we had AJ to guide us through most of it; even so, it was a massive learning curve for all five of us . . . albeit a very exciting one.

The scariest thing was, Total was one of the world's biggest music festivals and we really didn't have a lot of time to pull all this stuff together. It was less than two months away, and every hour that passed brought a new decision to be made, each more important than the last. First and foremost we had to announce to our viewers and to the world that we, GenNext, were taking over the Total Youth stage. There were plenty of rumours flying around already, but we felt, of course, that we needed to make an extra-big splash when we made it official, so Sai edited together a fast-paced video-teaser campaign that went out on our channel over five nights: a series of smart, vibrant moving collages that included music clips, TV shows, movie moments, newsreel footage and festival-crowd pano-ramas, all cut at breakneck speed with a blistering dance soundtrack and all ending with a new and exciting message.

As each day passed, Sai's videos went viral and the buzz grew. Then, on the sixth day, the Saturday, the message at the end read:

GENNEXT

THE
TOTAL YOUTH STAGE TAKEOVER.

TOTAL FESTIVAL.

AUGUST 2017 CALIFORNIA

From then on in you could pretty much say it was online carnage, with everyone trying to gather as much info about the event as they could, particularly our more loyal viewers, who'd been patiently hanging on all year to find out what our next big thing might be. It suddenly felt like everyone was talking about us, and once Total started previewing the festival on MTV, including a massive plug for our stage, they definitely were.

After that, there were the actual bands and artists to decide on. Most of the acts earmarked to play on the GenNext stage had been put forward by the festival organisers and then given our seal of approval, but we also wanted to bring two or three artists to the table that we'd chosen ourselves – 'wild cards', we called them. This was especially important to me. I wanted to make sure that our stage at Total felt like it was authentically GenNext and not just something we'd stuck our name on. Ella, meanwhile, was insistent that we come up with some sort of theme for the stage and the setting in which we'd conduct our exclusive post- or pre-show interviews. It was a good thought, and the suggestions for this were varied and . . . well, let's just call them interesting.

Sai was first in the queue with ideas at that particular breakfast brainstorming meeting. 'Let's rock a classic sci-fi-themed stage! Like *Alien* or *Star Wars*.'

'Right, because no one would be expecting a group of techy teenagers to think that one up,' Ava scoffed. 'Hey, we could go all out and wear Mr Spock ears.'

Ella's idea of a woodland theme was only slightly better received.

'What, trees and shrubs and that? I suppose it could work,' Sai said grudgingly.

'Nah, it's a bit Disney,' Austin disagreed, his mouth full

of bacon sandwich. 'I've got visions of Snow White and singing squirrels. What about a post-apocalyptic vibe? You know, we could factor in a few wandering zombies or something.'

'Yeah, 'cause that's really cheery,' I said. '"GenNext brings you death and destruction." Good one, mate.'

At that point everyone dissolved into laughter and the general consensus was that we needed to dedicate a little more thought to our chosen theme. Whatever it ended up being, I was certain of one thing: it had to have our signature off-the-wall, no-nonsense stamp all over it. *That* was the thing to make us shine bright in amongst all that festival magic.

There was plenty of other stuff to consider, too. Austin was obsessed with designing the perfect 'special edition' version of our GenNext logo for the stage banner and all the merchandise, badgering me with a new, minutely tweaked variation of the same thing every few hours until in the end I could hardly tell one from the other. Ava and Sai were keen to update some of our cameras and sound equipment and spent hours cooing and purring over various high-end audio-video websites for items we couldn't really afford. Ella, meanwhile, was all over the fashion, and with mood boards and Pinterest pages galore, she'd gathered together enough 'great looks' to take her and the rest of us well into our thirties. Added into the mix was the fact that AJ was in California for a week of meetings with the festival organisers and their lawyers, meaning that we were sort of on our own. Nothing could be left to chance; we all knew that. Everything had to be perfect.

There were late nights during those weeks when I think I was asleep before I even got into bed; early mornings when

I was down at HQ sitting in front of a screen before I'd woken up, and as for romantic interludes between Ella and me, well, they were on virtual freeze-frame. Still, despite how knackered and downright frazzled we felt, it was obvious we all loved it. It wasn't like A levels, where you worked your guts out for months and just got a piece of paper with a grade on it at the end of it all. This was something we were creating, something fantastic that we'd eventually unveil to the world. It was ours and it was going to be amazing. And as each day passed, the buzz of excitement was building. You could almost taste it in the air.

Still, there were a few moments when I felt like I was banging my head against a wall, especially when it came to locking in our wild-card artists. I don't know, perhaps I'd been a bit too cocky about the whole thing, naively assuming I'd be able to make a few calls to some record labels, music managers and sponsors, armed only with my cheery disposition and boundless charm, and everything would fall neatly into place. The world doesn't work like that, however. There are contracts and schedules and budgets to consider; there are nice people who just don't call you back and not-so-nice people who don't know who you are and who certainly don't care about your deadline . . . and however cool and spectacular you might think your big plans are, and however well you sell them, there are those people who just respond with a big fat 'NO!'

This cold, hard fact was bought home to me in a big way after a night-time flurry of WhatsApp messages on the 'GenNext Total' group, just one terrifyingly short month before the festival.

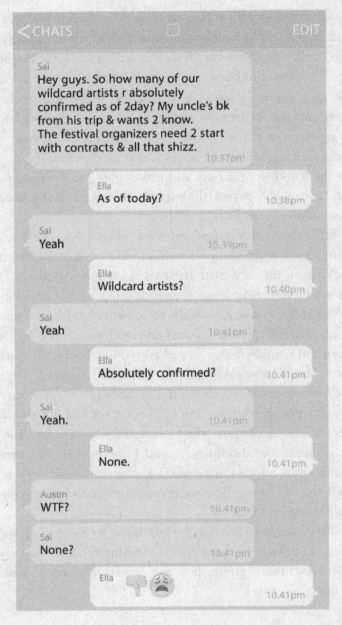

Sai
Hey guys. So how many of our wildcard artists r absolutely confirmed as of 2day? My uncle's bk from his trip & wants 2 know.
The festival organizers need 2 start with contracts & all that shizz.
10.37pm

Ella
As of today?
10.38pm

Sai
Yeah
10.39pm

Ella
Wildcard artists?
10.40pm

Sai
Yeah
10.41pm

Ella
Absolutely confirmed?
10.41pm

Sai
Yeah.
10.41pm

Ella
None.
10.41pm

Austin
WTF?
10.41pm

Sai
None?
10.41pm

Ella
👎😩
10.41pm

Sai
AJ isn't going to be happy. 10.41pm

Jack
Hang on, I thought Blossoms
were deffo on board. 10.41pm

Ella
They're an absolute no. :-(10.41pm

Austin
WTF? 10.42pm

Jack
What about The Chainsmokers?
The boys seemed really keen
on doing a DJ set. 10.42pm

Ella
They're not an ABSOLUTE no. 10.42pm

Jack
Well there u go then!!!! :-) 10.42pm

Ella
They're just a no. 10.42pm

Austin
WTF? 10.42pm

Jack
This is hard. 10.42pm

Ava
Jesus!!! All this beeping on my phone
is keeping me awake. I thought we
were having an early one, guys. I look
like an extra from The Walking Dead
as it is.
I NEED SLEEEEP!!!! 😭 😴 10.43pm

Ella
Sorry Babe! 🖤🖤🖤🖤 10.43pm

Ava
OK. Just read message thread. This is indeed grim but I have an idea. 10.43pm

Austin
Suicide? 10.43pm

Ava
Not that drastic, Austin. My EX!! 10.44pm

Sai
?????? 10.44pm

Ava
Suki will be able to help us out. She knows everyone!!! I'll call her tomorrow (Eek!!) 10.44pm

Ella
Brill idea!!! 🖤🖤🖤🖤 10.45pm

Ava
Thanks El! Now can we all please stop with the beeping? It's a well known fact that lesbians need more sleep than other people. 10.45pm

Sai
Really? I need loads of sleep. Is that true? 10.45pm

Ava
No. And I very much doubt you're a lesbian, Sai. 10.45pm

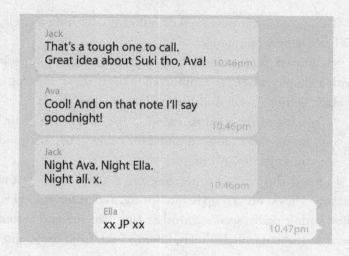

Jack
That's a tough one to call.
Great idea about Suki tho, Ava! 10.46pm

Ava
Cool! And on that note I'll say
goodnight! 10.46pm

Jack
Night Ava. Night Ella.
Night all. x. 10.46pm

Ella
xx JP xx 10.47pm

When I first met Suki, she'd been working for the record label that had signed our good friend Cooper, a singer-songwriter who'd since become a bloody humongous pop star in front of our eyes and who now spent half his time in America working with people like Calvin Harris and Drake. Yeah, I know! Suki went on to work for one of the biggest music management companies in the UK and, from what Ava told us, was poised and ready to break away from said company to look after her own client roster of talent. In other words, she knew what she was doing. When she breezed in through the door of HQ that next afternoon, I for one was very happy to see her. I'd always really liked Suki – in fact, despite being nearly three years older than us, she'd always fitted in with the gang really well. Certainly better than Jess had, anyway. We were all pretty gutted when she and Ava broke up. I could tell that Ava was pleased to see her too, even though she was clearly determined to act like it was no big deal.

'Hey, guys! Long time no see,' Suki said, flashing a smile. 'What's happening, gang?'

She looked as effortlessly cool as ever in a black jumpsuit with a chunky silver zip running all the way down the front, a black leather jacket and her trademark spiky heels.

'Sukes, it's really good to see you,' I said. 'Grab a chair.'

Suki sat down and looked round the room at us. 'It's good to see you guys too. All of you.'

I sensed she was a bit nervous and I knew Ava was the reason. They'd broken up in late spring, and as far as I knew, they hadn't really seen each other since. In the end it had been Ava who'd called it a day, leaving Suki, from the sounds of it, pretty upset. I must admit, I couldn't understand why Ava had broken it off at first. I mean, they'd seemed like such a great couple to me: always laughing, always affectionate. Then late one night a few weeks after their break-up, in a rare moment when I was alone with Ava at HQ, she'd subtly steered the conversation onto the subject of Suki, confiding to me that in the end she'd probably let her insecurities get the better of her.

'I think I had a weird freak-out with everything that was going on,' she said thoughtfully. 'All the pressure of coming out, GenNext taking off, revising for exams and then making the decision to defer uni for a year. God, trying to hold down a relationship on top of all that . . . it's a lot, Jack.'

She was perched on the end of my desk while I edited a couple of videos for the site and I got the feeling she'd been dying to get this off her chest for some time.

I stopped what I was doing and looked up at her. 'It is a

lot . . . but I'd have thought having someone to share it with would help, no?'

'Oh don't get me wrong, Suki was great at all that,' she said. 'Maybe *too* great if you want the truth.'

I smiled, slightly puzzled. 'How is someone too great?'

'Oh, you know: her lifestyle, her friends, her job, her general bloody fabulousness.' Ava laughed as if she knew how ridiculous it all sounded. 'I know she's only a couple of years older than me, but sometimes I felt like I was running to keep up with her, you know? Like I couldn't measure up to all that.'

'So that's why you ended it?'

She looked down at me with sad eyes. 'Maybe.'

'Have you told Ella any of this?' I asked.

She shook her head. 'I think I've only just figured it out myself, to be honest.'

'I hear you,' I said. 'And I think I know what you mean about running to keep up and all that stuff. I sometimes used to feel the same with Ella. Like I wasn't good enough for her or some crap . . . It's stupid, I know.'

I could see Ava's mouth twitching as she stifled a smile, but in the end she couldn't stop herself.

'It's not stupid at all,' she said. 'You're really *not* good enough. Always remember that, Penman.'

We both laughed loud and I knew that she'd said all she wanted to say on the subject for the time being.

Now, Ava and Suki were face to face in the same room for the first time in a good couple of months, and no one quite knew how it was going to go down.

'So, what's going on with you freaks?' Suki said, sitting

back in her chair and looking a bit more comfortable. 'Exciting things on the horizon, I hear. Total Festival! How good is that?'

'On the scarily close horizon,' Austin said. 'What about you, Sukes?'

'Me? I'm on a sabbatical from my job, trying to decide whether I'm brave enough to go it alone as a manager.'

'Really? That's exciting,' Ella said. 'Do you think you will? I mean, do you think you're ready?'

Suki smiled and shrugged, but then Ava chimed in. 'Oh, she's definitely ready. Come on, Suki; you know it's the logical next step. You'll kill it!'

Suki looked a little embarrassed by Ava's sudden outpouring of praise. 'Well, it's nice to see you have faith in me, Ava.'

'Always,' Ava said.

'Not always,' Suki replied softly.

There were a few seconds of uncomfortable silence so I decided to jump right in. 'Well, we could really use your expertise as a manager, Sukes. How's that for a start?'

'Intriguing,' Suki said. 'Tell me more.'

'We've got a few wild-card slots to fill for the festival. Artists or DJs that we've selected and brought in off our own bat,' Ella said.

'It was me who pushed for it so we could really put our stamp on it,' I added. 'Now I'm not sure it was such a brilliant idea.'

'Why the hell not?' Suki said, sitting forward. 'I think it's vital that you have a big say in what goes on on your stage – surely that's the essence of GenNext. What's the problem?'

Austin sent Miles out to get some coffees while I waxed

lyrical about the difficulty we were having securing bands and artists at such short notice, plus the pitfalls of dealing with uncooperative managers and potential sponsors who needed to know they were going to get their money's worth. Suki pursed her lips and nodded throughout, looking very businesslike. I wondered if maybe that was a cool front for the benefit of Ava, who'd kept a neutral, fixed smile on her face since the minute Suki walked in and clearly wasn't going to let it drop any time soon. As my diatribe came to an end, Suki was grinning and shaking her head.

'Yeah, we're a pretty tricky bunch, us management types; I feel your pain, Jack,' she said. 'But aren't AJ and *your* management team helping with all this stuff?'

'They are, but this last week AJ's been out in LA dealing with the festival organisers and sponsors and God knows what. I'm really conscious of time and . . . I don't know. It's just much bloody harder than I thought it would be.'

Ava stepped forward. 'You have such a great roster of artists at your disposal, Suki, and you know everyone . . .'

'Not everyone, just most people.' Suki laughed. 'So what do you need, guys? I mean, I could help you with ideas and maybe pull some favours with the artists I know. How does that sound?'

'It sounds pretty decent,' Austin said.

'I'd have to look into it all,' Suki went on, 'but why don't we start with me sitting down with Jack, and you could talk me through some of the artists you're thinking about. Go from there. Look, I'm absolutely certain we can get a couple of great acts on board. It's what I'm good at.'

That was one of the things I liked about Suki – her

confidence. She knew her strengths and she wasn't afraid to let people know exactly what they were. It's something I still didn't totally have a grasp of, even after everything that had happened the previous year. Sure, I was getting much better at it. Better at believing in myself. But sometimes – just sometimes – when I felt like I was roaming a little too far out of my comfort zone, I still sensed the shadow of that insecure, bullied kid who had to start all over again at a new school. I just didn't let any of the others see it, that's all.

Ella leaned over and grabbed Suki in a hug, with Ava nervously following suit.

'That's great, Suki,' Ella said. 'There's just so much to think about, and maybe we're a bit out of practice with all the madness.'

'Out of practice how?' Suki said, jumping out of her chair. 'God, the amount you lot have achieved on your own is incredible. Don't lose sight of that.'

'What Ella means is we let go of the reins to a large extent during exams,' Austin said. 'Yeah, we did a couple of great interviews to keep the profile up, but . . . I don't know. Maybe we're just not going in with enough confidence. Maybe the people we're talking to consider GenNext to be last year's big thing and now they're looking for something new.'

'Oh God, we're Myspace,' Sai said.

'Shut up! We are *not* last year's news,' I said, defusing what was fast becoming a major panic. 'Ella's right, though. We've been resting on our laurels a little bit, but let's leave that in the past. With Suki's help we'll be rocking again, right?'

Suki grabbed her jacket off the back of her chair. 'Jack's right. This Total Festival is totally my thing, excuse the pun.

OK, I've got to dash off to meet a mate now, but I'll deffo plunder my contacts later. I reckon I've got a couple of artists on my roster that could generate huge interest and help make the GenNext Total Youth stage *the* place to be at the festival.'

'Any big names?' Sai said, his eyebrows shooting up and down.

'You really only need one reasonably big name, Sai, just for the kudos and the publicity and to pull in the sponsors,' Suki said. 'And let's face it, the super-big names are going to be on the main stage anyway.'

'True dat,' Austin said.

Suki's eager brown eyes darted from one of us to the next. When they landed on Ava, I'm pretty sure I noticed Suki's cheeks redden slightly. 'OK, that's all settled then.'

'Great,' Ava said, rather too breezily, and I wondered if she really meant it.

Once Suki had exited HQ, the five of us forged ahead with even more purpose. Ava and Sai busied themselves with ideas for the big announcement to our viewers, and Austin finally unveiled his brilliant new special edition GenNext logo.

After a string of late nights, however, I was running on fumes by mid-afternoon, and it was only when I felt Ella gently shaking me that I realised I'd fallen asleep in the middle of writing an email.

'Why don't you call it a day?' she said as I prised my cheek away from the glass top of my desk. 'You're no good to anyone like this.'

I puffed out a massive sigh and shook my head. 'Too much to finish. Besides, it's not fair with everyone else doing their bit, is it?'

She grabbed a nearby chair and sat down close to me, smiling wearily. 'I'm as knackered as you are, Jack. Maybe if we both go home, we could have a power nap and then I could come over to yours and watch some Netflix. Get take-away. Just do something normal for once.'

'You mean like a date night?'

Ella wiggled her eyebrows. 'Exactly.'

'And can I choose the box set?' I said, sleepily.

'You can choose the box set,' Ella said.

'And can I have a kebab?'

'You cannot have a kebab,' Ella said. 'But I'll allow Domino's or, if you're very good, Nando's.'

Ella's idea sounded deliciously appealing, but then I glanced around the room: Austin printing out dozens of his new logos and plastering them all over the wall; Ava on the phone giving hell to a merchandise company; Sai banging away at his keyboard with a very intense expression on his face, writing God knows what. When I looked back at Ella, I suspected she was thinking the same thing as I was. 'It's not going to happen, is it, this date night?'

'I fear not,' she said, pushing her long blonde hair out of her eyes and flipping it back over her shoulder. 'It's a nice dream, but . . .'

'. . . but let's get on with our work, right?'

Ella nodded, kissed me softly on the mouth and then wheeled herself backwards towards her desk a few feet away.

As it turned out, I got home even later than usual that night. The house was in darkness so I crept in, quietly slipping off my trainers and dropping my bag gently in the hall in case I woke Mum and Dad. Half asleep, I grabbed a glass of water from the kitchen, but as I made for the door to head upstairs, the security light in the garden flashed on. I imagined it was probably a fox that had set it off, but I wanted to make sure. As I turned back towards the garden, I noticed that the patio doors were slightly ajar. Putting down my glass, I stepped outside, to find Dad sitting in one of his brand-new garden recliners. He was obviously miles away, because he didn't hear me approaching.

'Dad?' Given his regular early starts, he was the last person I expected to see stargazing at 3 a.m. 'What are you doing sitting out here? It's not even that warm.'

He looked like he'd been shaken out of a daze; almost like he was as surprised to see me in our own back garden as I was him. 'Oh! Hello, Jack. I didn't . . . You're late.'

'I'm always late these days. It's the festival preparations,' I said. 'But you should be in bed, shouldn't you? You're up in about four hours.'

He did a little half-laugh. 'Oi, I'm supposed to be the dad here.' Then I watched as his face fell back into a sombre stare.

'Is everything all right, Dad? Have you had a row with Mum or something? Is that why you're out here?'

Dad shook his head. 'Don't be daft; when do we ever row?'

This was true; they were more likely to be seen having a cheeky vomit-inducing smooch in the corner than an argument. Then an unsettling notion began worming its way into my mind. 'It's not anything to do with Mum's health, is it, Dad? There hasn't been any . . . any news?'

'No, son, not at all.' Dad shook his head. 'Your mother's fine; please don't worry about that. I just couldn't sleep, that's all.'

I muttered a silent thank you, relief sweeping through me. It was then I noticed the semi-crumpled letter in Dad's hand, the white envelope in his lap.

'What's that, a tax bill?' I said.

He looked down at the letter and then back up at me. 'Oh . . . no. This is just . . . some bloody irritating client who's giving me grief about . . . something that's really nothing to do with me, to be honest.'

There was something strangely vague about his manner, but he didn't look like he was in the mood to be pushed.

'A client writing a letter instead of an email; that's pretty old-school, isn't it?' I said. 'Couldn't he at least upgrade to a fax machine?'

Dad managed a smile and then got up from the chair. 'You're right – I should be asleep, and so should you. Night, Jack; make sure you get to bed soon.'

'I will do, Dad. Night.' I watched him as he drifted into the kitchen. He seemed a bit more . . . weary than usual. It was weird.

As tired as I was, it took me ages to get to sleep after that. I was unsettled but I couldn't put my finger on why. I mean, Dad's explanation of why he was sitting outside at three in the morning was straightforward enough – he couldn't sleep, right? The only thing was, he was fully dressed, so it looked like he hadn't even tried. A year ago I probably wouldn't even have given it a second thought, but after Mum's cancer I found it difficult to take anything at face value. Her illness had rocked my otherwise strong sense of security and reassurance as far as my parents were concerned, and sometimes I wondered whether I'd ever fully get it back.

Eventually I drifted off and had a good long sleep, and by the time I left the house the following morning, heading for HQ, I'd decided to put Dad's odd behaviour and post-midnight weirdness out of my mind. Let's face it, with the festival looming and still so much to achieve, I had quite enough on my plate.

THE COUNTDOWN

The festival was upon us so fast that it made my head spin. It was getting hotter and hotter outside, with summer well under way, but true to form, the GenNext crew barely saw daylight as we continued to pull everything together. The month of brainstorming, liaising and negotiating felt like it was happening on fast forward, but at the same time I don't think I'd ever felt more alive.

Suki settled back in with the gang brilliantly, and my initial concerns about her and Ava being all weird and ex-coupley around one another turned out to be unfounded – as far as I could tell they were getting along just fine. Suki proved her worth right off the bat, securing a couple of our wild-card bands – Beautiful Creatures and The Way We Live – super-fast, via her contacts. OK, so they weren't superstar names yet, but both bands had been getting a hell of a lot of media attention and had recently received the Zane Lowe seal of approval on Beats 1, which was good enough for me. In fact, the online announcement about these additions to our Total Youth line-up was the catalyst for a whole slew of amazing stuff.

Just two and a half nail-biting weeks before the festival, what started out like any other Tuesday turned out to be the day everything ramped up a notch – several notches.

It seemed like a pretty standard start to the morning as I headed along the hall towards Austin's basement, the sound of Miles's customary grumbling about the amount of coffee runs he'd been sent on the previous day drifting up the stairs as I descended.

'Seven times, Austin! Seven!' Miles, still in his pyjamas, was marching around the room after his brother, who couldn't have looked less interested. 'Is that all I am to you people, a tea boy or a kitchen maid? Yeah, that's it . . . I'm a maid. It's like *Downton Abbey* around here.'

'Morning, guys, everything all right?' I said, still trying to wake up. 'Is there any coffee?'

Miles gave me the stink eye. 'You lot need to find me some other stuff to do or I'm staging a one-man mutiny.'

'I'm not in the mood for this, Miles,' Austin said, not even looking around at his brother. 'If you don't want to be involved, then don't be.'

Miles spun around and stalked towards the door, snarling up at me as he pushed past. 'Good luck with him today; he's had a massive row with you-know-who.'

'Jess?' I suggested.

'No, Jack, Kim Kardashian,' he said and swept out of the room.

AJ was back at the helm by then, and by the time he and the rest of the crew made it down to HQ that morning, it was so full of the boxes of promotional GenNext T-shirts we'd had especially made that we could hardly move. I was just attempting to clear a space around my desk when I heard the ping go off on Suki's MacBook. That was when things started getting crazy.

First off, Ava took a look at the email over Suki's shoulder and then started bouncing up and down like a maniac.

'OH. MY. GOD.' Her eyes were out on stalks.

'What?' Sai said, jumping up. 'What's going on?'

'Only *Laura Harris*!' Ava shrieked.

'Oh, now that's cool,' Ella said approvingly. 'Very cool.'

'Who?' Austin said, scratching his chin.

'She's an Aussie EDM DJ-producer based in LA,' Suki said. She wasn't leaping around like Ava was, but I could tell she was pretty happy with what she'd just read. 'She's supported The Weeknd and Disclosure . . . she's played at all the big dance festivals . . .'

'And she's *hot*,' Ava said. Suki raised an eyebrow but didn't comment.

'And she's in?' I said.

'Yep! She's in,' Suki said.

AJ narrowed his eyes and smiled. 'Are you sure you're not after my job, Suki?'

Suki winked and blew him a kiss. 'You'd better stay on your toes, old man.'

'I'm twenty-nine!' AJ laughed.

Austin shrugged like he was unimpressed by it all. 'Yeah, but this Laura bird; is she big enough to be our big name?'

'She's pretty bloody big, Austin,' Suki said, clearly unimpressed by his attitude.

'Well, I haven't heard of her,' he said, killing everyone's buzz.

'It's not all about Justin and Kanye, Austin,' Ava snapped. 'For a start, artists of that magnitude are never going to play on the third biggest stage at a festival, even if it is a massively famous one, and besides that, we need a more boutique feel to the Total Youth stage; something more cutting-edge. That's the whole point! It's about having artists that speak to our audience.'

'She's right, mate,' I said. 'This is all good.'

He shrugged and turned his back on the rest of us. 'OK! You all know best, apparently.'

I watched as he kicked aside a few boxes of merchandise and sat down at his computer. Obviously the latest row with Jess had left its mark, but to be honest, it was hard to keep up with them. I mean, only a couple of days earlier he'd been telling me about the romantic night in he'd spent with her – with way too much detail, I might add. Maybe he was just extra tired. I made a mental note to grab a quiet moment with him later and make sure he was OK, before the Total Festival mania completely took over my brain again.

By five that afternoon I was knackered and ready for some fresh air; a brief escape from the windowless whitewashed rectangle I felt as though I'd been living in for the past few weeks. Ella followed me up the stairs and outside, and when I sat on the front wall of Austin's house, she sat down next to me, resting her head on my shoulder.

'So what's been your main task of the day?' I asked, putting my arm around her.

'Oh, I've mostly been looking at shoes,' Ella laughed.

'Of course you have.'

37

'And holidays,' she went on. 'I looked at holidays. Because after all this is done, I want to go on a really awesome expensive holiday.'

'Oh yeah?'

'Yes. Somewhere exotic; just the two of us, Jack. Somewhere there's sand, sea and a beautiful beach dwelling of some description.'

'What, no internet?'

She gave me a playful head-butt. 'Where's your sense of romance?'

'I think I left it in the back of an Uber about a week ago,' I grinned.

Ella looked up at me, the bridge of her nose crinkling in that incredibly sexy way it did. 'It is going to work, isn't it – all this? We will be able to pull it off?'

'Of course we will,' I said. 'Although some days I do feel like we've bitten off more than we can chew, you know?'

Ella nodded, her head moving against my shoulder. 'You're not worried, though?'

'No. Why, do I look it?'

'Not as such – but you do seem a bit distracted at times,' she said.

My mind flashed back to Dad sitting in the garden in the middle of the night, acting all weird. I'd done my best to shove thoughts of it to some deep, dark corner of my mind, but there had been something distinctly off about his behaviour ever since. It was like he had this constant faraway look in his eye, and it was bugging me. But was it that obvious? Was this the distraction Ella was seeing in me? I don't know why I was surprised she'd noticed. Ella was just about the most perceptive person I'd ever met. That was what was so great about our relationship: nothing got past her, and whenever I felt a bit low or crappy, she always said exactly the thing I wanted to hear before I even knew I wanted to hear it.

'Actually, if I'm distracted, it's nothing to do with GenNext or the festival,' I said.

'Then what?'

'Well, Austin for a start,' I said, deflecting the real issue. 'I don't know what's going on with him and Jess but he's being really negative today. It's not great for general morale, is it?'

'And what else?' she said, immediately sussing that I wasn't telling her the whole story. 'Come on, you can tell me.'

'My dad's been acting a bit . . . off,' I admitted hesitantly.

'Your dad? That's random. What kind of off?'

'Well, a week or so ago I found him reading a letter in the garden at three in the morning, looking all stressed, and since then he's been really . . . I don't know . . . cagey. I can't put my finger on it, Ella.'

'What, and you think the letter and the caginess are connected?' Ella said, lifting her head off my shoulder.

I shrugged. 'I don't know. Maybe I'm reading too much into it. Forget I said anything; I'm probably just knackered.'

'Are you worried he might be ill or something?' Ella said.

'I'm not even going to follow that train of thought,' I said. 'Not after last year. Actually let's not talk about it now, eh?'

She put her hands on my shoulders and gently pulled me around to face her. 'You've got such a good relationship with your mum and dad, Jack. Just talk to him. Ask him straight if he's got something on his mind. I bet it's nothing to worry about.'

I smiled, pulling her in for a kiss. 'And what makes you so bloody wise?'

'I'm afraid I can't impart the secret of great wisdom to any old dumb-ass,' she said, kissing me back.

'You cheeky—'

We were interrupted by Sai, who'd come up to get us. He was bouncing around like an excitable puppy in the light streaming out of the front door.

'Guys! Downstairs. Quick!'

Back down in HQ, AJ was on the phone – and he had a really weird expression on his face. It was impossible to tell whether he'd won the lottery or his cat had died, or anything in between. Everyone else was gathered around him in a hushed circle, waiting expectantly. After a few yeses and noes and one very firm 'Of course!' he held his iPhone out to me, still looking bemused.

'Someone wants to speak to you, Jack.'

I took the phone, wondering who it might be to provoke such intense curiosity from the entire crew. 'Hey! Jack Penman here.'

'Hey, Jack, what's going on?' It was a voice I recognised instantly: that soft, sexy Texan twang. I nearly dropped the phone. It was Harriet Rushworth! The major international pop artist Austin and I had interviewed in LA the previous year. An interview that had gone so monumentally wrong that it had almost brought about the end of GenNext. Harriet was cool, though – she didn't hold the screw-up against us, and we'd left things on good terms with her. Still, I hadn't expected her to be calling me up to shoot the breeze any time soon. Since that first encounter, she'd become more and more of a star. If her rise to fame had been meteoric, she'd now hit the stratosphere. I was on the phone to a major A-lister.

'It's Harriet Rushworth here. Remember me, sugar?' she said.

As if I wouldn't remember her. 'Of course I do . . .' I said, suddenly realising that I had absolutely no saliva in my mouth whatsoever. 'How are you, Harriet?'

'I'm fabulous, Jack. What about you? How's it all going with that website of yours?'

I gesticulated madly across the room, mouthing the words 'IT'S HARRIET!' to the rest of the team, who clearly already knew and were now all staring at me expectantly, wondering why one of the world's most sought-after stars was calling me for a chinwag.

Harriet didn't wait for my answer. 'Listen, I've been talking with your lovely manager, AJ. I could have gone through my management but I thought the personal touch was in order after what happened with y'all last year when we met . . .'

I felt myself get hot thinking about that disastrous interview. I just knew that my face was turning the colour of a ripe tomato. 'Well, that's nice of you, Harriet.'

'The long and the short of it is, I wanna play on your stage at Total,' she said.

I nearly dropped the phone. 'You . . . you . . . you . . .'

'See the thing is, the main stage is gonna be a minefield as far as I'm concerned: Ariana one night, Taylor the next, and honey, I ain't stepping on no stage unless I'm headlining the damn thing, you hear what I'm saying?'

'I do. I do hear. I hear perfectly.' Oh God, I was babbling.

'And I'll be honest, I admire the way you guys have pulled yourselves up by your Calvin Kleins and got yourselves a stage at the festival. Y'all have an ambitious streak. And I always liked you, Jack, I did. You were a little wet behind the ears when we met before, but I'm confident that has all changed. Tell me if I'm wrong . . .'

I started to speak again but I didn't get far. 'Well—'

'And another thing, Jack Penman,' she motored over me, 'I think your Total Youth stage is going to be where it's damn well at. It'll be a little more edgy, and that's what I'm looking for; nothing too corporate, if you get my drift. I mean, do I need to be walking on stage waving a bottle of sugar-infused fizzy crap just because some sponsor tells me that's what I should be doing? I do not.'

She was a piece of work, this girl, but I had to admire her for it. In amongst all the bull-crap about us getting GenNext back on track and how cool and edgy our stage was going to be, the crux of the matter was that Harriet didn't want to be just another big female solo artist on the main stage and end up being compared to all the others. If she performed on the Total Youth stage, she'd be a massive fish in a relatively small pond. Smart, but I wasn't complaining. Having Harriet Rushworth on our stage was exactly what we needed – it was the last piece of the puzzle snapping into place.

'Harriet, we'd love to have you, you know that,' I said, finally getting a sentence in. 'It's good to know that you trust us again after . . . you know.'

'Hell, I'll even throw in some exclusive behind-the-scenes stuff for the channel . . . that's if you're *real* nice to me, Jack,' she added, and I felt myself redden again, glancing over at Ella and hoping to God she couldn't hear what Harriet was saying.

'That would be amazing,' I said as calmly as humanly possible.

'OK, so can I hand it over to my management team to finalise everything? Good. That's settled. I'll see y'all in a couple of weeks. Be good now!'

'Thanks, Harriet, I . . .' But she was gone.

I looked over at the expectant faces of the team: Sai, Suki, Ava, AJ and Ella. Even Austin looked more excited than he had done all day.

'I guess you know what that was all about,' I grinned, handing AJ back his phone.

'Not really,' Sai said. 'The conversation was a little one-sided and you only said about three words, dude.'

'Well, let's just put it this way,' I said, slapping Sai on the shoulder. 'We're sorted. Done. We have our line-up and our big headliner. The Total Youth stage is going to be huge.'

Austin's mum's basement became a cacophony of cheers and whoops, like a newsroom that had just broken the biggest story of the year.

'Right, guys, what are we going to do to celebrate?' I said, attempting to calm the noise. 'Hit a club, open some champagne . . . what?'

'I know,' Ava said. 'Let's just all go home early, for Christ's sake.'

Ella let out a sigh. 'Oh babe, I love you for that.'

'Really?' I was semi-horrified.

'Really, Jack. It's time for the Nando's and the box set. Let's go, buddy.'

Ava was right, of course. Whatever mayhem we inflicted on ourselves by way of a celebration that night was only going to come back to haunt us in the morning. And God, there was still so much to do. But that was OK, because now I felt like we were really on our way. We were flying.

THE ARRIVAL

As our trio of black Cadillac SUVs streaked along, an enormous brightly coloured city seemed to spring up before our eyes, smack bang in the middle of the Nevada desert. That's what the Total Festival looked like anyway – a crazy metropolis, growing by the minute as we got closer and closer. It was a spectacular sight.

I was travelling in the first car along with Ella, Sai, Paulo the driver and enough luggage for a six-month trip around the world – mostly Ella's, of course. Behind us in the second car were Ava, Suki, AJ and his dazzlingly attractive twenty-two-year-old assistant Lily. Lily had been a total godsend so far, parking herself next to Sai, who was a horribly nervous flyer, on the plane and somehow managing to keep him calm throughout the ten-hour flight from London to LA. Austin, meanwhile, had chosen to ride in the third car with a couple of the American crew who were going to be working alongside us at the festival. He told us that he just wanted to zone out and listen to music. It was a little bit odd, but to be honest, he hadn't seemed himself since the gang had all met up at Heathrow. I wondered if perhaps it was a guilty conscience at having left Jess back in Hertfordshire, which hadn't been the easiest of tasks. Ella reckoned he'd had to promise to FaceTime her every hour on the hour throughout the entire trip, just so she'd let him on the bloody plane.

As the sprawling vision of Total got ever closer, Ella smiled nervously at me. 'Here we go then,' she said. 'Are we ready for this, Jack? Like, really ready?'

'We are,' I said, with a confidence I was trying to make myself feel. 'We definitely are.'

As far as I was concerned, there was no room for uncertainty. It was in moments of self-doubt that my mind traitorously played back GenNext's car crash of an interview with Harriet the previous year, when I'd totally blanked, live on air, in front of millions of people. I wasn't going to let that vision creep into my head. Not today.

'Although,' I added, shaking off the memory, 'I've never been to a festival before, so I don't really know what to expect.'

'Let's put it this way,' Ella said. 'When I went to V Festival a few years back, the toilets were uber grim and it poured with rain the whole time. It took me a week to get the mud out of my hair.'

'I think the toilets will be a lot more glamorous in the VIP areas here,' Sai said from the front seat.

'Well, it's always nice to have something to look forward to,' I said.

'And what about those sick tent jobs we're staying in on site?' he went on.

'Yurts! They're luxury yurts,' Ella said, turning to me.

'And I'm still not convinced we shouldn't just be staying in a nice dry hotel with multiple plug sockets, babe.'

'We'll be fine. We'll embrace the adventure together,' I said, laughing.

Staring out of the window, mesmerised by the red and orange sandstone rock of the desert, it suddenly dawned on me that in all the excitement of arriving in LA, I'd completely forgotten to text Mum and Dad – and I'd landed a good four hours ago.

'Crap!' I said out loud, and as I fumbled in my pocket for my phone, my mind flashed back to the drive to Heathrow with Mum and Dad. They'd both been unusually quiet, with me riding shotgun and Mum in the back seat, staring out of the window with a distant look in her eye. It was weird. Mum always had so much to say to me before I left for even the shortest trip: Have you remembered to pack this, Jack? Do you need that, Jack? Don't forget to take loads of pictures, Jack. But there was none of that today: just some stilted chit-chat about how lucky we'd been with the traffic. In the end I had to turn up Scott Mills just to cut through the atmosphere.

Before I jumped out at the drop-off point, ready to head into the terminal to meet the rest of the crew, Mum leaned over and hugged me tight, planting a fond kiss on my cheek. 'I'll miss you, love.' Was it just me, or did she seem more emotional than usual?

'We *both* will,' Dad said, like it was a competition. 'Have a fantastic time, Jack. And be careful.'

'Of course he'll be careful,' Mum said dismissively. 'Keep me up to date with what's happening when you get the chance, won't you? And text me when you land in LA!'

'Yes, Jack, fire me a quick text too,' Dad said.

I promised I'd send them both messages the moment I landed. Then I gave them both another hug and they waved me goodbye as I walked into the airport, although they were standing about five feet apart from each other.

What was up with those two? It was unlike them to be snappy with one another. It seemed obvious to me, as I wheeled my case through the terminal towards the bag drop, that whatever had been making Dad act so strange lately was having an impact on how he and Mum were getting on. I know what you're thinking: why hadn't I confronted them about it? Why didn't I just come out and say, 'What's going on with you two?' The truth was, after Mum's cancer diagnosis last year, I was worried about what their answer might be. OK, so Dad had told me that it wasn't anything to do with Mum's health, and of course I believed him, but I couldn't bear the thought that something else could be wrong.

Right at that moment, I was just about to get on a transatlantic flight. I was about to embark on something important and amazing, and I owed it to myself and my friends to be on form.

I'd tackle Mum and Dad once I got back to Hertfordshire.

'Jack! Look, we're almost there.' Ella's excited voice shook me out of my thoughts and I glanced up from my phone and out of the front window.

'Bloody hell, that was a quicker journey than I thought,' I said.

'Yeah, I'm pretty pleased about that; I'm feeling a bit queasy,' Sai said, looking slightly grey in the face.

Ella leaned over and patted his shoulder. 'You really don't travel well, do you, Sai?'

Sai shook his head sadly, and I looked back down at my iPhone at the text message I'd composed.

> Hi guys, arrived safely.
> Really good flight and got some sleep.
> Driving through the desert now
> and it's amazing. Will give you
> a shout once I get settled at
> the festival. Love you.

That was OK, wasn't it? Yeah. I'd send the same text to both of them. Keep it simple.

Pulling up at the artists' entrance to the festival site in front of two enormous metal gates, AJ and Lily jumped out of their car to be met by a uniformed man who carefully checked each of our names off on a clipboard, while a more casually dressed dude in a Coldplay T-shirt handed Lily a wad of laminated passes and stickers. Eventually the guy in uniform signalled the opening of the gates, and our convoy was directed through along a dusty, bumpy trail to one of the backstage parking zones. We were there!

I got out of the SUV and looked around, feeling the warm breeze on my face. The site looked epic. Through the hazy desert sun I could make out all the crews hard at work: hooking up light rigs, securing tents, setting up food stalls, and generally putting the finishing touches to everything, ready for the festival opening the following day.

'OK! I'm going to find someone to show us where our yurts are and help transport our luggage,' Lily said. 'Do you guys want to have a look around and I'll call you when I know what's going on?'

'Sure thing, Lily,' I said. 'Shall we find the Total Youth stage? Make sure it isn't looking like the water park at Alton Towers. It could go either way with palm trees.'

After all the heated discussions and a lengthy afternoon steering Sai away from the idea of recreating the bridge of the Starship frickin' *Enterprise*, we'd eventually agreed on Ella's idea of a twisted jungle wonderland theme for our stage, with rose-gold-coloured trees, hanging vines of light and these amazing hybrid-animal sculptures: a wolf with the wings of an eagle, a zebra with a lion's head, a snake with a panther's body – you get the idea. Suki had sweet-talked one of her set-designer friends into pulling it together for us super-fast and within our allocated festival budget, plus they had it all made in California so we didn't have to spend thousands shipping it. Now we just had to hope it had all arrived in one piece – and that it looked as amazing as we'd imagined when we drew up the designs back in GenNext's HQ.

'Sounds good, Jack,' AJ said, looking down at his phone. 'Actually, Jason Croft wants us to meet him over at the Youth stage anyway. He's a nice guy; one of the festival's owners. He'll show us what's what.'

'Cool, let's all go,' Ava said. Her arm was casually linked through Suki's, I noticed. 'The sooner we do a recce, the sooner we'll have a feel for the festival, and what we're dealing with.'

'OK, why don't you guys go meet Jason, and I'll go with Lily and scope out the living quarters,' Sai said. 'She probably needs a hand.' Ella and I raised eyebrows at each other and I had to stop myself from grinning. It was clear that Sai had taken a bit of a shine to Lily after the plane journey, despite having his head in a sick bag for most of it. It was no real shocker, I guess. Lily seemed like a really cool girl, and she was as striking as she was pretty, with dyed silver-white hair, twisted up in dreads, and this massive septum piercing through her nose, which on anyone else would have looked insane but which on her looked amazing.

'Talking of our stage, where the flippin' hell is it?' Austin piped up. 'This place is massive.'

Lily rifled amongst the passes and envelopes she'd been handed at the gate. 'There are a few site maps here somewhere . . .'

'I can show you where it is, if you like.'

A skinny, mousy-haired dude in cargo shorts and a checked shirt appeared from behind a white van parked adjacent to one of our cars. 'You're GenNext, aren't you? Total Youth stage?'

'That's us,' AJ said as the guy started walking towards us.

He was around our age, quietly spoken, with an English accent, and he had a pair of Pioneer headphones slung around his neck.

'I was just over at your stage, it's very nice. Would you like me to take you there?'

Ava strode forward to shake the dude's hand. 'That would be really helpful, thank you. I'm Ava.'

'Ethan; pleased to meet you.'

'And you're from the UK,' Ava said.

'Well spotted,' he smiled. 'But I've been living and working out here for the last few months.'

'Are you working here at the festival?' I asked, stepping forward. I felt like I'd seen him somewhere before but couldn't for the life of me think where.

'Sort of. I work on a TV show and we're doing some filming at Total.' He shook my outstretched hand. 'It's very nice to meet you, Jack.'

I was taken aback that he knew my name, and must have looked it.

'I've seen the GenNext channel, of course,' he said. 'You're something of a legend, Jack.' He looked over my shoulder, his polite smile widening. 'And you're Ella, right? Wow – you're even more stunning in real life.'

There was something a little slimy about this guy, I thought.

'I'll take that,' Ella said, smiling. She shook Ethan's hand too, the others following, and then we split: Sai and Lily heading off towards the yurts, and Ethan leading us out of the parking zone and into the festival grounds.

'This is vast,' Austin said in wonder as we all trailed along behind Ethan. He seemed more animated by the sight of the festival than he'd been by anything else since we left Heathrow. 'I mean, did you imagine it was going to be like this, J?'

I shook my head. To be honest, I didn't really know what I'd been expecting, but to me the festival seemed like another planet, with its food markets, futuristic fairground rides, brightly coloured circus tents and huge abstract art installations in silvers and whites, all contrasting with the cloudless desert sky. On the ground, makeshift pavements of slatted wood covered the sand, marking out clear pathways to the main areas, and from the route we were taking I could see at least two of the incredible-looking stages – was one of them ours perhaps? All around us people were either running like crazy or just heads-down busy, building something or setting up stalls. And behind me, on the highway, I could see lines of cars: everything from battered hatchbacks to camper vans to souped-up, pimped-out vehicles that looked like they were built to drive on Mars. Most of them were laden with camping gear and all of them were heading towards Total. It was four in the afternoon and time to let the masses in, where they'd set up home for the following three days and nights in this insane new city.

I'd seen all the plans for our stage and I knew what the dimensions were, but I still wasn't prepared for just how big it was in real life. It was obvious to all of us that this was a serious set-up and we were going to have to pull out all the stops if we were going to do it justice.

'What do you think?' AJ said, holding his arms aloft. 'Will it do?'

'I've got chills just looking at it,' Ella said. 'Look at the size of the GenNext logo on the backdrop.'

'Yeah, and it's going to be even more superb when it's all lit up with lasers,' Suki added, capturing a shot on her iPhone. 'We should upload a few before-and-after pics on the GenNext Instagram.'

I moved closer to the huge stage and tried to envisage myself up there tomorrow, addressing a large crowd, my stomach completing a Tom Daley-style backwards-triple-somersault dive at the thought. 'Yeah, it'll do, AJ. Very nicely.'

After a quick reconnaissance of the backstage area, with its Portakabin dressing rooms, catering area and – Ella was relieved to find – beautifully clean toilets, we headed back out to the front of the stage to wait for Jason. It was swelteringly hot, so we made our way over to one of the two huge pavilions constructed of recycled paper and rope and parked ourselves in its magnificent shade on giant chairs and couches.

Ava put her hands behind her head and lay back with her eyes closed. 'OK, I can't bloody wait for tomorrow now.'

'I won't sleep, you watch,' Austin added.

'I told you it was amazing.' Ethan appeared, seemingly from nowhere again. 'I've just been checking out all your merchandise stalls going up over there. You guys have got some really cool stuff.'

'You should take a free T-shirt,' Ella said with a smile.

'That's really nice of you,' he said, sitting down next to me. 'You OK, Jack?'

'Yeah, I'm good, thanks.'

'So what kind of TV show do you work on, Ethan?' AJ said. 'Like, a reality show or something?'

'No, I work for a show on Owl TV. We showcase new acts and do interviews. It's not a million miles away from what you guys do, I suppose.'

I could just imagine the type of show it was. Since GenNext had taken off, I'd seen a fair few music-based programmes that had either been inspired by our style or just plain ripped it off. I'd never really let them worry me, though; in fact I took it as a compliment rather than letting it annoy me.

'So are you a presenter?' Ava said.

Ethan shook his head. 'Oh, no! I'm just an assistant producer. I source content and stories for the show. Actually,

I was going through some of this week's rushes in my van when you guys turned up.'

'That sounds awesome, though, working for Owl TV,' Ella said.

Ethan shrugged. 'Yeah, it's cool. Eventually I'd like to do some on-screen stuff, but, you know . . . we'll see.'

'I reckon you'd be great, Ethan,' Ava said, sitting up. 'Let's face it, if Jack can do it, anyone can.'

'Oi!' I said, as Ethan turned to look at me.

'I think Jack's very good,' he said seriously, like Ava had meant it.

Ava laughed. 'Yeah, you wouldn't say that if you'd watched him fluff his questions during an interview. And how's it been, living in America? Do you like it?'

'Yeah, it's good to shake things up, I reckon. Plus it's a chance to meet new people, get some proper sun.'

Sun? The dude was milk white.

'What about you guys?' he said, looking around at all of us. 'Would you ever consider moving over here to work or live?'

Ella and I answered at exactly the same time, only I said, 'Yes,' and she said, 'Oh God, no.'

I turned to look at her, surprised by her emphatic answer – I'd always thought she was in agreement that if GenNext continued to grow, anything was possible. 'Well, I'd at least consider it,' I said with a smile, trying to make the moment less awkward. Ella looked like she was about to discuss it further when AJ's phone pinged twice.

'OK, Jason says he's sorry but he's tied up for the next hour and will come find us later. Lily says the yurts are amazing, and she'll meet us at the parking zone and take us over to where they are,' AJ said, reading from his phone. 'So why don't we go find out where we'll be laying our weary heads tonight, eh?'

'We might as well,' Austin said. 'There's not going to be much more to see here until later on, is there?'

As we started to head back towards the artists' parking zone, Ethan stuck close and I wondered if we might have acquired a shadow for the duration of the festival. I hung back from the group for a while, watching him laughing and chatting with Ella and Ava, and I hoped not. There was something a bit weird about the dude. It was like he was too eager to please all the time. And that kind of person always put me on edge.

THE VIP EXPERIENCE

'Our luxury yurt was quite cosy, wasn't it, Austin?' Sai was collecting more than his fair share of crispy bacon as we lined up at the impressive breakfast buffet laid on in the artists' glamping area on that first morning of Total. 'Bedside tables, lamps, even a sheepskin rug. Very nice!'

'It was a little *too* cosy for my liking,' Austin said, queuing behind Sai, bleary-eyed and settling for a cup of black coffee. 'I'll be pulling those bunks a bit further apart tonight.'

'Is he a snorer, Austin?' I said.

'That's rich coming from you, Penman,' Ella laughed, loading scrambled eggs onto her plate. 'You snored most of the way here on the plane. I could have dropped my complimentary moist towelette in your mouth and you wouldn't have stirred.'

'It wasn't so much the snoring,' Austin went on. 'It was the fact that I woke up at five a.m. to find we were practically spooning.'

We headed over to a long table set up in a clearing amongst the yurts and tents and sat down. Suki, Ava, Lily and AJ were right behind us.

'Don't listen to Austin, he's exaggerating,' Sai protested. 'My arm just flopped over, that's all. I'm a very physical sleeper.'

Austin peered over his coffee cup. 'Yeah, that's what worries me.'

'Well, our yurt was like a beautiful Bedouin tent with loads of plush throws and pillows,' Ella said, sipping her tea. 'I felt like Khaleesi from *Game of Thrones*.'

When we headed back to the Total Youth stage after breakfast, my stubborn body clock was insisting that it was still the middle of the night. In fact, the whole team were looking decidedly bleary-eyed, despite the Styrofoam cups of strong coffee that we were all clutching. The stage was complete, and our tech team – overseen by Lily – were industriously preparing it for our big launch at five o'clock that evening, and doing an amazing job by the looks of it. The first sight of the finished article brought a collective gasp from the GenNext crew as we gazed up at our dazzling, other-worldly jungle set, flanked by towering PA systems and two enormous video screens that would mirror everything that we broadcast on the GenNext channel.

'It's truly magnificent,' Ava said.

Ella nodded enthusiastically. 'I know! You picture it in your head, don't you? Then you see the 3D mock-ups. But you just can't imagine how fantastic it all is until you actually see it for real.'

High above the stage, a young woman wearing a tool belt and standing on a scarily tall ladder positioned the lights on the batten while her colleague on the lighting desk focused them one by one, guiding her through each intricate movement via a radio headset. Meanwhile, our two-person camera crew were moving around the front of the stage, finding the best positions and lining up potential shots. Once all that was done, Ella and I met our sound team and then headed up onto the stage for a quick microphone check. AJ remained quiet through the entire process, wandering around the stage looking deep in thought and very serious. I suspected he was as apprehensive as the rest of us; he just didn't want to let us see it. Once Ella and I had finished our sound check, he called the rest of the team up to join us on the stage. I could feel a speech coming on.

'Gather round,' he said, beckoning us all towards him. 'I have something to say.'

Ava rolled her eyes and giggled. 'This isn't one of those weird prayer circles, is it?'

AJ laughed. 'OK, no big speech. I just think we should all take a minute to be on the stage together. Once it kicks off, we won't get the chance. I want us to take a moment to appreciate what this all means and what you've achieved.'

'You know what, AJ, you're right,' Suki said. 'We spend so much of our time looking at things on a screen, we *do* sometimes need to stop and be in the moment.'

We all stared out over the vast area around our stage and the festival beyond. Once the stage was open, it would be utter madness, but for now it was all reasonably calm until—

'You're a bunch of bloody hippies!' Sai yelled, and everyone cracked up.

'All right, let's get out of here and let the crew finish up,' AJ said. 'We've got a few hours until we launch, so I say we get changed and go and explore the festival.'

'I was hoping you'd suggest that, AJ,' I said, grabbing Ella's hand. 'Let's go and get a taste of the VIP experience.'

By mid-afternoon the place was alive and full of noise as even more people poured through the gates. As we weaved our way in and out of the crowd, heading towards the main stage, I felt as if the warm sand under my feet was vibrating with the thump of distant music like some tribal signal. As far as dress code went, there seemed to be no limits. From girls in nothing but cut-off denim shorts and bikini tops to people with the most elaborate face paint and freaky fancy dress, it was a case of anything goes: native American head-dresses, Mexican death mask make-up, feathers, fur, a full-length coat like a mirrored disco ball, scrap-metal warriors and giant-winged fairies.

Closer to the main stage, giant sculptures rose out of the ground and towered above us, while below them people danced and ate and drank while they waited for their favourite artists to come on. And while Ella and the girls cooed in amazement over a giant multicoloured moving butterfly, Sai, Austin and I stood in awe underneath a forty-foot-tall LED-illuminated dancer made of stainless-steel rods, cable and mesh. Looming in front of us was the main stage, where Ariana Grande, Major Lazer and Disclosure, amongst others, were due to appear that day, and blinking into the sunlight to the left of me I could see rows of palm trees overshadowed by a giant Ferris wheel. It was spectacular.

'I've never seen anything like this,' Ella said, doing a 360 twirl. 'It makes some of the music festivals I've been to back home look like car-boot sales.'

She looked incredible at that moment, dressed in a lacy off-the-shoulder top, a flowing burnt-orange skirt and a gold-and-silver Aztec-style necklace, topped off with a garland of flowers in her hair. With her trademark silver rings and her nose hoop, she was like some beautiful hippy goddess. Man, I was going to be the envy of half the male population at that festival – I just knew it.

'I feel like I've landed on another planet,' I said, grabbing her hand. 'It's utterly crazy.'

'I feel a bit underdressed actually,' Sai said, pulling a face.

'I know what you mean,' Austin agreed.

Us boys were all in cut-off denim shorts and T-shirts plus Aviators and matching black and white bandanas. Except AJ, that is, who was in his customary summer attire of cream linen suit and pale blue shirt. We thought we'd nailed festival chic, but looking around, I sort of wished that I'd thought to pack a giant metal spider outfit and some glitter.

'I think you guys all look very sexy,' Ava said, without a hint of sarcasm.

'Which is a massive compliment, coming from her,' Suki said, laughing. Suki herself was radiating cool, as she always did, in some sort of dark-gold sheath dress and flicked-out gold liquid eyeliner. I could see Ava giving her subtle approving glances every so often, when she thought no one else was looking.

'Cool but understated. That's the GenNext way, right?' Ella said.

'Exactly,' AJ smiled.

'So should I go with the rhinestone G-string tonight or not?' Sai said, his eyebrows moving up and down quickly.

'Not!' I said. 'I know you like to get your muscles out, Sai, but nobody's ready for that; not even *this* crowd.'

We headed across the site to the left of the main stage, where Steve Aoki was whipping the crowd up into a frenzy, and were directed into the VIP hospitality area at the back of the stage.

'Oh yes, boys and girls,' I smiled. 'AAA is most definitely the way forward.'

Sai looked puzzled. 'What's that then?'

'Access all areas, baby,' Suki laughed. 'That's what this is.'

Within the enclosure there were a couple of bars, including one sponsored by and exclusively serving Cristal champagne, plus several stands serving everything from sushi to South American street food. It was already pretty busy, even though it was relatively early in the day, and in one brief scan around the main seating area, which languished under fairy-lit Bedouin-style tents scattered with plush white-cushioned couches, giant beanbags and seagrass coffee tables, I spotted Cara Delevingne chatting to Gigi Hadid along with Calvin Harris, who was due to play a set later that evening. The vibe was very definitely upscale festival chic; almost everyone I looked at either was, or surely could have been, a model or a rock star or some type of industry hotshot.

'I think I want to stay here forever,' I heard Sai say dreamily.

'Yeah, I'll second that,' echoed Ava.

I turned my attention back to our group to find that Jason Croft, one of the festival's big guns, had joined us. He seemed like a pretty cool bloke.

'It's good, huh?' he smiled. 'Are you vibing, gang?'

'We are very definitely vibing, Jason,' Ava said with a grin. 'It's actually a shame we have to work, because I'd quite like to hang out here with the celebs.'

Jason put his arm around her shoulder. 'Don't you worry, honey; remember you guys have your own VIP hospitality area right next to the Total Youth stage.'

'God, we've been so busy we haven't even had a chance to check it out since it's all been set up,' Ella said. 'Is it anything like this?'

'Not exactly like this, but there's a bar and a couple of great food vendors, including a Mighty Quinn's BBQ, which is frickin' *awesome*. We've called your hospitality area the Gen Pen. Get it? Gen as in GenNext?'

'Amazing,' Ava said, clearly unimpressed.

'I'm happy with a bar and barbecue,' I said, laughing. 'Just make sure you steer Cara and Gigi over there at some point, will you?'

Ella shot me a look, which I returned with a wink. Then I spotted Austin, standing a few feet away from the rest of the group, looking around the VIP area on his own.

'You OK, mate?' I said.

He looked startled, as if he was surprised to hear my voice. 'Oh yeah, J, I'm fine. I was just thinking about getting something to drink at the bar.'

'Cool, I'll go with you and get a round in,' I said.

I was eager to grab a moment alone with Austin. He wasn't himself and I wanted to know why. Once we'd reached the bar, he folded his arms on the counter top and rested his chin on them.

'I'll just have a water,' I said to the bartender.

'Party animal,' Austin said, lifting his head, and I thought I almost saw a smile.

'What are you having?' I asked.

He shrugged. 'Maybe I'll join you in that water.'

Once our drinks had been served, I turned to him. 'You sure you're all right, mate?'

'Yeah, why?'

''Cause you've been, like, really quiet and un-Austin-like the last few days. What's going on?' I said.

Austin sucked in a long breath of air and then puffed it out slowly. 'Er . . . if I'm being really honest with you, J, I've been feeling a bit down about the whole Jess situation.'

'OK . . .' I said, waiting for him to continue. He was silent again for a couple of moments.

'I mean, Jess is Jess,' he said eventually. 'I literally can't do anything right and it's not been great for a while. Still, I thought coming away to the festival would help me think a bit more clearly about everything, but . . .'

'What? You can tell me, mate.'

For a moment his eyes glazed over and I thought he might cry.

'Austin, what is it?'

'I'm sorry I've been so quiet so far on this trip. It's nothing to do with you guys, it's . . . I've actually been getting really anxious about everything we're doing here. It sounds stupid, but I've been, like, worrying about whether we can even pull it off, do you know what I mean?'

I knew exactly what he meant, but it was a shock hearing it from Austin. He was the one who seemed to have the endless supply of confidence. He'd always been the one to deliver a shot of self-belief when I needed it.

'We all go through moments like that, don't we?' I said. 'I get nervous too, but at the end of the day I know we'll pull it off because we're a brilliant team.'

Austin nodded. 'Deep down I know that, but . . .'

'And you're the brains of that team, Austin, as scary as that sounds.' I laughed, trying to lighten the moment. 'You can't let all this negative stuff with Jess cloud that, mate.'

Austin looked down at his feet. 'You know, Jess is my first real girlfriend. Most of the way through school I was, like, the nerdy one who none of the girls were interested in.'

'I get that,' I said. 'But to be honest, it's probably her making you feel crap about yourself all the time that's causing a lot of this anxiety about the festival. So if you're not happy with her, then maybe it's time to call it a day.'

'The problem is, I can't bring myself to think about doing that at the moment, J. It does my head in even considering it.'

'OK, fair enough,' I said. 'It's hard, but maybe for the moment, the best thing would be to put all the Jess stuff out of your mind. Just focus on the task at hand.'

He nodded thoughtfully. 'I'm certainly gonna try.'

'OK. Shall we get some drinks for everyone and head back?' I said, glancing at my phone. 'We've got just under three hours till we launch. How mad is that?'

As I collected some bottled waters and turned to leave, Austin grabbed my arm and looked at me with a determined expression on his face. 'Look, Jack, I'm not going to make this a miserable experience for you guys – no way! Whatever is going on in my head is going to stay there until we've done this. I promise.'

'That's cool,' I said. 'But I'd prefer it if you told me when you're feeling crap, rather than bottling it all up for everyone else's sake. You know I'm always here if you need me – we all are. You deserve to enjoy this Total Youth takeover as much as the rest of us, do you hear me?'

'I hear you, J,' he said, breaking into a grin. 'Now let's go kick some festival ass!'

As I followed Austin back towards the group, I wondered where all this might lead. I'd never known him to let stuff get on top of him like this, and I hated the thought that it was all happening while he was supposed to be having the time of his life and living the dream. I just hoped he could take his mind off it for the duration of Total, for all our sakes.

The gang hung out with Jason Croft for an hour or so, laughing and joking with one another and soaking up the glamour of the VIP area for as long as we dared – a relaxed moment before the madness, I guess you'd call it. Pretty soon, though, as the sun was beginning to lower in the sky, a massive roar went up from the main stage as the first live act headed out to perform. That was when the butterflies started fluttering around in my stomach and I knew it was time. Time to make our way over to the Total Youth stage; time to launch our much-heralded GenNext takeover; time, as Austin had so succinctly put it, to go kick some festival ass.

THE LAUNCH

It's hard to imagine the euphoria of walking onto a stage and addressing thousands of people. And that afternoon, fifteen minutes before the Total Youth stage was about to go live, imagining it was about all we could do – because our audience was barely scraping a hundred.

'Where is everyone?' Sai hissed as we huddled around the stairs leading up to the back of the stage. 'I thought it would be rammo?'

Suki poked her head above the stage to get a better view of the audience. 'OK, it is a little sparse, but it's still early, and there are more people gathering as we speak. Don't forget, Sia's just done the main stage so everyone's been over there for her.'

AJ appeared behind us, grinning and rubbing his hands together. 'OK, are we set? Where's everyone supposed to be right now?'

Lily was at his side, her arms full of bottled water. 'Grab one each, guys,' she said. 'I'm going to put some on the stage for the first band.'

'Everything is ready to go live from our end, AJ,' Ava said. 'Crew, cameras, audio. I've got a couple of Total's cameramen out front with me and Austin is doing the onstage hand-held stuff.'

By now, Sai had hit the ground for some pre-show push-ups at the bottom of the stairs. 'I'm going to be in the broadcast van directing the shots with Suki,' he said, breathlessly. 'Lily is going to get some of the live Tweets rolling across the screen during the performances. The sound guy knows his stuff so he doesn't need me looking over his shoulder.'

'Our crew is on it, AJ,' Austin added. To anyone else he would have sounded totally confident, but after the conversation we'd had earlier, I could hear the nervous edge to his voice. He was doing an amazing job of keeping his anxiety under wraps, though; maybe just getting his worries off his chest earlier had done him some good. 'It's running pretty smoothly,' he continued. 'The second Jack and Ella go out on stage to kick things off, we'll be streaming live on GenNext exclusively.'

'Well, I'm really proud of you all,' AJ said.

'Thank you, AJ,' I said. 'If it weren't for you . . .'

AJ smiled and winked at me. 'I know, Jack, I know.'

The audience in front of the stage was waiting with a hushed expectancy that seemed unnervingly polite. Meanwhile, I could hear the thumps, beats and roars echoing from other stages and wondered if we could achieve the same kind of atmosphere at Total Youth. Could we? Would we? I felt slightly queasy, and the smell of popcorn and candyfloss drifting over from the audience fused with the deep tangy aroma of the backstage barbecue pit wasn't helping. I slugged down half the bottle of water that Lily had given me and tried to breathe deeply.

Ella squeezed my arm excitedly. 'It's bloody amazing, isn't it? Can you actually believe we're doing this?'

I shook my head, fear rising in my throat. The truth was, I really couldn't believe it. Not in the slightest. Ella was pretty much born to be in front of a camera and never seemed to get nervous no matter how big the potential audience. She didn't seem fazed by the fact that we were about to broadcast our takeover all around the globe. I, on the other hand, had some stage fright that I needed to deal with. Sure, I knew that with Ella up there with me I could go a good job – that was why we'd ended up doing most of the on-screen stuff for GenNext, while the others preferred the behind-the-scenes action – but I still had to banish the niggling memory of my monumental screw-up in front of the entire world at last year's interview with Harriet. I took a few deep breaths. You can do this, Penman.

Austin slapped my shoulder as he and Ava moved to their camera positions for filming. 'Break a leg, Jack and Ella!'

I looked over at Suki, who blew me a kiss. 'The crowds will come, Jack, trust me,' she said as she headed off to the broadcast van with Sai and Lily.

I wasn't convinced that they would for our first band, it had to be said. The Revenants were a trio of New Yorkers who looked like they needed a good bath and played post-emo rock. They'd been booked by Jason and the festival organisers, but it was us who had to walk out onto the stage once our opening DJ had finished and announce them to their small army of young, tattooed fans.

'So, are you ready to officially open our stage, Jack?' AJ said, looking at his watch as The Revenants gathered behind us at the bottom of the stairs, all of them dressed in black and with chin-length tangled hair hanging over their faces. I wondered, momentarily, if they'd even be able to see their way onto the stage.

I grabbed the handrail tight, ready to ascend. 'Can I wear my Aviators, AJ? Just something to hide the nervous twitch in my eye.' I was bricking it.

AJ laughed. 'Of course you can.'

'You'll be fine, and I'll be right beside you,' Ella said. 'You know how brilliant you are once you get into performance mode.'

'I'm better in front of a camera with no crowd,' I said with a smile. 'But if I'm going to do this, I'm bloody glad you're doing it with me.'

In a flash, Ella and I were bounding out onto the stage to a surprisingly enthusiastic reception, gripping our mics tightly. The crowd, who only minutes before had seemed scarily subdued, suddenly lit up, and a small sea of happy, eager faces welcomed us. I moved cautiously through the amps and guitars, all set up and ready for the band, and came to a halt centre stage to a soundtrack of shouts and cheers. Then the lights hit my eyes and a rush of adrenalin shot through my body like forked lightning. Nervous and excited all at once, I looked to my left at a beaming but slightly shell-shocked Ella. I was certain she felt the same.

'Hi, everyone, welcome to the Total Youth stage!' Her voice boomed out across the crowd, which was growing by the second. 'I'm Ella Foster, and this is . . .'

'I'm Jack Penman and— Whoa!' The deafening whistle of feedback from the mic threw me, but it was all under control in a matter of seconds. 'I'm Jack Penman and we are GenNext' – more cheers went up, stronger now, chasing some of my jangling nerves away – 'and this is the first night of our takeover of the Total Youth stage. We'll be here for the whole festival.'

'OK! We reckon this is gonna be the biggest and best Total ever,' Ella said, her spiel perfectly rehearsed. 'What do you say?'

The crowd called out a resounding 'Yeah!' so I moved further forward towards the front of the stage, slowly coming to terms with the idea that they didn't actually want to kill me. 'And the Total Youth stage is where it's all happening, right?'

Cue more cheering and a bit of light whooping. I looked over at Ella and she gave me a reassuring smile. This was all so different from the straight-to-camera stuff we'd done in the past. The reaction was so immediate, and even though I was starting to enjoy it, part of me still felt vulnerable and exposed. It was like the stress dream I'd had a few months back where I was stark naked, performing on *The X Factor*.

'OK, we'll be back out here later, and there's loads more amazing stuff happening,' Ella said. 'But right now we'd like to introduce our first band. Please welcome, from New York . . .'

And in unison we yelled, 'The Revenants!'

Suki was right. By the time The Revs were halfway through their third number, the crowd had almost tripled in size, much to our relief. When the second act hit the stage – a good-looking boy/girl duo called Pan, who sang fiercely catchy pop melodies over pulsing, funky electro beats – our audience was looking more than respectable and my nerves had completely disappeared. As soon as one act finished, they were whisked backstage to our fairy-lit tree house over-looking the hospitality area, where we'd set up to record the post-show interviews. Ella and I took it turns to conduct the interviews, while the other one handled the intros and anything that was happening on stage. It was crazily fast-paced, but really seemed to be working. Three acts in, and we were both having a great time. The show seemed to be running without a hitch and the audience were loving it. I just hoped the rest of the team were enjoying it as much as we were.

'Jeez, The Revenants didn't have much to say for them-selves during the interview,' Ella said as we crossed paths backstage in a brief lull in the proceedings.

'Well, the people watching on GenNext seemed to like it,' I said. 'Didn't you see Sai's WhatsApps from the broadcast van? Apparently the Twitter and Facebook pages were going off and he's had all the comments scrolling across the video screens either side of the stage.'

'Well, that's a relief, because they were positively mono-syllabic.' Ella grabbed a tiny mirror out of her pocket and checked her make-up. 'If the singer was any more laid-back, he'd be a corpse with a guitar welded to him.'

'The trick is to get them all to drink some of those blue cocktails in the half-coconuts they're dishing out at the VIP bar,' I said. 'They seem to contain some magical tongue-loosening drug. The girl from Pan was very forthcoming.'

'Oh she was, was she?' Ella raised an eyebrow, then grinned and gave me a quick kiss on the mouth. 'I shall keep that in mind. Right, I've got to go; I'm about to give away some merchandise to the hottest kissing couple. They've been tweeting in photos of themselves.'

'God, is that the best we could come up with for our first giveaway?' I said.

Ella giggled. 'It was Sai's idea, and . . .'

'. . . and he's a pervert,' I said.

'Exactly!' And she was gone.

Ava had the unenviable task of going into the crowd in between acts to get some feedback from the revellers. This seemed to start reasonably well, but as time went on and the crowd really got into the party spirit, her messages to the WhatsApp group became a little more frantic.

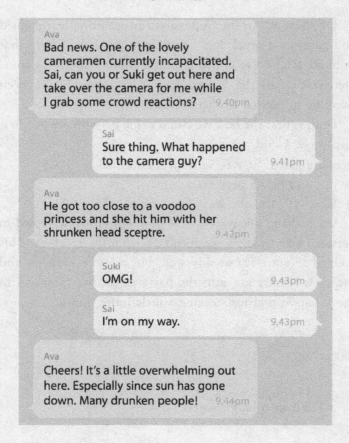

Ava
Bad news. One of the lovely cameramen currently incapacitated. Sai, can you or Suki get out here and take over the camera for me while I grab some crowd reactions? 9.40pm

Sai
Sure thing. What happened to the camera guy? 9.41pm

Ava
He got too close to a voodoo princess and she hit him with her shrunken head sceptre. 9.42pm

Suki
OMG! 9.43pm

Sai
I'm on my way. 9.43pm

Ava
Cheers! It's a little overwhelming out here. Especially since sun has gone down. Many drunken people! 9.44pm

An hour later, a very pissed-off Sai came storming towards Austin, Ella and me in the backstage area, just as Ella was getting ready to head on stage to introduce the final act of the evening.

'Some drunk idiot was sick on my shoes,' he said.

Austin was halfway through a particularly messy chilli dog. 'Oh man, that's just gross.'

'Your interview technique is enough to make anyone sick,

Sai; I told you to let me do it,' Ava laughed, sweeping towards us and handing Austin the camera. 'Right, people, I'm going front-of-house to make sure my one uninjured camera operator is all set to shoot Laura Harris's set. Who's coming to watch?'

'Absolutely!' I said. 'As soon as Ella's done the intro we'll follow you out – and then I'm ready to party.'

'Er . . . you've still got to interview Laura afterwards, so keep a lid on it for a while, Penman,' Ella said.

'But they're Nike special edition,' Sai said miserably.

I patted him on the shoulder. 'Come on, mate. We'll get you some nice new free trainers from one of the festival sponsors tomorrow. Go back to the truck and see if Suki can come out and join us for some of Laura's set.'

'TOTAL FESTIVAL! TOTAL YOUTH STAGE! HOW YOU FEELING RIGHT NOW?'

Laura Harris's voice soared over the crowd, and after a moody, swelling synth overture, the beats of her first track cracked through the night air just as every one of the palm trees, hanging vines and jungle animals on our stage burst into their multicoloured, twinkling LED glory. Ella and I grabbed a cheeky kiss at the side of the stage and then made our way to the press pit at the front, where Ava, Suki, Sai and Austin were already jumping up and down. I looked out at the crowd, which had now swollen massively, transforming into a noisy, bobbing throng of excited revellers.

Ella grabbed me, talking loudly into my ear over the music. 'How many people do you think are here now?'

'I dunno. A thousand maybe?' I said.

'I'd say more,' Austin shouted, the other side of me. 'Definitely more.'

'And hundreds of thousands tuning in online,' Suki added. 'Plus Austin's backstage live Facebook videos are going down a storm.'

'I've been interviewing people coming out of the toilet,' Austin said proudly.

I nodded along to the beat, grinning like an idiot. 'And we did this.'

'We did,' Ella said. 'God knows how, but we did it. Let's hope we can keep it up tomorrow.'

But I didn't want to think about tomorrow right then. I was on a natural high. We all were: riding on the sound of Laura's blistering set and the love of the crowd, who were going nuts. All I wanted to do at that moment was enjoy myself . . . and dance with Ella.

THE TROUBLE

It was well after midnight by the time we all came down off the ceiling and started bringing the post-show debriefing to a close. We were crammed into our allocated Portakabin-cum-changing-room: AJ, Suki, the whole GenNext team, the exhausted tech crew, and Lily, who was efficiently scribbling notes about anything we might need to rethink the following day. There wasn't much. As far as I was concerned everything had gone pretty smoothly. Up till then, that is. The night wasn't over yet.

'I would call it a rousing success!' AJ was in the middle of his third summing-up of the day, while we were all itching to get changed into our glad rags and hit the aftershow. I mean, it *was* our very first aftershow in our very own VIP area after all, and the various rumours about all sorts of big names dropping in and hanging out there had been filling my ears all afternoon. We didn't want to miss any of that, did we?

Still, AJ had a habit of saying everything in triplicate – just to make sure we'd all heard it. 'As I said, the viewing numbers on the live feed were more than we could have imagined, and Jason said he's never seen anything like the buzz that the Total Youth stage has created this year. Now, Lily is making a note of anything that needs looking at and can be improved upon tomorrow, but as I said, you all did just brilliantly.'

There was an enthusiastic chorus of 'Thanks, AJ!' as the crew filed out while the rest of us shifted to various corners of the cabin and struggled into our party clothes: Ava and Suki totally owning the night, with Ava rocking a short, deep-red punky dress, black biker boots and a bowler hat, and Suki in a black leather strapless corset with metallic patterns, a black skirt slashed to the thigh and some very cool Roman-type sandals with criss-cross ties up her calves. It was funny, they weren't a couple any more, but they still seemed to complement one another in so many ways – they just looked right together. And although they spent half the time acting all cool and businesslike with each other, sometimes they'd forget themselves and slip back into being all coupley again – just for a few seconds – before snapping out of it and hoping no one else had noticed.

'And one more thing,' AJ called out as I took Ella's hand, all geared up to storm the bar and BBQ. 'Let's not overdo it at the aftershow, people. We've got an even bigger day tomorrow. We need to be fresh.'

Another chorus, slightly less enthusiastic. 'Yes, AJ!'

Then Ella yelled, 'Let's do this!'

By the time we got to our VIP hospitality enclosure (Ava had threatened anyone who called it the Gen Pen with certain and instantaneous death), the party was well under way, with what looked like an alien drag queen on the decks spinning some old-school funk and disco. OK, so it wasn't a huge space or anywhere near as fancy as the VIP area at the main stage, but all lit up it looked beautiful. I glanced around, taking in the fairy-lit jungle oasis we'd created: the silver palm trees, the twinkling vines, the glowing storm lanterns and the little tiki-hut seating booths with the African-drum bar stools. I marvelled at the crazy, diverse crowd with their gold body tattoos, showgirl headdresses and smeared and faded face paint. It was amazing. Everyone was having the time of their lives.

It was about half an hour into the proceedings that I noticed the two young guys. Loud and staggering slightly, they were clearly quite drunk – or maybe they'd had one too many herbal cigarettes. There was something about their demeanour and behaviour that sent a warning flickering across my frontal lobes. I kept a cautious eye on them for a while, eventually deciding I was being paranoid and needed to relax. Yeah, they were a tad obnoxious but nobody else seemed to care that much, so why should I?

Ten minutes later, I was chatting to Ava at the bar when . . .

'Jack, can you come help us out?' It was Suki, her voice brittle and panicky. 'Ella's having some trouble.'

I went cold and Ava stopped what she was saying mid-sentence, her eyes darting up to meet mine.

It was then that I heard Ella shouting, her voice sailing above the noise of the crowd during a sudden drop in the beat of the music. 'WILL YOU GET OFF ME?!'

I sprinted towards the commotion, adrenalin spiking through my body, with Ava and Suki on my tail.

When I found Ella, one of the messed-up looking dudes I'd seen earlier – a guy in a cowboy hat with a narrow, leering face – was holding her wrist, refusing to let go as she tried to wriggle free. His bulkier friend was standing next to them, laughing. My temper rose instantly at the sight of this idiot manhandling my girlfriend. As I got closer, I heard him mouthing off: 'I just wanted to have a dance with you, you stuck up little—'

That was when I grabbed his shoulder and spun him around to face me.

'What the hell do you think you're doing?'

He released Ella from his grip, a surprised expression on his weaselly features, and I shoved him, sending him staggering back against the metal fence that bordered the VIP enclosure, anger coursing through my veins. I'm not a violent person, but I've never wanted to hit someone as much as I did in that moment.

'Jack, stop!' Ava cried. 'The security guard's on his way . . .'

With a massive effort I pulled myself back and turned to Ella to see if she was all right. She was holding her wrist, furious.

'I told you I didn't want to dance, you jerk,' she shouted at the guy. 'Can't you take no for an answer?'

Suddenly I felt myself flying forward through the air, not knowing what the hell was going on. After that everything happened fast. I went down face first in the sand and it took me a few painful seconds to realise that the cowboy's mate had jumped me from behind, winding me completely. The guy landed on top of me, trying to put his hands round my throat. I could hear Ella, Ava and Suki shouting – and all I kept thinking as I struggled to throw the guy off me was, where the hell is Sai and his bloody Tiger Claw kung fu when you need him? Seconds later I felt the weight lift as the guy was forcibly dragged off me. I rolled over and looked up, momentarily blinded by sand. A security guy in the nick of time, I assumed, but no . . . it was bloody Ethan standing over me.

'Are you hurt?'

He held his hand out to me and I lay there looking up at him for a moment before I took it and he pulled me to my feet.

'Jack!' Ella had her hands over her mouth. 'Jesus, are you OK?'

As far as I could tell I didn't have any broken bones, but my brand-new shirt was a mess. The security guard had turned up and the two drunk guys, meanwhile, were being frogmarched out of the area, hopefully on their way to being ejected from Total once and for all.

Once I was on my feet again, Ethan shook his head. 'Wow! That could have been nasty, right?'

'Yeah, thanks for that, mate,' I muttered, dusting myself down.

'Don't mention it,' Ethan said. 'Glad to be of service.'

I managed a smile but felt weirdly annoyed . . . or frustrated . . . I didn't know. Did it have to be him who came to the rescue?

I looked over at Ella. 'Are you OK, babe?'

'A bit shaken up, but yeah, I'm OK,' she said. 'I might need to sit down for a minute, though.'

A moment later, Austin and Sai were by my side; Austin's

ketchup moustache a dead giveaway that they'd been chowing down at the hospitality barbecue while I was scrapping with the locals.

'Dude, what the hell happened?' Sai said. 'Suki said there was a fight.'

'Nothing to see here,' Ava intervened. 'All over now and Ethan here saved the day.'

'Yeah, thanks, Ethan,' Ella added. 'You were a hero there.'

'Oh, hardly,' Ethan said, laughing as if the whole incident was no big deal. It was weird; he didn't even seem shaken up about it when the truth was we both could have got our heads kicked in or worse if the security guards hadn't arrived when they did. If I'm honest, I was a bit put out at Ava making out that Ethan had come flying in like Batman, not to mention Ella joining in with the hero worship. Was I being unreasonable?

'Anyway, it's a good story to tell my friends back home,' Ethan said, blushing slightly. 'That I got to help out *the* Jack Penman of GenNext.'

'Are you sure about that?' Sai laughed.

'Of course,' Ethan said. 'Listen, I've got to go and meet a couple of work colleagues I'm here with. But shall I come and find you guys later? Jack, maybe we could get a drink or something? It'd be nice to hang out.'

'Erm . . . sure,' I said.

'Why don't you bring your friends over, too?' Ella said.

'OK, I'll do that,' he smiled.

I watched Ethan as he disappeared into the crowd. What was it about him that didn't sit right with me? There was definitely something. Or was I being unfair? I mean, he had just saved me from a potential beating, right? Had I sounded rude? Ungracious? Still, there was something . . .

'He's a decent bloke, that Ethan, isn't he?' Sai said. 'A bit awkward, but—'

'I'm just glad he turned up when he did,' Suki interrupted. 'Let's make sure security is here at all times from now on.'

'Too right!' I said, dusting the remaining sand off my clothes. 'Now let's go and get another drink. I don't think I can stand any more excitement for one night.'

THE ARGUMENT

My ribs hurt the next morning; a throbbing reminder of my undignified first-night scrap in the middle of the Total Youth hospitality area. Some bloody hospitality! It wasn't a moment I wanted to savour, particularly the part where I was rescued from a potential beating by someone who looked like he couldn't bitch-slap his way out of a soggy McDonald's bag. So I necked a couple of ibuprofen and got on with it, trying not to visibly wince whenever Ella hugged me or I had to get up from a chair.

By 11 a.m. the GenNext crew were all gathered at a special brunch thrown by Jason Croft and his team in the main VIP area, strictly for artists and invited guests. 'What happened to the bacon sandwiches?' Austin said, picking pink pomegranate seeds off his plate and flicking them at Sai across the table. 'Oi, Sai, do you want my fruit?'

Austin was looking more like himself this morning, I was relieved to see. Maybe the success of the first night had done him good, plus I'd overheard him FaceTiming Jess before breakfast, and the conversation had sounded pretty relaxed – none of the usual 'yes, Jess, no, Jess, sorry, Jess' stuff. Maybe she was actually allowing him to have fun without her for once. Anyway, he seemed more alert today, more confident. And a bit more cocky. Yeah, back to normal, I'd say.

'Just get your breakfast down you,' Sai told him, dodging the pomegranate seeds. 'You need to bulk up that skinny body.' He pulled his own T-shirt sleeve up and flexed his guns, presumably to show Austin what he should be aiming for. Suki, who was sitting opposite, screwed up her face in horror.

'Not at the table, dude, I'm eating,' she laughed. 'Anyway, where were you and your big guns when poor old Jack was being wrestled to the floor by drunken idiots?'

'I wasn't wrestled to the floor,' I said huffily. 'I was shoved!'

'It's all right, Jack. There's no shame in being rescued by another dude,' Austin said, punching my arm. 'No shame at all.'

I was still quietly annoyed about how everything had gone down, but I figured that any display of resentment would look like sour grapes, so I decided it was best if I just kept my mouth shut.

Ava was rubbernecking all around her, checking out who was on the other table or further along the one we were sitting at. 'I don't see many artists enjoying "artists' brunch",' she said, raising an eyebrow.

'What were you expecting to see? Ariana Grande nibbling a cheese toastie?' Ella laughed.

'Shawn Mendes chowing down on a jumbo sausage?' I joined in, but my laughter was cut short when I saw Ethan approaching our table. He had that same friendly, pleasant smile on his face.

'All right, guys?' he said. 'You don't mind me crashing the party, do you?'

'Of course not. Grab a seat,' Ella said. She looked pleased to see him, I noticed. 'There's room next to Sai.'

'You saved the day last night, mate,' Austin said, leaning over the table to shake Ethan's hand. 'You got Jack here out of a tight spot.'

'Seriously, it was nothing,' Ethan said humbly. 'Anyone would have done the same.'

'Oh my God, is that a black eye?' Suki said, peering at Ethan's face. 'What the hell happened?'

'I think Jack caught me with his elbow when I pulled him off that drunken creep,' he said. 'I didn't feel it at the time, but this morning I looked like I'd gone a round with Floyd Mayweather.'

'God, sorry about that, mate,' I said.

Ethan smiled generously. 'No hard feelings, Jack, I know it was an accident. That guy knocked you for six; you didn't know *what* you were doing.'

Seriously? I had absolutely no recollection of my elbow making contact with Ethan, but for a brief moment I was glad that I'd given him a black eye, even if it was an accident. Then I quickly decided that I was a terrible person.

'What I need is a few kung fu sessions from you, Sai,' Ethan went on, looking down at his own lanky frame. 'I'd kill for muscles like yours.'

Sai's face lit up with pride, whilst next to him Austin groaned. 'Oh God, don't encourage him.'

'No, really,' Ethan said. 'I've got so much admiration for people who can dedicate themselves to something like that.'

The dude was seriously trying to kiss Sai's ass.

'Ethan, I am more than happy to share my skills,' Sai said eagerly. He was almost rabid in his enthusiasm to discuss his love of martial arts at any given moment. 'It's all very controlled. No crazy violence. It's a real discipline, you know?'

'It's bloody boring, that's what it is.' Austin flicked another pomegranate seed Sai's way.

'I'd really appreciate that, Sai,' Ethan said sincerely.

Ava waved a hand dismissively. 'Nah! You don't need kung fu lessons, Ethan. I'd say it was pretty badass the way you pulled that guy off Jack.'

'Yeah, well, my boss doesn't think so. She wasn't all that impressed with the black eye, unfortunately,' Ethan said. 'Olympia's a bit of a tough cookie. Said it looked unprofessional.'

'Oh God, I'm so sorry, Ethan,' Ella said. Really? Was she actually apologising on my behalf?

Suki dropped her fork and looked up, wide-eyed. 'Not Olympia Shaw? I thought Owl TV sounded familiar; that's where she works, right? Is she your boss?'

Ethan nodded. 'You know her?'

'I think most people involved in music TV know her,' Suki smiled. 'We were on the same media course at uni but I haven't been in contact with her for ages. Not since she went all big-time, anyway. You'll have to bring her over to say hello later and have a drink with us.'

I caught Ava rolling her eyes as if to say, of *course* Suki knows Ethan's boss.

'I'd be happy to,' Ethan smiled. 'I already mentioned you guys to Olympia and she's a big fan. I'm sure she'd love to meet you.'

It looked like we were going to be spending even more time with Ethan, then. Awesome.

As the artists' brunch wound down, it was almost time for us to head over to the Total Youth stage and start preparing for day two. AJ and Lily joined us to talk through the schedule. As Lily sat down at the table, Sai drew his stomach in and flexed his muscles again. Subtle, mate.

'So, the flash giveaways and competitions,' AJ said sternly. 'I think some of yesterday's got a bit out of hand, don't you?'

Ella giggled and I tried to look as innocent as possible. There'd been an oversight when we'd asked people to tweet us their sexiest costume pictures so that Sai could slideshow them across the video screens and broadcast them live on the GenNext channel. It was well after 10 p.m. by then, and some of the pictures that slipped through the net were . . . well, let's just say they were more sexy than they were costume.

'Why don't we try something more in the GenNext tradition?' Ava suggested.

'Like what?' I asked.

'We could get some of the festival-goers to send us Instagram or Snapchat videos of themselves doing mini interviews of their mates, and then get one or two of the best ones up on stage with you guys in between the acts.'

'I'm not sure about that,' Austin said. 'Remember when we ran that viewer competition earlier this year? Getting people to send in their own interviews is a nightmare!'

Of course I remembered; it was a disaster. We'd all been in the midst of A-level mayhem at the time and desperately needed an extra body to do a bit of on-camera stuff while Ella and I were indisposed doing our exams – just to keep GenNext up, running and relevant. The idea had been to hire the competition winner temporarily, someone amazing and quirky from our own audience. We'd encouraged people to send in videos of themselves conducting a one-minute interview. We were inundated with the bloody things and only managed to sift through about half of them in the end.

'Oh God! That awful girl we ended up using for one gig report, who swore at anyone who didn't like Little Mix,' Ava laughed.

'Yeah, *and* she bloody trolled me on Twitter after we told her that her services were no longer required,' Ella said. 'She was a total nut-job, Ethan, I'm telling you.'

'A lot of the videos were pretty lame,' Ava said. 'It wasn't our best idea.'

I noticed that Ethan was suddenly looking weirdly uncomfortable: his face and neck had flushed an ugly red. 'Actually, I sent in one of the lame videos you received,' he said awkwardly.

There was a moment of silence. Ava looked mortified.

'No way,' Sai said. 'You entered our competition?'

'Yes, I did,' Ethan admitted, still blushing. 'Bit embarrassing. I wasn't going to say anything, but since you brought the whole thing up . . .'

'I don't remember seeing your video,' Ella said, her brow wrinkled. 'I sat through loads of them.'

'Actually, it was Jack who emailed me with a very polite "thanks but no thanks",' Ethan said. He gave a what-can-you-do sort of shrug. Everyone turned to look at me.

'Harsh, Penman, harsh,' Austin said with a laugh.

So *that* must be why Ethan looked so familiar to me. The competition.

'Oh, I emailed you? Well . . . that's because your entry was definitely one of the better ones,' I said, thinking fast and trying to dig myself out of an embarrassing hole 'I don't think we emailed many people, did we, Ella?'

Ella shook her head, also clearly mortified. 'We didn't have time with everything that was going on. I mean, we would have, but—'

'Honestly, it's fine,' Ethan said. 'I wish I hadn't brought it up now.'

'Don't be embarrassed about it, Ethan,' Ava said. 'It was clearly our loss.'

'Absolutely! Look where you are now; working in real TV,' Ella said. 'I'd love to be doing that.'

Now that stung. So what we were doing wasn't real TV? Was that what Ella was implying? Wow! Why not just kick me in the—

'Cheers, Ella. Maybe I wasn't destined for presenting anyway,' Ethan said. 'It's pretty much impossible to match up to you guys.'

Oh, please.

As breakfast went on and the gang continued to chat and laugh with Ethan, generally making it clear that they thought he was the dog's gonads, I tried to figure out what it was about him that put me on edge. That constant handing-out of compliments seemed a bit off to me, for one thing. And popping up like Sooty as soon as we arrived and knowing exactly where our stage was, coming to the rescue when we were in trouble, having a mutual friend with Suki and now telling us he'd entered our competition months ago . . . There was definitely something a bit shady about it all. Why couldn't the others see it? Why couldn't Ella?

After brunch, we hit the Total Youth stage for round two. The second day of the takeover was shaping up to be even better than the first. I guess word must have spread, because the crowd was bigger and much noisier, even early on in the day. We had to make sure there was something happening constantly on the stage, so Suki came up with the genius idea of having these random retro singalong sections, hosted by Ella and me, with the best moments of well-loved songs blasting out over the crowd and the lyrics flashing across the video screens. They actually went down better than any of us expected, and not just the cooler ones, either: the Britney Spears singalong was insane, with hundreds of festival-goers singing their heads off to 'Hit Me Baby One More Time' – reliving their musical childhood memories under the blazing sun.

It was just after one of these mad moments that Ella and I managed to grab our first five minutes of the day alone together. Ella had just introduced The Daughters and we met back in our dressing room, both sweaty after a huge crowd singalong and eager to change into dry clothes. OK, so I admit it: the comment she'd made at brunch had really got to me. And yes, I know it's better not to just blurt something out after you've been turning it over in your mind and winding yourself up about it, but . . .

'So, you don't think what we're doing is as good as "real TV" then?' I was doing my utmost to sound light-hearted, but Ella could read me like a book.

'Oh, I *knew* you'd take that the wrong way,' she said, pulling on a fresh T-shirt. 'I didn't mean it like that.'

'I just thought it was slightly dismissive of what we do, that's all.'

'Come on, babe, you know that GenNext is everything to me, especially the fact that we get to do it together.' She gave me the sort of smile a mother might give a stroppy toddler she was trying to appease. 'I mean, you know I'd love to get into TV presenting eventually. We've talked about that.'

We had, sort of. Ella had made no secret of the fact that she wanted to make a career out of her natural abilities in front of a camera. But I'd thought she meant that her career would stay with GenNext.

'You have, but I suppose I assumed—'

'I've actually been thinking about going to acting classes too,' she went on. 'I loved acting when I was younger but with everything else going on I've let it go. I used to dream all the time about going to drama school, you know? I've been thinking that maybe I could get on to a part-time course or something.'

It struck me suddenly that I wasn't quite as aware of Ella's ambitions as I should be. Or maybe I'd been so wrapped up in what we were both doing with GenNext I'd chosen not to hear them. I'd just assumed that we wanted exactly the same things.

'Right,' I said.

Ella could read the doubt on my face. 'I'd make it work with GenNext, Jack. I'm totally committed to it, you know that, I just want to explore the other things I'm passionate about, too. Ava's going to uni next year, so things are going to change with the group anyway – we'll have to adjust, but we'll still be just as strong . . .'

Her words didn't particularly reassure me, and I couldn't help mentioning the other worry that had been swimming around my head. 'What about taking GenNext to America in the next couple of years? I thought we always said we'd do that if the right opportunity came up – and then the other day, you said—'

Ella stopped in the middle of brushing her hair. 'Have you been stewing on that for the last two days?'

'No. Yes. I've always thought it was on the cards, and then you go and tell Ethan that you'd never want to work out here. I just felt like I could have done with some prior warning before you announced it to the whole group . . .'

Outside I could the roar of the crowd as The Daughters finished another song. It suddenly seemed ridiculous to be standing in a Portakabin having an intense discussion about things that were mostly hypothetical when all that magical stuff was happening outside, but the brakes were off and we were rolling down the hill at speed.

'Look, I've spent my whole life moving around because of my dad's job. I like where I am now,' Ella said. 'I don't know if I can up sticks and move to another country again, just when I'm feeling settled. I finally have good friends and I don't want to leave them. I know it's what you want to do, but I'm not sure it's the right decision for me.'

I got it, I did, but it was so far from where I'd thought we were going that I just couldn't get my head straight. 'But . . . what happened to taking GenNext all the way?'

'I love GenNext, you know I do. But I have other ambitions too . . .'

The next words just spilled out of my mouth. 'What about us?'

Ella put her hands on her hips. 'There's no reason for anything to affect *us* unless we let it, Jack.'

'Isn't there?' I said. I knew I was pushing the argument too far, but I felt totally blindsided. How had I failed to notice that Ella and I wanted different things?

We stood staring at each other for a few moments. 'I'd better get back out there; The Daughters have almost finished their set,' I said.

Ella nodded and turned away. 'I'll see you later, then.'

I walked out of the cabin and instantly felt horrible. Ella and I never argued – it just didn't happen. Why hadn't I waited until we had a quiet moment to discuss all that stuff, instead of blurting it out while we were rushing to get ready? I half turned to go back in and say sorry, but I could hear the final song of The Daughters' set on stage. I'd send Ella an apologetic WhatsApp for now – and then I'd sort things out with her properly later. Total had been amazing so far, and I wasn't going to let my own idiocy ruin it.

THE BURRITO

My day didn't get any better after that. Later that evening – up on stage and chucking a few GenNext T-shirts and caps out to the crowd – I wasn't feeling so great. In fact, I was feeling worse by the second. The problem seemed to be in the pit of my stomach. Cramps. Pain. Not good. Maybe I shouldn't have had a second burrito that afternoon, but man, they were just so tasty.

I looked around to see if the DJ was anywhere near ready or if Ella was somewhere in the vicinity to take my place on stage. No sign. By now, I was sweating like a pig in a sausage factory. In a split second my stomach fell like a plunging elevator in a disaster movie and I had the sudden terrible conviction that I was going to throw up.

In the end, I tossed an armful of T-shirts into the cheering crowd, waved half-heartedly at them and then walked as quickly as I could to the stairs at the back of the stage. Once I was out of sight, I tore towards the loos like my life depended on it.

Ella found me in our Portakabin fifteen minutes later. I

was sitting on a chair in front of the mirror where the girls did their make-up, panting like I'd run a half-marathon.

If she was still annoyed about our earlier discussion, the sight of me looking so pathetic seemed to put it – temporarily at least – out of her mind. 'Jack, what's happened?' she said. 'You look awful.'

I dropped my head toward my knees, because holding it up was making me feel dizzy. 'I think I've got food poisoning.'

She knelt down next to me, lifted my head and examined my face, just as Ava, Suki and Austin crashed through the door of the cabin. To my annoyance, Ethan was with them.

'Is he OK?' Austin said.

Ava rushed to Ella's side. 'Oh my God, Jack. We need to get a doctor.'

I wanted to lift my head and tell them that I'd be fine and that they were all being overly dramatic, as per, but a sudden attack of violent stomach cramps put paid to that.

'It does sound like food poisoning,' Austin said. 'I think you're done for today, mate. You need to rest up.'

'What about the schedule?' I pulled a crumpled piece of paper from my pocket. 'I'm supposed to be interviewing Beautiful Creatures as soon as they come off stage, and then—'

'Don't worry about the bloody schedule,' Ava said. 'We'll sort something out between us.'

As I sat doubled over in agony, Ella rubbing my back, I could hear the others talking quietly behind me about what they were going to do.

'There's no way I can do any presenting,' Ava said. 'Or Sai. I'm doing most of the filming and liaising with the camera crew, and Sai's covering the broadcast. Austin, what about—'

'Me? Ava, come on. You know I'm a behind-the-scenes man. Plus I've got all the hand-held stuff to do.' I could hear the panic in Austin's voice. He'd done bits and pieces of presenting for GenNext in the past, but I knew that getting up in front of a huge crowd of people was his worst nightmare.

'I think I might have an idea.' That was Ethan, cutting in smoothly. 'I pretty much know your set list off by heart; I'd be more than happy to step into the breach.'

Ella's back-rub come to an abrupt halt.

'Ethan, that would be amazing!' she said. 'Are you sure?'

'Honestly, I'd love to help you out, Ella,' he said. 'If you think I'd be good enough.'

Hang on. What?!

'But don't you have your own job to do?' I managed to get out, trying to breathe through the pain in my gut. 'For Owl TV?'

'I've got nothing on for hours,' Ethan said. 'Free as a bird.'

'You'd be doing us a huge favour, mate,' Austin said gratefully. 'If you already know the set list, it's a massive help.'

'I do, and Ella can hold my hand and guide me through the rest of it, I'm sure.' I looked up and caught Ethan's eye as his mouth curled into a smile. It was a small, satisfied smirk and it was exclusively for me.

'Brilliant! Disaster averted,' Suki said.

Of course I wanted to object. Of course I wanted to jump up and shout, 'No way is this happening.' But I knew what they'd all think: that I was just being difficult or petty. Plus the fact that I didn't have the strength to argue, let alone jump up. I just wanted to sleep.

As my friends continued to formulate their plan of action – who was going to take me to the medical zone? What was happening next on stage? How were they going to explain my sudden departure to the fans online? – Ethan walked over to me, patting me on the shoulder. 'You just concentrate on getting better, Jack. I'll hold the fort with Ella.' Then he smiled and held out his hand, pointing to the black metal pack on my belt, which was attached to my in-ear monitors. 'I'll probably need that, won't I?'

The next hour was a blur. I spent half of it trying hard not to throw up, and the rest of it having my temperature and blood pressure taken and generally being prodded and poked by the on-site medical team. Then I was given some paracetamol to ease the pain. Eventually I started to feel a little better, and once my stomach had calmed down, Lily came to take me back to the yurt, leaving strict instructions for me to rest and drink lots of water. To be honest, I don't remember much after that. I think I was asleep before my head even hit the pillow.

When I woke up a few hours later, apart from my still-sore ribs from last night and feeling like I'd been winded, there was little sign of the bodily horror show I'd suffered earlier. I whispered a quick 'Thank God,' and reached for my iPhone on the bedside table. It was just after ten.

The first thing I saw was a lengthy message from Mum, asking me how it was all going, reminding me not to party too hard and telling me how annoying some of her customers had been that day at the hairdressing salon. Hmm, nothing out of the ordinary, then – but no mention of Dad either. God, I hoped everything had gone back to normal between them. I sent her a quick 'Love to you and Dad' message, and then fired Ella a WhatsApp to let her know I was feeling tons better. Then I drank half a bottle of water and sat back down on the bed, logging on to the GenNext channel just in time to see Ella and Ethan taking to the stage together.

I watched, transfixed, as Ella addressed the crowd. 'Hi, everyone! I'm very happy to report that our boy Jack is on the mend and will be back on the Total Youth stage, fighting fit, tomorrow.'

I consoled myself with the fact that there was a decent amount of cheering at her announcement, but then Ethan stepped forward, looking slightly awkward in a slim-cut suit and skinny tie. His hair was slicked back and he was wearing Clark Kent glasses.

'Right, ladies and gentlemen, we have a terrific band . . .'

Ladies and gentlemen? Terrific band? What the hell did he think he was presenting, the *Eurovision Song Contest*, 1964? I watched in stunned silence as he pulled a piece of paper from his back pocket and read from it, his face splashed, giant-size, across the video screens at the sides of the stage. 'They're all the way from Canada, and they're called The Outside Girl . . . I mean, Outside Girls . . .'

The audience laughed and cheered. How was it that they were finding his awkwardness so endearing? Why wasn't this guy getting booed off the stage? I slammed the computer shut, took a few deep breaths and fired off a message to the WhatsApp group.

> **Jack**
> Just watching footage. Is everyone
> happy with Ethan's performance?
> I'm feeling much better now. 10.10pm

Nobody replied except Lily, who just told me to get some rest, so I opened up my Mac again, eager to check out the GenNext Twitter feed. What did the fans have to say about all this? Quite a lot, at first glance.

> **@Ladyjazzminal2**
> @GenNextOnline What's happened to @JackGenNext? Not seen him for the last 2 hrs!! #Totalyouthtakeover

> **@Littlefish**
> Who's this clown on the stage with @EllaGenNext #awkward #Totalyouthtakeover @GenNextOnline

> **@JenGennextfan**
> Missing my evening helping of @JackGenNext. WTF? Not keen on the replacement @GenNextOnline!!!

Well, that was a relief at least.

But scrolling further forward on the Twitter feed, there seemed to be a worrying shift in opinions.

> **@JONNIBOY157**
> Check out @The EthanHarper on #Totalyouthtakeover @GenNextOnline! The dude cracks me up.

> **@Zadajonathan**
> LOVING @TheEthanHarper @GenNextOnline Total geek-chic! CUTE!!!

> **@Popprince**
> The @GenNextOnline #Totalyouthtakeover has been excellent so far; good work @JackGenNext @EllaGenNext Really enjoying @TheEthanHarper too

That last one was too much for me. @Popprince was Kevin Hughes, DJ and entertainment correspondent for all sorts of radio and TV shows, with God knows how many followers. I shut down my computer and stood up, ready to grab my shoes and head out to reclaim my place beside Ella on the stage for the final introduction of the night. That little weasel wasn't getting away with this. Then something stopped me. I'm not sure exactly what it was; let's just call it instinct. I'd already had one argument with Ella that day because I'd shot my mouth off without thinking; did I really want to go steaming in there shouting about Ethan and making it worse? In the end, I lay back down on the bed again and closed my eyes, breathing deeply. This is just for tonight, I told myself. You can sort it all out in the morning.

It was just after midnight when Ella came into the yurt. She tried not to make a noise, but I was wide awake anyway. I sat up in bed and smiled. 'How did it go?'

Ella sat down next to me. 'Oh God, Jack, it was bloody stressful. I was trying to do a good job, but I was so worried about you.'

'I'm loads better now,' I said. 'I'll be fine tomorrow.'

She took my hand. 'Thank God! I can't go through another day like that. Especially after we had that stupid row and . . . If it hadn't been for Ethan . . .'

'Yeah, about that.' I said it as matter-of-factly as I could manage. 'I imagined he was just going to help with interviews or something. I wasn't expecting a full-on co-presenting thing.'

'Oh, that was just . . . I mean, he literally knew our whole set list, so it made sense for him to co-present . . . He was a godsend, to be honest.'

'He was wearing a suit,' I said, grimacing.

'I know,' she laughed. 'But he is actually very funny. He comes across all dorky, but then he'll say something really dry that just cracks you up. I spent half the time giggling up there. It seemed like the more uncool he was, the more the audience liked him.'

'Is that right?

'Yeah . . . I mean . . . You're not pissed off about it, are you, Jack?'

There was an uncomfortable silence before I slowly shook my head. I wasn't sure what I felt, to be honest. The worst part of the entire episode was that I'd missed one whole night of the festival, and that really sucked. I would have to make up for it tomorrow for sure. After all, it was the final night.

THE FINAL NIGHT

I felt a hundred times better the next day. It's like my mum always says: everything looks better after a good night's sleep. And this was a big day: our main act was playing. Harriet Rushworth.

By the time the Total Youth stage opened that afternoon, I was buzzing again. Even the others ripping it out of me for 'coming over all faint' the night before couldn't take the edge off how excited I was for the final night. Plus, Ethan had made himself scare, and that was something to be happy about as far as I was concerned. The online appreciation of his cute geeky act was still pouring in, so I just didn't want to see the dude, and the thought of shaking his hand and thanking him (again) for helping out (again) made me want to punch something. Instead, I kept my focus on going over the programme for the evening with the group, keeping up my fluids, and giving the burritos a wide berth. Ella and I didn't even mention the angry words we'd exchanged the day before, and although there was the slightest undercurrent to our usual laughs and jokes, it was clear that both of us were ignoring it until we had time to talk about things properly – in private.

Our priority was to make that night amazing.

After Total Youth opened for the third and final time, Ella and I walked out on stage and the audience went nuts. I looked over at her, wide-eyed, as we headed towards the front amidst deafening cheering. If we thought the crowd had been massive over the past two nights, it had nothing on this. 'Look how many people there are already!'

'I reckon everyone wants to get a good spot for Harriet's set later,' she said in my ear. 'It's gonna bring the house down!'

Once our opening act of the afternoon was up and running, Sai, Ava and Austin came over to join Ella and me in the hospitality area, where we were setting up for the day's interviews in the tiki hut.

'Where's Suki?' I said.

Ava shrugged. 'She bumped into some girl from an indie band her company used to manage, and they got chatting. We'll see her later, I guess.' She was coming across all casual, but I could tell she was a bit miffed. She'd had the same look on her face the day before, when Suki was all lit up talking to Ethan about that Olympia chick. It made me wonder if maybe Suki's history with Olympia went deeper than just being uni mates and Ava knew it. It was funny, Ava and Suki seemed to have been getting on really well over the festival, but now Ava was starting to act all distant and annoyed again, just like she did after they broke up.

'How are you getting on anyway, Penman?' she went on. 'You sure you'll be able to manage the rest of the evening?'

'I'm good,' I said. 'Never better. I'm not going to let you freaks replace me with Ethan for a second day!' I'd meant it as a joke, but I could tell by the way Austin caught Ava's eye that it had come out wrong.

Ella sighed. 'Oh, here we go.'

'Come on, mate,' Austin said. 'You know how much we had going on last night.'

'I know, but . . . *Ethan*? He looked pretty awkward up there.'

'He was a bit awkward at first,' Sai admitted. 'But then he got loads better.'

'He actually ended up doing a really good job,' Ava said. 'We were lucky he was there.'

'Apparently his Twitter followers went up by about ten thousand over the course of the evening,' Austin said.

'No way!' Sai said with a laugh. 'That's mad.'

I looked at my friends, all raving about Ethan's triumph on the Total stage. 'And you guys don't think it's just a little bit weird that he happened to know our set list off by heart?'

'What are you saying, Jack?' Ella said.

'Methinks Jack is worried about how easily he was replaced,' Ava laughed.

'And all that chemistry between Ethan and Ella on stage . . . ooh yeah, baby!' This was Sai, who I could have cheerfully punched at that moment, but I laughed through gritted teeth instead.

A voice from the doorway of the hut stopped everyone in their tracks. 'Oh come on, you guys, that's rubbish and you know it!' It was Ethan. I wondered how long he'd been standing there; how much he'd heard. 'Jack, don't listen to them; they're winding you up,' he said, walking into the hut. 'I could never have done as good a job as you.'

I looked at him closely. Something about him was different from the day we'd met him. He'd changed his clothes; shed the skinny-geek gear in favour of a nicer outfit, a patterned shirt open over a white T-shirt and denim cut-offs. It was the sort of gear I wore . . . in fact it was almost the same thing I'd worn on the first day! What the hell was this guy playing at?

'Don't do yourself down,' Ella said. 'You were a real life-saver.'

'You were amazing!' Ava added.

I'd had enough.

'Look, sorry, guys, I've got an interview in five minutes – can we clear the space, please?'

'Yeah, we'd best get back as well, troops,' Ava said, prodding Sai and Austin and herding them out of the door.

Ethan had this strange expression on his face. 'Oh, OK! I just came by because I had something I wanted to tell you guys. It's just an idea at the moment, but . . .'

'Can it wait till later, mate?' I said.

He looked pissed off for a moment. 'Sure, Jack,' he said, as he followed the others out of the hut. 'Later.'

The last night of Total Youth was as epic as I'd hoped. Finally, it was time for Harriet Rushworth, our headline act of the festival, our big star name. As the crowd in front of our stage swelled, so did the excitement. It was totally crazy. So much so that I started to wonder if there could be anyone left at any of the other stages. Our audience looked and sounded like it was made up of every single person at the festival: a swaying mass of smiling faces, raised arms and bright colours. It was amazing.

Only fifteen minutes before she was due to go on, I still hadn't had a chance to speak to Harriet. I'd caught a little bit of her soundcheck, earlier in the afternoon, but had to dash off to do a quick interview for MTV about the GenNext stage. And right after that, I got majorly distracted when I decided to check the Totalyouthtakeover hashtag, only to discover an online Twitter poll posing the question 'Who's hotter: Jack or Ethan?' (I decided not to check the results for the preservation of my sanity.) To be honest, I was also quite nervous about meeting Harriet again, and who could blame me? I mean, the last time she saw me in the flesh I'd just made a total prat of myself in front of a live audience of millions. Sure, we'd talked on the phone since then and everything seemed to be fine, but looking her in the eye was going to be another thing. She was one of the world's biggest pop stars, after all.

Ella and I waited for Harriet to join us at the bottom of the steps leading up to the stage, excited, but also a little bit sad that our final act marked the end of our stage take-over.

'I can't believe this is our last act,' Ella said. 'Don't you feel like you want to do it all over again?'

'Apart from the bit where I was spewing my guts up, yeah!' I laughed. 'Anyway, we've still got Harriet to go, and the final after-party. That looks like it's going to be pretty amazing.'

When Harriet finally appeared from her cabin, she was wearing a beaming grin as she strode towards us, and all my nervousness instantly melted away. She looked incredible: her long red hair had been teased into massive wild curls, and she was dressed in an epic jungle-themed outfit to match our stage, with leopard print, feathers, rips and sequins everywhere. There was even a giant tail fanning out from the back of the dress, like a peacock's.

'Why, Jack Penman, I do declare: you're even more hand-some than I remember.' She was playing that Southern charm for all it was worth – and I didn't mind a bit. 'And you must be Ella. Gosh, I feel like I know y'all so well already.'

I'd never seen Ella look star-struck, but there it was, right in front of my eyes. Harriet kissed her on both cheeks and she went the colour of a strawberry.

'Harriet . . . Wow! It's so good to meet you. And so good of you to do this for us . . . really.'

'Oh please, honey, I'm doing it for myself,' she laughed, smoothing down the fabric of her crazy outfit. 'I *know* what my young fans are watching, and it's not *American Idol*. They're all tuning in to GenNext. You guys are hot property. So thank *you* for having *me*, baby.'

'Harriet, I really think you should come and be the GenNext spokeswoman,' Ella said.

'Keep the job offer open, and if my next album bombs I'll know where to come,' Harriet said with a wink.

Bloody hell, I was in awe of Harriet Rushworth. I mean, she wasn't much older than us, but she just had this way about her. Total confidence, total charm.

'OK, are we ready?' she said, just as a crew member dashed up and handed her a radio mic.

'We are if you are,' I said.

A cacophony of cheers and excited screams broke out amongst the crowd; they knew what was coming and they were totally up for it. Ella and I looked at one another and nodded.

'Let's do this,' I said, and up we went.

It was no surprise that Harriet nailed it. Her hour-long set was a smart mix of the best tracks from her new album plus all the hit singles the crowd were dying to hear – and she held them in the palm of her hand all the way. Nearing the end of her performance, she called out over a sea of happy faces and illuminated phone screens: 'So how are y'all feeling about the GenNext Total Youth takeover?'

A roar of approval filled the air, just as Harriet launched headlong into her final encore, belting out her biggest hit of all, 'Jeopardy', with the audience singing along at such a volume that you could barely hear her over the top of them. As she took her bows, she thanked her slick young band and her backing singers. Then she dived straight back into a final chorus of 'Jeopardy', spinning around the stage and giving it every last drop of energy she had, while the lights strobed and lasers fired from the eyes of our other-worldly jungle creatures above the heads of the crowd. On the final chord, Ella and I bolted in from the side of the stage just in time to see the glitter cannons fire into the sky, showering everyone below.

'HOW WAS THAT, PEOPLE?' I shouted over the mic. 'GIVE IT UP FOR HARRIET RUSHWORTH!'

Another mass cheer went up. Harriet smiled and blew kisses at the crowd. Then we were joined on stage by Austin,

Sai, Ava, Suki, AJ and even Lily, all waving and whooping like crazy, eager to celebrate this amazing moment as a team: the epic finale of our three-day takeover. Unprompted, Harriet shouted into her own mic.

'Hey, y'all! Put your hands together for our amazing hosts: Generation Next!'

The crowd went mental; the noise was completely deafening. By now, I had a lump in my throat and my eyes were stinging. I looked around at the team, who were all grinning from ear to ear, totally buzzing. We had smashed it.

As the noise continued and the GenNext team took their bows and waved at the audience, AJ sidled over and shouted into Ella's ear. 'Ethan's over there at the back of the stage. He won't come on; says it's our moment, but I think he should, don't you?'

'Leave it to me,' she said, and I watched her run over to where Ethan was standing clapping politely. I was just telling myself that I didn't care and that even bloody Ethan couldn't ruin this moment when Harriet grabbed hold of my hand and pulled me to the front of the stage.

'Let's hear it for the gorgeous Jack Penman!' she squealed, lifting my arm up like I'd just won a world heavyweight title. Then she leaned forward and pecked me on the lips. I felt myself redden, and turned away just in time to see Ella leading Ethan by the hand towards the front of the stage.

Ethan smiled and did an old-fashioned little bow, and a short chorus of chants went up: 'Ethan! Ethan!' Then he bowed to Ella; she smiled and curtsied back. And although Harriet's arm was still slung around me, I felt my teeth grind together.

The crowd's cheering grew and grew as Ella gave shout-outs to all the members of GenNext, and finally we all stepped forward for one more bow.

'Thank you, Total Festival!' I had to shout into my microphone to be heard over the cacophony. 'We are GenNext. Keep watching!'

And that was it. The Total Youth stage takeover was done.

THE AFTERSHOW AFTERSHOCK

If there was one thing I could say about Jason Croft, it was that he knew how to throw an after-party. Behind the main stage, where Drake had just finished the final set of the festival, the VIP area was a mad, mesmerising utopia, full of the most eclectic mix of people I'd ever seen gathered in one place. Jason wasted no time in coming to find us as we all gathered around a cluster of seagrass chairs and couches, grabbing glasses of fizz from passing waiters.

'Boy oh boy!' he said, shaking his head. 'I am *so* frickin' glad that I decided to stagger Harriet's set and Drake's show. If they'd happened at the same time I would have been in trouble. I mean, yeah, they're both popular acts, but the buzz on the atmosphere over at Total Youth was insane. I think you would have stolen most of my crowd.'

Ava raised her glass and smiled. 'I reckon we'd have taken all of it, Jason.'

'Look, I couldn't be happier,' Jason said, shaking hands with us in turn. 'I think we should talk about next year asap.'

'Seriously?' Sai said.

'Absolutely!' Jason replied, gradually disappearing backwards into the throng. 'I'll catch you guys later and we can discuss it, OK?'

AJ pulled a couch and a couple of the chairs closer to a large bamboo coffee table so we could set our drinks down, then we kicked back, ready to toast our success with all the hard work behind us. I guess you could say we were on a massive high after the epic finale to our show, which had been an incredible moment for all of us. Now all we wanted to do was celebrate together. I'd even been granted a temporary Ethan reprieve, as he'd been called away to do something for Owl TV after the show had finished, so that made me doubly happy. It would have been cool to celebrate with Harriet too, but naturally she had other places to be and was jetting off to somewhere in Europe immediately after the set. She'd been delighted with how her performance had gone, though, especially after Sai showed her some of the incredible online feedback. She'd given each and every one of GenNext a massive hug and kiss to say goodbye – including AJ, who tried his hardest to act cool, but I could tell that even he was dazzled.

As I got comfortable, Ella, sitting next to me, gave me a sharp nudge with her elbow. Glancing to my left, I caught the improbable sight of Sai and Lily, over near the bar, in the midst of what they obviously thought was a clandestine kiss . . . Well, it wasn't all that clandestine, because everyone saw and collective jaws dropped around the table. For a few seconds nobody said a word. I don't think any of us had ever seen Sai kiss anyone, ever.

Once they'd separated, they arrived at the table to find

us all looking somewhat stunned. It was obvious to both of them that we'd witnessed their snog, and they blushed in tandem. Ava was the one to break the silence. 'Er . . . exactly when did all this happen, guys?'

'Yes, you've certainly kept it under wraps, oh nephew and trusted employee.' AJ raised an eyebrow, but he was laughing. Probably as pleased as the rest of us to see Sai getting a bit of action.

Lily looked down, her dreads falling over her face. 'Well, what can I say? I've been locked in a truck with him for the best part of three days; I guess he wore me down.'

'Yeah, they call that Stockholm syndrome, where a kidnap victim falls for their captor,' I said, causing Austin to spit some of his drink out and launch into a half-coughing, half-laughing fit.

'I think it's lovely,' Ella said. 'Sai, it's about time you had a . . . dare I say, girlfriend?'

Sai and Lily looked shyly at one another. The little sneak. He hadn't said a word to me, or Austin as far as I knew.

'So the muscles finally paid off,' Austin said, holding his champagne up. 'Cheers, mate!'

'Shut it, Austin! Lily likes me for my intellect, OK?' Sai said.

'That's right,' Lily agreed, putting her arm around him. Mystifyingly, this very cool and beautiful girl did indeed appear to be really quite into Sai.

I clocked Ava looking at Sai and Lily reflectively. She'd been lounging across the back of Suki's chair, but now she sat up, as if she'd somehow been reminded that she and Suki weren't actually a couple any more. Austin, meanwhile, was staring down at the floor, looking a little sad. I wondered if he was thinking about Jess. He hadn't really said much about her since our conversation at the bar on the first day of the festival. His phone seemed to be lighting up every five minutes with a new WhatsApp message, which I'm sure were all from Jess, but he didn't read any of them.

I was about to ask Sai and Lily a few more questions when Suki spotted someone in the crowd and suddenly jumped up, her eyes bright. 'Oh look! There's Olympia Shaw.' She waved frantically at a young woman standing a few feet away from us, tall and freckly with a mass of glossy chestnut curls. 'Olympia! Olympia! Limpy, over here!'

Ava looked at Ella and me. 'Really? *Limpy?*' she whispered, rolling her eyes.

Olympia finally turned, lighting up as soon as she saw Suki and heading over to where we were sitting.

They hugged like long-lost family and then Olympia sat down with us. 'Oh my God, Suki. How long has it been?' she said.

'Three years at least, and now look at you,' Suki smiled.

'And you, too. You've done such amazing things and you look beautiful, as always,' Olympia said. 'I was so excited when Ethan told me you were here with GenNext.'

'I know; it's wonderful to see you!' Suki said. 'Has Owl TV been covering the whole festival? You must have been crazy busy!'

'I've got a good team on board,' Olympia said with a smile. 'Ethan in particular has been working really hard. I've trained him well.'

Suki shook her head and grinned. 'I'll bet. I know what

a hard taskmaster you are when you're in charge of a project. Oh my God! Do you remember when . . .'

As Suki launched into reminiscences about some project she and Olympia had worked on at university, I noticed that Ava had a familiar expression on her face: the slight frown she always wore when she was trying to process information. As if she were trying to work out what the deal was, or perhaps once had been, between Suki and Olympia. They certainly seemed pretty familiar with each other. And it probably didn't help matters that Olympia was very easy on the eye.

'And how about you guys!' Olympia said, eventually turning her attention away from Suki towards the rest of us. 'What you've done is just so fantastic. I was at the Total Youth stage earlier and it was *incredible*.'

'They're a smart bunch, Miss Shaw,' AJ smiled. 'It's good to meet you – I'm AJ.'

'We had a brilliant time up there,' I added. 'I'm Jack, by the way.' I leaned across to shake her hand, and the others followed suit – including Ava, who was still frowning. Once we'd done the introductions, Olympia got her phone out. 'I must text Ethan to come find us. I'd been hoping to find you all tonight, actually. We've got something we want to run past you guys.'

'Oh really?' Ella said, sitting forward. 'What is it?'

Olympia raised her eyebrows and smiled mysteriously. 'It was Ethan's idea, so let's wait for him to arrive.'

I wasn't sure I liked the sound of this. Ten minutes later, Ethan was on the scene again like a recurring bad smell. He sat down on the arm of Ella's chair, so close that his thigh was pressed up against her shoulder, and smiled over at me. 'Hey, Jack.'

I nodded. 'Ethan.'

'Wasn't the finale a buzz?' he said. 'I'm so grateful to you all for letting me be involved. Being part of GenNext – even for a couple of days – just feels special, you know?'

'It was a pleasure to have you on board, mate,' said Austin. Beside him, Sai and Ava were nodding vigorously. I stifled the urge to stick my fingers down my throat and gag.

Ella jumped in eagerly. 'So what's this idea of yours then, Ethan?'

Ethan smiled. 'I was going to bring it up earlier, but Jack was in such a massive rush that I decided to save it for tonight.' He winked at me like he was just kidding, like there wasn't an edge to his words.

As I opened my mouth to explain, he cut me off again. 'You know that Olympia has been overseeing all Owl TV's coverage of Total, including the Total Youth stage?'

'It's been the best Total Youth stage I've ever seen,' Olympia said. 'What I like most about you guys is that you're cool, but you're accessible, too. That's why we think you might be perfect for our next project. Back to you, Ethan.'

I was intrigued and alarmed all at once. Where the hell was all this leading?

'So, Owl TV is making a big new show called *Emerge* in partnership with Channel 4, and Olympia is exec-producing,' Ethan said.

'That's seriously amazing, Limpy,' Suki said, and Olympia smiled and patted Suki's knee. I saw Ava's eyes widen.

'The show is all about fresh new artists,' Ethan went on.

'It'll be a cross between a documentary and a competition. We'll follow five chosen acts over five episodes, really getting into the nitty-gritty of their lives, looking at how they're working towards achieving their dreams and how tough it can be breaking into the music business.'

'Sounds very solid,' AJ said.

'It is,' Ethan agreed. 'The sixth and final episode will be a massive live show – prime time – where viewers vote for their favourite act. The ultimate winner will be featured in a full televised live showcase gig, all promoted, paid for and filmed by Owl TV, plus they'll get a deal with Island Records, who are helping sponsor the show.'

'It sounds bloody awesome,' Ella said, with everybody nodding enthusiastically.

I had to know where this was going. 'So what did you mean when you said we'd be perfect?' I asked, looking from Ethan to Olympia.

'We mean perfect for hosting the show,' Ethan said, like it was nothing.

'Are you kidding?' Sai said. Actually, it was more of a squeal.

'We really need to get the tone right with this show,' Olympia cut in, her manner suddenly more businesslike. 'This is not *The X Factor*; we want to do something more edgy. I need a great team to help me shape it, and that means all of you. Plus, as Ethan says, I need hosts.'

'What, us? Me and Ella?' I said.

'Well, if we have to take you to get Ella, we will,' Ethan said, deadpan.

'That's so exciting, Ethan,' Ella said. She was beaming

– I could tell that the prospect of 'real TV' had totally wowed her.

Ava, meanwhile, looked stunned more than anything. 'This sounds . . .' She looked at Olympia, who still had her hand resting on Suki's knee, and frowned. 'I mean, this is a bit of a bolt from the blue, isn't it?'

'But an amazing one, right?' Suki said. 'I think you guys working with Owl would be such a perfect match, especially with Olympia at the helm. What do you think, AJ?'

'I think I need to sit down with Ms Shaw and talk logistics,' AJ said, his manager's brain clearly whirring away. 'But it sounds like it could be fantastic.'

'We're just ironing out the finer details with Channel 4, but it's likely to kick off pretty soon – filming in London – *if* you guys come on board,' Ethan said. 'We've already found the potential acts, but we've been looking for the right hosts for ages – and after working with you guys at Total, well. You're perfect.'

Sai looked at Austin and then Lily. 'What do you guys think?'

'I think it's wonderful for you all,' Lily said, squeezing his hand.

'And it's a big yes from me,' Austin said, grinning.

The next few minutes were a blur of excited jabbering, with everyone asking questions and talking over each other. Meanwhile I was feeling massively conflicted. Of course I could see how incredible this was: GenNext partnering not only with Owl TV but with Channel 4. Bloody hell! Still, as fantastic as it sounded, I just had this horrible sinking feeling. I mean, working with Ethan back in the UK? Sure,

Olympia seemed cool enough, but I wouldn't have trusted Ethan as far as I could throw him. Plus, it all seemed very well thought out and orchestrated on his part; not at all like a spur-of-the-moment idea he'd formed over the last three days.

Olympia broke in over the excited chatter. 'As I said, there's lots for AJ and me to discuss, but I'm really excited about Ethan's idea, and after what I saw on the Total Youth stage, you three would make such a strong presenting team – so quirky!'

'Three?' I said.

'Well, Ethan would mostly be heading up the day-to-day production of the show, but there's so much to cover, it'd be criminal not to give him some screen time too, after his success here.' She looked over at Ethan and raised a perfectly plucked eyebrow. 'From what I can gather, he's a bit of an internet heart-throb all of a sudden, God help us.'

'I am not,' he laughed. 'The only reason people even noticed me at all is because I was standing next to Ella.'

Ella blushed. 'Flatterer!'

Meanwhile I was ready to throw up my champagne.

So this was it: our chance to take GenNext to another level. But it was all hinging on an association with someone I disliked intensely. I looked around at my friends, all smiling and toasting each other, clearly thrilled with this new idea, and I knew that this wasn't the right time to air my doubts. Total had been incredible, and I wasn't about to burst the bubble.

Excusing myself by saying I was going to the loo, I got

up and left the group, heading over towards one of the bars. The sweetness of the champagne was making me feel a little queasy, and right at that moment I wanted a glass of water and some time out to think over the events of the evening. I'd been at the bar for a few minutes when I felt a tap on my shoulder.

'Jack, there you are. I'm off, heading back to my yurt.' It was Olympia, her brown curls bouncing around her face. Her curls and freckles made her look younger than Suki, more like our age, but there was this air of authority and experience about her. It was easy to see how she'd got to where she was at such a young age. 'I think this partnership could be so good for both Owl and GenNext, you know. I'm having breakfast with AJ in the morning to discuss all the details.'

'Yeah, it's . . . it's really . . .'

'It was all Ethan's idea,' she said. 'He adores you guys. Especially you, Jack.'

'Yeah, about Ethan—'

'Mind you, you'll have to keep an eye on him,' she cut in.

'Why? What do you mean?' I wondered if she was about to confirm my suspicions that there was something a bit peculiar about this guy.

'Oh, he's just such a perfectionist,' she laughed. 'And he's very determined too, which is mostly a great thing, but sometimes he goes too far. Did he tell you he fell out of a tree the other morning? He was totally adamant that he'd get a shot of the sunrise over the festival for us because the regular cameraman couldn't get up there.' She laughed and shook her head.

'No, he didn't,' I said, confused.

'Oh yeah! Gave himself a black eye into the bargain. Just lucky he didn't break the camera and a few bones.'

'No, he didn't mention that at all,' I said.

After saying goodnight to Olympia, I drifted back towards the gang, the party now in full swing around me. So Ethan had fallen out of a tree and given himself a black eye. Why did he lie and say that I'd given it to him? To make me look bad?

I had no idea what was going on with this dude, but I knew I had to be careful around him. With a seemingly perfect new opportunity on the table for GenNext, it wasn't exactly going to be a piece of cake persuading the others that as long as Ethan was involved, we should proceed with the utmost caution.

THE RETURN

The clouds above Heathrow hung heavy on the Tuesday morning we touched down, and the look on everyone's face said it all. Back. To. Reality. I'd slept for a few hours on the flight, so as we trailed through the arrivals hall towards the luggage carousel, I was feeling reasonably bright, not to mention happy because I hadn't clapped eyes on Ethan for the last fifteen hours. We'd left him behind in California – at least for the time being.

There was a hold-up with the luggage so we had to wait ages at the baggage carousel, which didn't help anyone's mood.

'Don't look so glum, guys,' AJ said, looking around at all of us.

'You say that, AJ, but it's pretty grim coming back here after all that,' Austin said. 'I need time to adjust.' I also suspected that he was feeling more than a little nervous about having to face the music with Jess.

AJ laughed. 'You won't have time to be bloody miserable, Austin. You've got post-festival vlogs to work on, and once the contracts are sorted, we're straight back into this new project.'

Yes, it was official: AJ and Olympia Shaw had had their business breakfast, and the GenNext/Owl TV partnership was going ahead just as soon as all the contractual stuff had been agreed. The others were over the moon about it, and couldn't stop gushing about how wonderful Olympia and Ethan both were, while I was still trying to get my head round the pros and cons of having such an amazing opportunity at the cost of spending more time with someone whose intentions I couldn't for the life of me work out.

Suki grabbed her suitcase first; she was going back to her flat in London, rather than to Hertfordshire like the rest of us. 'I'm going to get the Heathrow Express and then jump in a cab from Paddington. Thank you, guys; it's been amazing! You did such an incredible job; you should be really proud.'

'Thank you for everything, Suki,' I said.

We each gave her a massive hug. When it came to Ava's turn, she seemed a little hesitant.

'When will I be seeing you again?' she asked apprehensively.

'Hopefully soon, Aves. You'll have to let me know if you need my expertise for your new venture,' Suki said.

'Are you kidding?' Ava said. 'If it weren't for you, it probably wouldn't even be happening. You're our good-luck charm!'

Suki smiled and blushed slightly. 'That's really nice to hear, Ava. Thanks.'

They hugged, somewhat awkwardly it must be said, and once Suki had left, all eyes were on Ava, who was clearly a bit choked up.

'You need to sort this out, Ava,' I said, dragging my own

backpack off the carousel. 'It's so obvious you two should be together – what's the matter with you both?'

'I know it doesn't happen often, but Jack's right, babe,' Ella said.

'I know, I know.' Ava ran her hands through her hair. 'It's just that every time I think it's the right time to . . . I don't know . . . say or do something, there's always something stopping me. I mean, I was all ready to broach the subject at the after-party and bloody Olympia turned up with her fabulous job and her cute freckles and . . . That's the way it always is with Suki and me. You know what I'm saying, Jack, right?'

I nodded. 'I know, but just because they were mates at uni, it doesn't mean there was anything between them. You should talk to her.'

'Yes, oh wise one,' Ava smiled. 'I promise I will.'

As we headed out of the baggage reclaim towards the exit, I turned my attention to Austin. 'And while I'm doing my best agony-aunt impersonation, how are you feeling about seeing Jess now you're back?'

'He's anxious,' Sai shouted from behind us, hand in hand with Lily.

'I can speak for myself, thank you, Sai,' Austin said. 'I'm anxious. The last time we FaceTimed she said I was being distant and evasive.'

'So normal, then,' Sai said.

'The thing is, I haven't missed her at all, J,' Austin said, looking down at the floor. 'What am I supposed to do with that realisation?'

'I don't know, mate, I really don't. But remember what I

said. Whatever happens, I'm always around if you need someone to bitch and moan to.'

'You're top of my list for bitching and moaning,' he laughed.

In the people carrier on the way back to Hertfordshire, AJ dozed off in the front while the rest of us scrolled through our phones, catching up on anything that might have happened in the world while we were in the air. It was funny really; away from of the atmosphere of Total and back on my own turf, so to speak, the unease I'd felt the day before seemed to have evaporated. I mean, what exactly was I worried about anyway? We'd smashed the festival gig, then been offered the chance of a lifetime immediately afterwards. But there I was focusing my thoughts on Ethan. It seemed a bit daft in the cold light of day.

'Oh my God, have you seen this?' Ella said, holding out her phone. 'Really? Is this all people have got to write about?' She shoved the phone close to my face and a photograph loomed towards me. It was of Harriet kissing me on stage at the end of her show.

Brilliant. Ella had seen Harriet grab me on the last night and peck me on the lips. It wasn't a big deal – Harriet was a very physical person – but I didn't exactly want it splashed all over the media.

'What site is that?' I asked.

'The Mail Online, of all things' Ella said. 'The headline is: "Harriet Rushworth gets over cheating ex with sexy young internet star Jack Penman at Total Festival".'

There was laughter from the others, but Ella didn't crack a smile.

'There's more on BuzzFeed,' Austin said, leaning over from behind us and reading from his phone. '"While gorgeous Ella Foster was cosying up to new presenting partner Ethan Harper, her boyfriend Jack Penman was getting busy with superstar Harriet Rushworth. Is Jack doing the dirty on Ella?" Same picture, and there's one of Ella holding hands with Ethan on stage.'

'Twitter's rife with it,' Ava said, looking up from her own phone. 'All speculating on whether you two are still on, or seeking pastures new.'

I swallowed hard. Just the mere mention of Ella and Ethan in the same sentence made me feel a little bit sick.

'Pastures new! Oh for God's sake,' I said.

'Look, I know it's crap and you probably didn't invite Harriet to kiss you,' Ella said. 'It's just not very nice to see it all over the internet.'

'*Probably* didn't invite her to kiss me?' I said. 'Of course I didn't invite her – as if! Come on Ella, you know I didn't. She just got carried away – it was a split-second peck on the mouth.'

Ella's eyes narrowed. 'Yes, a quick peck on the mouth that the media has turned into a massive scandal. Brilliant.'

Of course we both knew it was all crap, didn't we? One of those stupid rumours that would be forgotten in two days. Still, Ella was quiet for the rest of the journey, and when she got out of the car at her place, her goodbye kiss on the cheek was fleeting and cold.

I was the final drop-off, and the sight of home stirred up a few mixed feelings. Sure, I was glad to be back, but it had been days since I'd thought about Dad's odd behaviour or the tension between him and Mum before I left for California. I'd had to push it to the back of my mind so I could concentrate on the festival. Now that I was walking up the front path towards our house, it was something I was going to have to face again. What *had* been going on? Was it still going on? I opened the front door and dropped my massive suitcase in the hall. As soon as I shut the door behind me, Mum poked her head out of the living room.

'Jack, you're home!'

She seemed happy to see me, and hugged me so tight that my ribs hurt all over again.

'Hey, Jack!' Dad was right behind her.

I was a little surprised to see him, given that it was the middle of a weekday. 'Dad, hi! Day off?'

'Sort of,' he said, looking a bit awkward.

'Your dad just wanted to be here when you got home,' Mum added.

'Right,' I said, slightly confused. Dad never came home in the middle of the day; it was all a bit suspect. Still, so far there was no sign of the tension that had been there between them before I left – so that was a good thing.

'Come on, I'll make you a coffee,' Mum said. 'I've been watching the festival online and you did so well, love. I want to hear everything.'

'There's loads to tell,' I said, following her and Dad into the kitchen. 'We got some pretty exciting news at the end of the festival. You're going to freak out when I tell you!'

I clocked a nervous glance flash between them as I sat down at the breakfast bar.

'Come on then,' Dad said. 'Let's have it.'

They both seemed to be with me all the way for about the first ten minutes of me regaling them with my desert adventures, but as I went on, it was impossible not to notice a look of distraction on both their faces. They kept looking at one other as if they were waiting for me to finish because they had something to say. Mum was chewing her lip, which was always a sign that she was nervous. In the end, I stopped mid-sentence, unable to carry on jabbering about all the fun I'd had when there was obviously something else going on. Time to call them out on all this weirdness.

'Look,' I said, 'it's clear that you two are on another planet. What's going on?'

Both of them looked distinctly awkward. Dad opened his mouth and closed it again, evidently unsure how to broach whatever it was that they needed to tell me.

'Right, love,' Mum said eventually. 'This is going to come as a bit of a bolt from the blue . . .'

My stomach turned over.

'You might have noticed that things were a bit odd before you left for America,' Dad said.

'You think?' I laughed nervously.

'I'd had some news that was . . . unexpected,' Dad went on. 'That's probably the best way to describe it. And your mum and I didn't really want to lay it all out in front of you until we'd discussed it together. It's a big thing, son.'

'It was a real shock at first – for both of us – and that's probably why you noticed a bit of tension between me and your dad.' Mum said this with a smile, making it clear that whatever tension there had been had now vanished. 'We've talked and talked about this, though, and everything's fine between us now. We're just not sure how you're going to feel about the news, that's all.'

'*What* news?' Whatever they were about to tell me, it was clearly something major. I noticed that Dad's hands were shaking slightly and that Mum put her hand over his.

'Dad, can we just get this explanation under way, please?' I said. 'I feel sick.'

Dad took a deep breath and leaned back against the sink. 'OK. I just need to give you the background first. Before I met your mum, I was going out with this other girl for a bit, Trisha Martin. We weren't together for very long; she was making plans to travel around the Far East for a year, so we both knew that it was going to be a short-lived romance, you know?'

I nodded. Where was this going? 'OK . . .'

Dad looked down at the floor. 'So Trisha went abroad, and I met your mum fairly shortly afterwards, and that was that. I hadn't heard from Trisha in years. And then, a few weeks ago, I got a letter from her out of the blue.'

Ah yes, that would be the 3 a.m. in the garden letter.

'It was . . . Well, it contained some surprising news. Trisha had written to confess that there was something she'd kept from me all these years. And she probably would have kept it from me forever but . . . he wanted to make contact, you see, and she couldn't stop him, you know?' Dad was rambling. 'I mean, it was a complete shock, honestly.'

'It *was* a shock at first,' Mum cut in – the voice of calm. 'But now we've both had a chance to process it, we think this could be something exciting – something wonderful, even – for our family.'

'*What* was a shock? *What* are you excited about?' I was probably sounding slightly hysterical by now, but as soon as the question left my lips, I knew what the answer was going to be. 'Oh!'

Dad looked me in the eye, a hesitant smile on his face. 'Jack . . . you have a brother.'

THE BROTHER

Lewis. Lewis, my brother. My brother . . . Lewis. No matter how many times I repeated the words, they just didn't seem connected to me somehow. I couldn't get my head around the revelation that I had a brother I'd never even heard about before now, let alone met. Lewis, who, according to Dad, was twenty and lived in Cornwall, and who'd dropped out of university and spent most of his time riding a surfboard. Lewis, whose Facebook page I'd been unable to resist a sly peek at when curiosity got the better of me – not that it gave much away – and who now wanted to come and meet Mum and Dad, and me.

On the one hand, I was relieved that Mum and Dad were united and back on the same page, especially after all that strange behaviour before I left for Total. On the other hand, the news was a massive curveball; one that had left me feeling unsettled.

A couple of days later, once I'd slept off my epic jet lag, I told Ella about Lewis. We were sitting on the grass at 'our spot' in the park, the sun was warm, the birds were singing and everything was right with the world. Except that to me, everything felt like it was upside down. As I spilled the story, Ella's mouth fell open. She took hold of my hand and held it, tight. 'Oh my God! Why didn't you call me when you first found out?'

I shrugged. 'I just needed a bit of time to take it in, and to talk it through with Mum and Dad.'

The truth was, I'd felt like things had been more than a little frosty between Ella and me after the stuff with Ethan and the pictures of Harriet and me all over the internet. I wanted to give that some distance before I moved on to a whole new drama.

'How come nobody knew about him?' Ella asked.

'That's the insane part,' I said. 'Trisha, Dad's ex-girlfriend, found out that she was pregnant really late on, and she didn't tell Dad. By then she'd met someone new on her travels, and she ended up marrying him. Lewis grew up thinking his stepdad was his real dad. And then his stepdad was killed in Iraq when Lewis was twelve.'

'God, that's so sad,' Ella said. 'Poor Lewis.'

We were both silent for a few moments. Then she said, 'Jack, this is crazy! But . . . in a good way, right? I mean, I can't believe you've spent your whole life thinking you were an only child – and all along you've had a brother living just a few hours away!'

I was a little taken aback by her enthusiasm. 'I suppose . . . I mean, Mum and Dad are really excited about it. And I'm curious, I guess.'

'Of course,' Ella said. 'Who wouldn't be?'

'I've been wondering if he's anything like me, you

know? I found him on Facebook and he doesn't *look* like me.'

'Maybe he takes after his mum,' Ella ventured. 'Plus he's a bit older.'

'He's not that much older,' I said. 'He's only twenty.' I lay back on the grass and put my hands behind my head. 'I'm not sure I know how I feel about it yet. I mean, I'm happy for Dad and everything . . . It's just weird, you know?'

Ella lay down next to me. 'You must be a bit excited, though. Are you going to meet him?'

'He's coming up to Hertfordshire soon, so . . . I guess I am,' I said.

I thought back to the conversation I'd had with Dad that morning. The one where he'd told me that Lewis wanted to meet us all. He'd tried to play it down, but I could hear the excitement in his voice. Now that it was out in the open, he wanted to get to know Lewis – of course he did. Lewis was his son, after all.

'I have to say, I'm a little bit jealous,' Ella said, shaking me out of my thoughts. 'I've always wanted a brother or sister. You must have too, when you were growing up?'

'Not really. The idea of having a sibling just didn't occur to me,' I said. 'I was always happy with it being me, Mum and Dad.'

'Well, I think it's awesome,' she said. 'He's probably a really lovely guy. Maybe meeting him will be like . . . I don't know, making a new best friend or something.'

'Yeah, maybe.'

'Try not to be negative about it, babe. This is a good thing!'

'I'm not being negative,' I said, annoyed. 'I'm just . . . still working out how I feel about it.'

I wanted to be enthusiastic about Lewis, I really did, but I couldn't shake the weird feeling that a stranger had just been dropped into the midst of our family. Ella was usually so intuitive that I didn't have to explain how I was feeling to her; she always got it. But as far as this topic went, we were in different postcodes.

'Look, let's not say anything to the others about it,' I said. 'We've got so much other stuff to concentrate on and there's no need for me to cause any more drama. We all need clear heads when we start filming with Owl TV next week.'

Ella leaned down and kissed me on the nose. 'OK, babe.'

We sat for a little while longer in the park. We were both silent, lost in our thoughts, which was unusual; normally we couldn't stop talking. I found myself thinking about how Lewis might feel about all this. Was he angry that Trisha hadn't told him about Dad sooner? Was he genuinely excited to meet us? It sounded, from what Dad had said, that he was. Would this feel like a new beginning for him? I needed to see it as a new beginning too, I knew that. But I couldn't shake how strange the whole thing felt. Almost like an invasion.

Twenty minutes after we left the park, Ella and I arrived at Austin's place for our first big meet since Total. On the agenda today: the battle plan for *Emerge*, GenNext's first venture into the world of television. *This* was why I needed a clear head.

Miles greeted us at the front door with a dramatic eye-roll/ head-shake combo.

'Thank God you're here,' he said. 'He's getting on my nerves.'

'Who is?' I laughed, and he motioned towards the kitchen.

'My brother. I think he's losing it. Do what you can, Jack, but all hope might be lost.'

'And the others?' I asked.

Miles shrugged. 'They're all downstairs.'

Ella looked at me and raised an eyebrow. 'Jack, why don't you go and see what's up with Austin? I'll head down and see what the gang are up to.'

'That doesn't exactly sound like a fair deal to me!' I said, but she'd already disappeared down the stairs.

Poking my head round the kitchen door, I discovered Austin at the table, still in his pyjama bottoms and a Clash T-shirt, drinking a giant mug of coffee and staring into space. I stepped in and cleared my throat.

'Oh hey, J,' he said. 'I was going to come down to the meeting soon.' He looked pale and bleary-eyed. Tired? Or had he been crying?

'In your pyjamas?' I asked.

He looked down at his rumpled clothes. 'Sorry. I guess I'm not really in the right frame of mind at the moment for loads of gushing about the new TV show.'

'Has something happened?' I asked. 'No offence, but you look kind of . . . rough.'

'Long story, but me and Jess are no more.' He swallowed hard.

'Oh mate. I'm sorry.'

'And before you ask, it was me who ended it.'

I pulled out a chair and sat opposite him. His head was down and he was staring at the table, looking totally miserable. I was still feeling pretty emotionally raw myself, but Austin was clearly in pain; I needed to step up and be a good friend to him.

'So why did you end it?' I said gently. 'I mean, I knew it was on the cards after our conversation at the festival. How did Jess take it? Was she OK?'

'Not really,' he said, pouring himself yet another mug of coffee. 'When we got back from California, I just felt like I didn't have the energy for it any more. It was too intense, Jack. Every conversation between us felt like a battle. The trouble is, now I've actually done it, I've got all this guilt for hurting her and I feel . . . Oh, I don't know.'

'Go on, mate. You can say what you like to me; I'm not going to judge you,' I said.

'I feel a bit ashamed, J. Like I'm a massive screw-up and a failure for not being able to make it work. She was my first proper girlfriend, you know? I still don't know if I've done the right thing.'

'You're not a screw-up, Austin,' I said softly. 'It's not your fault that things didn't work out between you. Sometimes it's just . . . it's just not meant to be, that's all.'

Austin nodded slowly. He didn't look convinced. 'I know you're right. It's just . . . on top of that I've been feeling really anxious and uncertain again since we got back from Total, especially after a few of the choice things Jess said to me when we broke up.'

'Like?'

'Like I'm a loser and I can't see anything through and probably never will.'

'Nice.'

'Everything seemed so great out there in California, but being back in the UK, and just about to start work with Owl TV . . . I don't feel like I've got any confidence at the moment.'

We were both quiet while I tried to think of what I could say to guide him out of the horrible place he was stuck in.

'Look, why don't we go out this week?' I suggested. 'Not with everyone; just the two of us. We haven't done that for ages.'

It was true. Over the past year, since we'd both had girl-friends, we'd hardly ever hung out like we used to. The light came on in his eyes at my suggestion, as if somebody had just flicked a switch.

'Yeah, that sounds cool,' he said. 'I'm not sure if I'll be amazing company, though.'

'Hey, what's new?' I cracked, and he finally raised a smile.

'Look, why don't you get dressed, and then we'll go and see what the score is with our new TV show. We should get down there before Sai and the girls start calling all the shots.'

Austin slid his chair out from under him, drained the last of his coffee and stood up. 'Good call, J. We don't want that, do we? I'll see you down there.'

As I headed along the hall, I could hear the voices of my friends, loud and animated, coming from HQ. They were making plans, eagerly plotting our next moves, and of course, I was expected to be a part of that. I *wanted* to be a part of it. It was just that there was so much uncertainty flying around in my head at that moment: uncertainty about Owl TV and what it might mean for GenNext, about the surprise new addition to my family, and about my best friend, who was clearly dealing with a lot more than he'd originally let on. And yes, I was even feeling a bit weird about me and Ella. I told myself it was nothing serious, but I'd always felt like we were on the same page, and now suddenly it seemed like . . . like we weren't.

I took a deep breath as I descended the stairs.

It's going to be fine, Jack.

THE VISITOR

On the Sunday of Lewis's visit, I felt twitchy. Unsettled. Up in my bedroom, sitting on my bed and intently focused on my MacBook, I flicked from one YouTube video to another: funny, silly, annoying, informative. Anything to stop my mind running riot and worrying about how today was going to pan out. It was crazy, really. There was nothing I could do about the situation. This was happening whether I liked it or not . . . and it was happening at any minute. It wasn't just about me, either. Today was Dad's day and I wanted it to work out well for him, too. True, he and Lewis had spoken on the phone a fair bit by now, but meeting in person was different. Whatever happened, I intended to be supportive.

Finally I shut my computer off, got up and went to the mirror, looking critically at my reflection. I was wearing my favourite worn jeans and a 'GenNext Total Youth Takeover' T-shirt, and I had a couple of days' worth of stubble. Did I look OK? Decent, without looking too try-hard? What exactly was the right outfit for meeting your long-lost brother anyway? What would *he* be wearing? I was at a disadvantage,

I decided. I'd only seen a couple of photographs of him that Dad had shown me, and his minimalist Facebook page. Lewis, on the other hand, was bound to have looked at the GenNext channel. He'd probably made up his mind about me already.

A roar outside the house shook me out of my thoughts. Peering out of the window, I could see that a motorbike had stopped right outside our house. The rider dismounted, took off his helmet and strode towards our front gate. I pressed closer to the window to get a better look. Oh wow! This was him. This was my brother.

The doorbell rang. 'Come on in, Lewis,' I heard Dad say. 'We're so glad you could make it.'

By the time I got to the bottom of the stairs, Dad was shaking Lewis's hand warmly, and Mum was giving him a friendly peck on the cheek. Then Lewis glanced up, and I got my first proper look at my new brother.

The first thing I noticed was how slimly built he was, but sinewy and suntanned with it, his bleached blonde hair long and messy. He was wearing a flesh-tunnel earring in one ear and a silver ring in the other, and as he slipped off his leather jacket he revealed arms that were almost completely covered in brightly coloured tattoo sleeves, made up, for the most part, of sea, surf and beach designs.

'Hey. Jack, right?' he said.

'That's right,' I nodded, and shook his hand. 'Good to meet you, Lewis.'

'Likewise, man. Wow. I can't quite believe this, can you?' he said, looking around him. 'It's all a bit mental, right?'

'Yeah, it's pretty crazy,' I agreed.

There were a few seconds of awkward silence before Mum

suggested we all move through to the living room and sit somewhere more comfortable. Five minutes later we were swapping chit-chat about how nice our house was, how Lewis's journey from Cornwall had been (windy, from the sound of it), and just how much he looked like Dad. I looked from one to the other, trying to convince myself that it wasn't the case, but the truth was, they did look alike. I'd always been much more like my mum, but Lewis definitely took after Dad in his younger days. It was all a bit odd.

'Right,' Mum said, getting up from the armchair. 'I'm going to make a drink before you pass out from thirst, Lewis. What would everyone like?'

Dad and I said, 'Coffee' in unison.

'Do you have any herbal tea?' Lewis asked. 'I'm trying not to drink caffeine.'

'We might have some chamomile gathering dust at the back of the cupboard,' Mum said, wrinkling her brow. 'I don't tend to buy much herbal tea because the boys both think it tastes like dishwater, even though I like it.'

'I like to fuel my body with natural stuff wherever possible,' Lewis said. 'It's so important to be aware of what we're consuming, don't you think?' Mum and Dad both nodded seriously, as if they, too, were experts on health food rather than the caffeine and M&S ready-meal devotees I knew them to be.

'I've recently given up eating meat because I can't justify the slaughter of animals for food any more,' Lewis went on.

'But you're OK with it for leather jackets?' I said, smiling.

I'd meant it as a joke, but Lewis pursed his lips and said nothing.

Once Mum had distributed teas and coffees, she and Dad started asking Lewis all sorts of questions about where he lived and what he liked to do. He answered them with a relaxed smile that never left his face; in fact, he seemed totally comfortable, like he regularly drove up to see a new family he'd never met before. I, by contrast, was trying to stop my right foot from nervously tapping the floor.

'And did you bring the photos you mentioned?' Dad said. 'I'm dying to see those.'

'Oh yeah, man,' Lewis said. 'I've found some cool ones that you're gonna love.' He grabbed a handful of prints from his scuffed backpack and spread them out on the coffee table.

Dad smiled, looking down at them. 'These are great. God, look at you!'

I glanced down at the pictures. There were a few of Lewis as a young kid – one in a park with a man I assumed was his stepdad, one sitting on Santa's lap, where he looked comically miserable – plus a few teenage snaps with him and his mum, Trisha, and four or five more recent beach shots with Lewis proudly holding his surfboard. Dad was looking at them with an expression of awe, and it struck me how completely mad this must be for him, too.

As Mum and Dad leafed through the photos, I asked Lewis the question I'd been dying to know the answer to.

'So how did you feel, Lewis? You know, when your mum told you about Dad?'

Lewis sipped his herbal tea. 'I was really angry with her at first. I mean, I just couldn't understand why she hadn't told me before that Ian, the man I'd always thought was my dad, wasn't my natural father. I could understand her not telling me when I was a little kid, because it's just too much to take in, but Ian was such a good dad to me that she never wanted to rock the boat and so she just let the secret drift on. She said it never felt like the right time to tell me. Then, after Ian died, I was a little bit . . . well, troubled I suppose you'd call it, and she thought that telling me the truth then might make matters worse.'

'So why *did* she decide to tell you when she did?' I asked. 'Why now?'

'She actually told me about six months ago. I'd been going through a bit of a rough patch since I dropped out of uni. It just wasn't for me, you know? And I'd sort of lost my way. I didn't feel like I had any direction and I was going out and partying too much and . . . Well, Mum's a bit of a hippy at heart, and she thought it might help me spiritually.'

'And did it?' Dad asked.

'Not at first,' Lewis said with a laugh. 'I went even more nuts, finding out my dad wasn't my dad and that someone else was. Then one morning I woke up facedown on the beach, hung-over and freezing my arse off, and this thought just popped into my head. It was, like, Oh, OK! So I've got an old man I didn't know I had. I think I need to check him out. And that was it.'

'Yes, not so much of the old, thanks,' Dad laughed. 'Well, I'm glad that you did decide to check us out, Lewis.'

'And how are things now, with your mum?' Mum said. 'Finally telling you the truth – it must have been a very hard thing for you both to deal with.'

Lewis nodded. 'We're fine – we had a couple of really

good talks. Once I'd got in touch with Paul, the anger just went away. Me and Mum and are totally cool now, man.'

What was with all the 'man's? God, if Trisha was a bit of a hippy, then Lewis was definitely a chip off the old block.

Sunday lunch (a vegetarian roast, because Mum had thought to check ahead) was a reasonably relaxed affair. At first. It was when Dad brought up the subject of GenNext that things started to go a bit pear-shaped.

'Of course, Lewis, you must have seen Jack's stuff online. His videos, vlogs and everything. He's built up a brilliant business with his mates and we're really proud of him.' I knew what Dad was trying to do. We'd been talking about Lewis and his life since the moment he arrived, and this was his way of trying to make me feel included.

'Yeah, you mentioned that on the phone,' Lewis said, nodding. 'It sounds amazing, but I'm not really into all that stuff. I'm a bit of a technophobe, to be honest. Actually, I don't use a computer at all these days.'

'Really?' My voice shot up much higher than I'd have liked. 'You mean you just use your phone instead?'

'What, this?' Lewis dug around in his pocket and pulled out a piece of technology that looked like it should have been in the Science Museum. 'I haven't even got a smart-phone. I hate the bloody things. I just think people have become such slaves to the screen in the last ten years.'

'You're not wrong there, Lewis,' Mum laughed. 'The girls who work in my salon might as well have their phones surgically attached to their hands.'

'Yeah, but it's information, isn't it?' I said. 'It's how we know what's going on in the world and how we find enter-tainment and how we communicate.'

'Yes, or we could just read a book or talk to somebody face-to-face,' Lewis said assertively. 'I think we all need to look up a bit more. See what's actually going on with our own eyes, rather than through the lens of somebody else's phone camera. And shouldn't we be forming our own opin-ions rather than being bombarded with what other people think on Facebook and Twitter?'

'I can see what you mean by that,' I said, trying to be agreeable even though I could feel myself getting irritated, 'but there must be a happy medium. I mean, you're on Facebook, aren't you?'

'My page is up but I haven't updated it for aeons,' Lewis said. 'At one time I was actually really into technology and computers.' He laughed as though he was embarrassed. 'That's what I was studying at uni before I dropped out, and I was obsessed with it all.'

'So what changed your mind?' Dad asked.

Lewis shrugged. 'Academia wasn't for me, man. I fell behind with my studies, was always getting hassled by the lecturers for not turning in projects, and by then I'd spent so long in front of one screen or another, I felt like it was eating my soul or something. I just couldn't hack it any more and went completely the other way. Nowadays I'd rather wake up and look outside or gaze across a beach than at a computer screen.'

'Well, I think that's a very refreshing way to look at it, Lewis,' Mum said tactfully, glancing at me.

'You never said on the phone that you'd studied computers at uni,' Dad said. 'Jack has always been so brilliant with computers and technology, but I suppose it's a case of each to their own, right, Jack?'

'I suppose,' I said.

'I'm just over all that,' Lewis said, as if he'd evolved into a higher being. 'I get more joy out of being outdoors: riding a wave, or my motorbike.'

'Now that's something I can understand,' Dad said. 'I used to be bike crazy when I was your age. I had a Suzuki Katana. Very nice.'

'That's a cool ride,' Lewis said.

I wasn't sure exactly what a Suzuki Katana was, but I made a mental note to google it at the earliest opportunity. In fact, I knew nothing about motorbikes; they didn't interest me in the slightest, and I'd never paid that much attention whenever Dad started enthusing about them.

'That thing used to terrify the life out of me,' Mum said. 'If it wasn't for me, I think your dad would still be riding around on one now, Lewis.'

I was jarred by that. Mum using 'your dad' so casually like that to Lewis, in the way that she would to me.

'I'd love to go out and have a look at your bike, Lewis,' Dad said.

'Sure! You could take it for a spin up and down the street if you like,' Lewis said.

Dad's eyes lit up in response. 'I'd love that!' he said with more enthusiasm than I'd heard him express for anything in ages. He looked at Mum, who was clearing the plates away.

Mum rolled her eyes. 'Oh, here we go. Wear a helmet if you're going to get on that thing!' she said.

I watched Dad, smiling as he got up from the table and

headed towards the front door, with Lewis following, and I felt confused . . . maybe slightly jealous. On the one hand, the day was going really well. Dad had been apprehensive about meeting Lewis, but as it turned out I could tell that both he and Mum liked him a lot. On the other hand, Lewis and I had totally failed to find any common ground. In fact, we were as different as chalk and cheese. Now that Dad and Lewis had discovered a shared love of motorbikes, I felt this weird sensation that I was somehow on the outside, looking in, and it was growing by the second. Was it possible that Lewis would end up having more in common with Dad than I did?

Dad and Lewis were gone for ages. They'd taken the bike out for a proper spin, Mum said. Back up in my room, I lay on my bed, finger hovering over my phone as I sat mentally toing and froing with the notion of calling Ella to tell her about our family lunch. I'd already pinged a couple of WhatsApps to her earlier in the afternoon, and any other time when something of this magnitude was happening I'd have been straight on the phone to her, but right then and there, something was making me stall. Maybe I was worried because I knew she was going to ask me how I felt about it all, and I didn't have a definitive answer to that question yet. Or maybe I just wasn't ready for her enthusiasm about the whole thing while I still had doubts and concerns flying at me from all angles. Plus, we'd be together in London in a few days once filming started on *Emerge*. Maybe I should just wait till then.

'Jack! Jack, love!' There was no time to chew it over as Mum yelled at me from the bottom of the stairs. 'Your dad and Lewis are back. Do you want to come down for a cuppa?'

I exited my bedroom and headed down the stairs, plastering on a smile. 'How was the biking, guys? You didn't kill yourself or anyone else then, Dad?'

'It was pretty close,' Lewis laughed.

'Oh, you must be joking!' Dad punched Lewis's arm playfully. 'Admit it, you were impressed to see how well I can handle a bike.'

He put his arm around Lewis's shoulders and I felt myself freeze on the spot. The spin on Lewis's bike had clearly been a galvanising experience for both of them.

'Lewis is going to stay over tonight, Jack,' Dad said. 'It's too far to do that journey twice in one day.'

'Oh, OK!' I said, reaching the bottom of the stairs.

'Maybe the two of you could do something this evening,' Mum suggested, looking between me and Lewis. I sensed that she'd figured out we hadn't exactly clicked yet, and was trying to rectify the situation. 'Take Lewis for a walk around the town or something, Jack. Show him the area.'

'Er, yeah, why not? I could take you to one of the pubs I never go in, Lewis.' I had to make the effort, for Dad's sake more than my own, although I had no bloody idea what we were going to talk about, and I could see that Lewis wasn't exactly jumping up and down at the prospect of the two of us going out together either.

'Sure thing, man. That would be cool,' he said with a nod.

I swallowed hard. Yep. This was happening, all right. There was a new member of the family . . . and I was going to have to get used to it.

THE SHOW

3 Mills studios were built on the site of an old mill and disused distillery on an island in the middle of the river Lea in east London. And four days after Lewis's visit, there we all were, gathered in its swish reception at 7 a.m. on a bright Thursday morning in September, ready for the first day's shoot on our brand-new TV show: Ella, Ava, AJ, Austin, Sai and me. This was *very* cool.

Ava, as usual, was the brightest among us at that time of the morning. 'Another day, another adventure. Are we all feeling good about this, people?'

'I'm ready for anything,' Sai said. He was wearing a shirt so tight that literally every muscle was on display. Since he and Lily had got together, he'd become even more shameless about showing off his physique. Usually Austin would have been mercilessly ripping it out of him for the shirt, but he'd been pretty quiet today so far.

'I think I'll need a coffee or five before I know whether I'm feeling good about anything, Ava,' he said.

'Well, you won't have to be here this early *every* morning,'

AJ assured him. 'Plus the apartments are only fifteen minutes' walk from here, so it's not exactly a big commute, is it?'

AJ had found us two apartments on the same floor of a cool new building in Wapping, overlooking the water – one for the girls and one for us boys – and we were all set to live there for the duration of the show, to save us the hassle of travelling back and forth from Hertfordshire every day during a manic three weeks of filming. Mind you, moving out of my family home straight after Lewis's visit hadn't been the easiest thing in the world. I felt like it wasn't the best time to be leaving, with such a massive change happening in the family. Of course, Mum and Dad were totally cool with it, but being down in London, miles from them, I couldn't help but feel a little bit like I was bailing on the situation.

On the journey to London I'd had the chance to tell Ella about Lewis's visit, although I kept it all quite light and didn't go into too much detail about the awkwardness I'd felt between us.

'You see; I knew you'd be fine with him,' Ella had said, hugging me in the back of the car that was speeding us towards the metropolis. 'I bet you end up becoming really close.'

In the end, I'd smiled and agreed because I knew that was what she wanted to hear, and I really didn't want to start another disagreement. Not when we were just a few hours away from diving into the TV show. All that other stuff could wait.

'It's like the first day at a new school when you don't know what to expect,' Ella said now, as we followed one of the show runners through the massive studio building towards our set. She was right, and it was quite an exciting feeling. GenNext had done a ton of cool stuff since we'd started, but nothing like this. We were buzzing with anticipation – well, all of us except Austin. You'd think he was about to be wheeled into surgery for a major operation rather than embarking on his own TV show.

'Dude, relax,' Ava said, noticing his worryingly grey complexion. 'You're not even going to be on camera.'

Austin smiled nervously. 'Yeah, I know. It's all just very . . . big.'

'We'll be all right,' Sai said. 'If we can pull off a stage at a major festival, we can do this.'

I knew only too well that Austin's fears ran much deeper than just worrying about the show; it was something that he and I had been either talking or messaging about in the days leading up to our departure for London. I was trying hard to be a good mate and to build up his confidence, but he wasn't in a good place at the moment. The fact that he hadn't been able to work things out with Jess had left him doubting every other part of his life, and he was having trouble believing that he was good enough to be involved in a show like *Emerge*. I was hoping that working on the show would remind him of how good he was, like Total had. But I'd never seen him looking as anxious as he did today – about everything.

Ella, on the other hand, seemed totally at ease with being in the studio. Her eyes were shining and she looked at home and relaxed. I couldn't help thinking that maybe this really was where she belonged. In a proper studio, doing 'real TV'.

'Look, Austin, it's nothing that we haven't done a thousand

times before; just on a bigger scale,' she said, striding along confidently behind the runner. 'It'll be absolutely fine, I promise.'

'You're bang-on, Ella,' AJ agreed. 'I spoke to Olympia after the meeting last night and she has every confidence that *Emerge* is going to be a huge hit.'

I thought back to the previous night's get-together with Olympia and Ethan in the swanky surroundings of Ham Yard Hotel in Soho. Olympia had referred to the meeting as 'the big briefing', and it consisted of her talking us through every single thought and idea she had for what she called the 'tonality and trajectory' of the show, at lightning speed. I have to say, it all sounded pretty good, even with Ethan sitting by her side with a perpetual self-satisfied grin on his face.

'Guys, forget the fact that I'm the exec producer,' Olympia had told us. 'Don't be afraid to push your ideas forward; that's what I need from you. If I think what you're giving me is lame, I'll tell you straight and we move on. That way we don't waste time and everyone wins.'

There was something refreshingly honest about Olympia Shaw: she loved the GenNext brand and she wasn't afraid to admit she wanted a piece of it. And there was plenty of creative leeway for us, too. We discussed how the show would be shot and edited, and how GenNext should lead the way as far as online and social-media content went, and Olympia seemed agreeable to all of it. I guess that had been my main concern at the start of all this: that we'd end up getting pushed into something that wasn't really us. But by the end of that very long meeting, I was convinced that *Emerge* was going to work . . . and that despite my misgivings about Ethan, it was going to be awesome.

We all fell silent as the runner we were following led us out onto a full-size sound stage, surrounded by white brick walls with bars of light hanging from high ceilings, and massive cameras everywhere. It was somewhat bigger and grander than Austin's mum's basement, that was for sure. I felt dwarfed as I stared around the cavernous room, but I convinced myself I'd get used to it, just like I had the festival stage. One corner of the studio was set up like a smart lounge, with an expensive-looking L-shaped couch and some stylish armchairs. Lights and cables surrounded it, so I assumed this area was part of the set, rather than just some-where for us to hang out between takes – probably where some of the interviews would take place.

Standing in the midst of it all was Ethan, waving us over. He shook hands with me, AJ, Austin and Sai, and then gave Ava and Ella a hug, with Ella's hug including an unnecessary kiss on the cheek, I noticed.

As we all got settled on the various chairs in the lounge area to the side of the sound stage, Ethan held court in front of us. 'So, guys, listen up! I just want to run through what's happening today.'

I was sure he was loving this. The GenNext team, who'd once turned him down as a potential presenter, now under his direction. He seemed about a thousand times more confi-dent than he had when we'd first met him. He even looked different, with some decent clothes and a haircut a bit too similar to my own for my liking. It was clear that landing this gig and being able to rule the roost had given the guy a massive boost.

'You all met Glen, our director, at the briefing last night,' he went on, motioning towards the short man standing next to him, who was peering at us through a mop of teased black hair.

'Hey, guys! Fabulous to see you all again,' Glen said. 'I must say you're all looking great. Jack, loving the red shirt, babes. That's really gonna pop on camera.'

'Cheers, Glen,' I smiled.

Sai leaned towards me and stage-whispered, 'He wants you.' I elbowed him in the ribs before Ethan went on with his opening speech.

'Today we're seeing three artists and bands, and shooting two or three takes of each one. Ella and Jack, you'll be shooting intros, links and interviews with the artists.'

'In your own adorable style, of course,' Glen interjected.

'You just tell us where you need us to stand and we'll be fine,' Ella smiled.

Ethan continued, picking up momentum. 'Ava and Austin, obviously you'll be working with Glen on the overall look and feel of the show: camera shots, set-ups, that kind of thing, and Sai will be taking the reins in post-production and editing, along with our own team, of course. Does that all make sense?'

'Perfect sense,' Sai said. Austin nodded, too. The worried expression was still on his face, but he seemed to be relaxing just a bit. I hoped that working with Glen, who seemed like a good bloke, would help him to chill out.

Before we headed off to wardrobe and make-up, Ethan

finished rattling off the long list of details that we'd already gone over a dozen times in the meeting, but as he was obviously enjoying wielding power, I just smiled and kept my gob shut. To be honest, I was too busy wondering (a) how someone could have gone through such a massive personality transplant in such a short space of time and (b) how come nobody else apart from me seemed to have noticed this fact. I mean, this was in no way the same geek who'd conveniently run into us at the festival. Even the way he carried himself was completely different. Weird. Bloody weird.

By midday, I felt like I was getting into the swing of things. In fact, apart from being under the glaring lights of the studio and getting used to the stop-start-repeat nature of TV filming, it didn't really feel all that different from what we did at GenNext. After all, an interview was an interview, right? And Ella and I seemed to click quickly and neatly into our on-screen repartee with no problem at all, despite the awkward moments between us over the past couple of weeks.

We'd already filmed one artist – a girl called Ace Love, who played guitar and wrote all her own songs, which were very melancholic and made the average Adele ballad sound like a carnival tune. Still, she was super-talented and very sweet, and Ella nailed the post-performance interview with her, gently encouraging her to talk about the fact that she'd once been homeless and that music had been the thing that got her back on her feet. Olympia, who'd been scrutinising quietly in the background all morning, was very chuffed, telling us that that kind of interview was exactly what she was looking for. So all in all, I thought we were off to a pretty great start.

'OK! Jack, Ella, we're going to shoot the link in to the next band,' Ethan shouted over at me as I grabbed a coffee. 'Sai, are we all set up and ready?'

'Two minutes,' Sai called from where the three-piece band were setting up. 'Just fixing a couple of things.'

Glen was standing behind me at the coffee machine and he didn't look all that happy.

'You OK, mate?' I said, sipping my almond-milk latte. 'All going well?'

'Fine, dear,' he said. 'Apart from the fact that I'm not sure who's directing this bloody thing: me or the little prince over there.'

He motioned towards Ethan and I almost spat out my coffee. 'Oh, right. You don't think much of him, then?' It was a strange relief to find someone else who didn't think the sun shone out of Ethan's arse.

He shrugged. 'There's often a fine line between associate producers and directors on a show like this, but I tell you, this guy takes the—'

He was interrupted by Ethan calling across the room. 'Glen! Are you all set?'

Glen rolled his eyes at me and swept past me towards the set-up. 'And to think I turned down *The Great British Bake Off* for this,' he sighed.

The Getaway were a group of good-looking young guys from Liverpool. I'd watched a few of their videos on YouTube the previous night and thought they were very cool. They had a great raw sound that reminded me a bit of the Arctic

Monkeys, and it was obvious that girls tuning into the show were going to love them. The idea for the next link was that Ella and I would do it together, talking a bit about the band's formation and history before they launched into their first number. We were only about thirty seconds into it when—

'OK, CUT. Let's hold it there a moment!'

I was literally mid-sentence when Ethan yelled over at us.

'Can we just hold it for a sec? Thanks,' Glen added wearily.

'Jack, can I have a quick word?' Ethan said, beckoning me over.

'Yeah, of course.' I looked at Ella and shrugged, then headed over to where Ethan was standing peering into the monitor.

'What's up?' I said.

'We're thinking this intro link would be better if it was just you,' Ethan said.

'What, without Ella?' I said. I glanced over at Ava, who was standing behind the camera, but she looked as confused as I was.

Ethan nodded, narrowing his eyes. 'Mmm, I think so, yeah. That's what we were thinking, isn't it, Glen?'

Glen opened his mouth to speak, but just then Ella walked over.

'What's happening, Ethan?' she asked.

'It's just that we think Jack looks very strong here, but Ella, you're not really coming across.'

'Not really coming across how?' I said, irked.

'Don't get me wrong, I'm not casting aspersions on anyone's presenting skills,' Ethan said. 'That straight-to-the-point, robust sort of approach you're going for is great, Jack.

I just think it's making Ella's delivery seem a little bit quiet in comparison, and it'll be stronger if you do the link on your own.'

I looked at Ella, who was frowning.

'What do you reckon?' I asked.

'Well, you did talk over me a couple of times,' she said with a shrug. 'Maybe Ethan's got a point.'

'Did I?'

'You did, Jack,' Ethan nodded. I gritted my teeth.

Ella turned to Ethan and Glen. 'Look, I'm happy for Jack to present solo if you think it's stronger. I'm all about what's best for the show.'

'Sorry, Ella,' Ethan said, rubbing her shoulder.

'No worries,' Ella said, with another shrug.

'Ready to go again?' Glen asked.

I took a deep breath and headed back to my mark, a white gaffer-tape cross on the floor, a few feet in front of the band. 'I'm ready.'

'OK, rolling,' Ava shouted from behind the camera.

'When you're ready, Jack,' Glen said.

Once the band had done their bit, we all gathered in the lounge-style area to set up for the next shot. Olympia had arrived back at the studio after a lunch meeting. 'How's it all going, guys?'

'Really good,' Ava said, beaming. 'We got some great stuff this morning. We're just setting up to interview The Getaway after their performance.'

'I'm happy to see that you're keeping it quirky,' Olympia said.

'That's what we do best,' Sai replied, grinning.

'Fabulous! Loving the enthusiasm.'

'Actually, I've had a brainwave about this next section,' Ethan said, rubbing his stubble – another new acquisition of his since I'd let mine grow. 'Just thinking outside the box, as you'd say, Olympia. Why don't I step in and do some of the post-performance interviews with Ella?' Olympia raised an eyebrow, and Ethan glanced over at me. 'It's just that Jack is very dynamic on the intro links, whereas Ella has got that amazing way of relating to the artists, which I think the audience will love. If I co-present with her, I think her personality will really be able to shine through. After all, we made a pretty good team at Total.'

'Er . . . I'm not so sure about this,' I said. 'Everyone loves the way Ella and I do interviews together. It works because I go for the humour while she asks the more serious questions.'

'I totally get that,' Ethan said, 'but it means that sometimes Ella ends up looking like the straight woman to your funny-man routine.'

Funny man?

'I never really thought about it like that,' Ella said.

'Look, don't get me wrong,' Ethan went on. 'I think that works great online, but maybe it's time to mix things up.'

'You *are* looking especially fine on all the intro links, Jack,' Ava said. 'I say let's give it a go. If it doesn't work, then we'll go back to our usual way.'

'Fine by me,' Olympia said, turning to answer her constantly ringing phone.

'Great,' Ethan smiled.

I felt completely stumped. I knew that if I kicked off

about this I'd look like I was being difficult. I mean, it wasn't like Ethan was saying I was crap – in fact it was almost the opposite – but he'd somehow convinced everyone I was over-shadowing my girlfriend on camera and that he and Ella might be a better fit. I had to hand it to him: whatever he was up to, he was doing a bloody great job. I looked at Ella to gauge what her reaction was, but she was busy getting ready for her next shot.

Ethan smiled affably at me. 'Jack, you and Austin can pop off to catering and grab lunch now if you want to. You must be starving.'

'Actually, I am hungry,' Austin said, nudging me. 'Let's eat, J.'

At that moment, eating seemed preferable to watching Ethan cosying up on a couch next to my girlfriend, so I followed reluctantly.

As I passed Glen on my way out of the studio, he turned to me with a raised eyebrow and I nodded back at him. Yeah, I thought, Glen knows what I know. He knows that this isn't going to be easy for him . . . or for me.

THE BETRAYAL

And so it went on. For the next three days I flew solo with most of my filming while Ethan monopolised Ella. And was I dying to put a stop to it all and confront Ethan? Tell him that I was on to him? You bet I was . . . but that was easier said than done. First off, we had just under three weeks to film and edit five forty-five-minute episodes, and so far it was actually going pretty smoothly and the set-up was working. Ella was great at the interviews, and as much as I loathed him, I could see that Ethan made a pretty good wing man for her. And I was happy with what I was doing too: all the spiel about the bands and artists before they performed, peppered with a few quirky critiques and comments. I was having fun. Sort of. What did I have to complain about, aside from the fact that I wasn't standing next to my girl-friend in any of the shots? Which brings me to the second reason I didn't kick off. Ella. We still hadn't really got back into synch after Total and then the news about Lewis, so the last thing I wanted to do was rock the boat. Plus, Ethan had cleverly arranged things so that if I complained, I'd look like I didn't want Ella to shine on screen. So I bit my tongue and got on with it.

By some miracle, we finished filming at a reasonable time on Saturday night, but there were no big GenNext plans to party our way around London on our first weekend there, even though we had Sunday off – we were all too knackered. No, I was going to slump on the sumptuous cream couch in our riverside apartment and watch something unchallenging with mild violence on the enormous Samsung 4K: *Independence Day: Resurgence* or *Guardians of the Galaxy* – something like that. I just needed to crash and relax, big time.

That afternoon I'd left the studio before anyone else. Ella still had some filming to do and said she'd text me when she was finished, but that she and Ava had an evening lined up of face packs, nail varnishing and whatever they could find on Netflix featuring either – or preferably both – of the Hemsworth brothers. Yeah, I thought, I'll give that one a miss. Sai, meanwhile, was taking Lily for dinner at one of the restaurants in the Shard – very nice – so it would just be me and Austin in the apartment, which I was looking forward to. The night after Lewis's visit we'd had our boys' night out together back in Hertfordshire, and I think it had helped him to get a lot of his worries off his chest. Since we'd arrived in London he had got into the swing of things on set, but I could tell that he was still struggling a bit. It would be good to just hang out together and order some Thai food. Only . . . no Austin. Weird, as he'd said he was coming straight back to the apartment after filming, and my watch was telling me it was 8.40 p.m. By 9.30 I'd got used to the idea that I was going to be spending the evening on my own, semi-horizontal, watching Marvel superheroes battle it out.

It was just after 10 p.m. when the apartment door slammed shut suddenly, making me jump, and Austin walked into the living room, a strange expression on his face.

'You all right, Austin?' I said. 'Where have you been, mate? Have you eaten?'

'I'm not hungry,' he said abruptly.

Hang on – something was wrong here. I sat up on the sofa. 'Austin, what—'

'Well, cheers, mate. Thanks a million for that,' he said.

'What's the matter?' For a moment I thought he was going to cry, he looked so furious.

'Don't play all innocent, Jack. I know you said something,' he spat.

'Said something about what?' I was bewildered.

'To Ethan. I know you said something,' he said.

'Ethan? God, he's the last person I'd talk to about anything.'

'Clearly not in this case. It's bad enough feeling like this in the first place, but to end up with everyone talking about it behind my back . . . that's harsh, Jack.'

I got up and went over to him. 'Just tell me what Ethan said. I guarantee you this is all some sort of misunderstanding, whatever it is.'

'I don't think so.' Austin sidestepped me and sat down on the couch, arms folded, jaw tight, TV still raging in the background. 'He asked me if I was OK this afternoon. I don't know: maybe I wasn't on the best form, maybe I looked a bit fed up. Anyway, I said I hadn't been feeling great lately. He said he'd been chatting to you so he knew something was wrong.'

'What?!'

'He then went on to tell me that his Auntie Alison has mental-health issues. Apparently she had a nervous breakdown. Then he very kindly assured me it was nothing to be ashamed of and how impressed he was that I was working through it.'

I was gobsmacked. 'Austin, I swear—'

'Mental-health issues! I mean, God, who else have you been talking to? Ella, AJ?'

'No one! I never said anything to him, Austin. You've got to know that.'

Austin looked down at the floor, shaking his head. 'You must have, Jack, because I haven't said anything to another living soul. I don't get it. Do you realise how on the edge I've been while this show is going on?'

I was at a loss. Who else could have told Ethan about Austin's depression apart from me? Only it wasn't me. Jesus, I wouldn't trust that guy with my date of birth, let alone sensitive information about my best friend. I racked my brains for a moment when he might have heard Austin and me talking privately . . . but there was nothing.

'Look, Austin. Why don't we try to figure this out between us? Let's—'

'I'm not staying,' Austin said, getting up again. 'I just came back to tell you how pissed off I am.' He headed towards the door, shaking me off when I tried to grab his arm. 'Just keep out of my way for the time being.'

'Austin, this is all down to Ethan!' I said desperately. 'However he found out about this, it WASN'T from me!'

Austin spun around to face me. 'God, J, listen to yourself. Blaming Ethan is pretty low. You know, the weird thing is, he was really cool about it. Once I got over the fact that I was bloody mortified, we had a good chat. He actually sat down with me and tried to help me to understand why I'm feeling this way.'

'Austin, mate, you're not thinking straight. This is insane . . .' I almost bit my tongue.

'Perfect choice of words, Jack,' Austin said. And then he was out of the door, slamming it shut behind him.

I stood in the middle of the living room for a moment, trying to think straight. What the hell had just happened? In the whole time we'd been friends, Austin and I had never had a really big argument, not one that could hurt our friendship. I'd never seen him like that before: cold and angry, clearly hurt by my perceived betrayal. The thought that he believed I would betray his trust like that made me feel sick.

I sat back down on the couch, unsure what to do with myself. I WhatsApped Ella to see if she was awake, but the message went unread; clearly she and Ava had turned in early after their night of Hemsworth gorging. I tried calling Austin, but it went straight to voicemail. I WhatsApped him too, but like Ella the message went unread. He'd turned his phone off, or he was flat-out ignoring me.

God, how the hell had it come to this? How had Ethan managed to turn my best friend against me in one short afternoon? Something was very wrong with all this, and I needed to get to the bottom of it.

When I woke up the next morning, I felt like death. I'd been awake for hours tossing and turning after the scene with Austin, unable to believe that we'd fallen out, and that he could have trusted Ethan over me. I ended up drifting into an exhausted sleep, and by the time I got up it was after 11 a.m. A quick glance at the GenNext WhatsApp group informed me that Ella and Ava had headed into central London to grab brunch and do some shopping, and Sai was spending the morning with Lily. There was also a separate message from Ella saying, *Looking forward to seeing you later, sleepyhead!* ☺ ♥♥♥ This cheered me up slightly, until I noticed that Austin hadn't been in touch, and still hadn't even read my messages from the night before.

I came out of my room and looked around the flat. It was silent, and peeking into Austin's room I could see that his bed was still made. So he definitely hadn't come back after our argument, and it looked like I was spending at least the first half of my day off alone. Normally I would have been happy to have a bit of time to chill out, maybe catch up on some GenNext admin, but with the worry over my fight with Austin firmly lodged in my stomach, I was in serious need of distraction. Right, time to FaceTime Mum and Dad. I hadn't spoken to them for a couple of days, so I was due a catch-up. I wasn't sure I could bring myself to tell them about the argument – I knew that it would worry Mum – but maybe just chatting with them would cheer me up. I texted first to make sure they were at home and that they had the iPad on, gave them a couple of minutes, then sat at the desk in my room and called.

They were sitting in the kitchen at the breakfast bar when they picked up, both smiling happily, mugs of coffee in hand, and a pang of homesickness flickered through me.

'What's happening, Jack? Is it all going well?' Mum said

eagerly. 'I've seen your pictures on Instagram. It all looks very glamorous, I must say.'

'It's really good, Mum,' I said, not totally truthfully. 'The show's going well, and there's so much amazing talent.'

'That's terrific, son,' Dad said. 'You know how proud we are of you, don't you?'

I nodded, sensing a lump in my throat. 'I do, Dad.'

'Hey, your brother said to say hello, too,' he went on. Then he chuckled. 'That still sounds so weird, doesn't it? Brother? Anyway, Lewis says hi, and he hopes it's all going brilliantly.'

'Oh, right. That was nice of him. So what's he been up to down in Cornwall?' I asked nonchalantly.

'Well, we FaceTimed yesterday,' Mum said. 'He was in some surfing competition this week and he won, bless him.'

'Yeah, Christ knows where he gets all that athleticism from,' Dad laughed. 'Not from me, that's for sure.'

'That's great,' I said, trying to sound enthusiastic. 'Good for him.'

'It's brilliant, isn't it?' Dad said, with the same proud smile he'd given me moments before. 'Actually, Jack, I thought I might go down to visit him next weekend. There's a big biking rally on close to where he lives. What do you think?'

Even via an iPad screen, I could tell he was a little nervous, and that this was his way of subtly asking my permission and checking it was OK with me. I have to admit, I was slightly thrown by the idea of Dad visiting Lewis, and the two of them heading off to a sporting event together . . . but I could tell it meant a lot to Dad, and I was determined to support him in this, even if it did feel weird not to be the only son in his life any more.

'Whoa, Dad!' I said. 'A biking rally. That's different . . .'

'Oh, he's bound to break something, and by that I mean a limb,' Mum said, rolling her eyes.

'Yeah, I know,' Dad said, looking sheepish. 'But I miss that kind of thing.'

'Well then . . . you should go, of course,' I said. 'Go wild; rediscover your youth.'

'Hey – why don't you come, too?' Dad said suddenly, his eyes lighting up. 'Make it a real boys' weekend, both of us get to know Lewis better.'

'What, me?'

'Why not? Can you get off for a couple of days? I'm sure Lewis would love it if you came. And so would I.'

'Er . . . Well, I . . .'

I didn't know what to say. A bike rally with Dad and Lewis next weekend? With the schedule for *Emerge* as crazy busy as it was? If I took time out now, it was only going to make things worse with Austin, plus make Ethan look even more like the golden boy. And I knew that Dad was just being polite – thinking back to our first meeting, I highly doubted that Lewis would want me to come along, too.

'Dad, I wish I could, but there's just no way. You know what it's like when GenNext are in the middle of a project. It's crazy.'

'I thought as much,' Dad said disappointment flickering across his face. 'Just thought I'd ask.'

'Jack's got enough to think about, love' Mum said to him. 'Maybe next time, eh?'

After we'd said our goodbyes I ended the call, somewhat deflated. I mean, I hadn't really got the chance to tell them about *Emerge* in any great detail. And then hearing that Dad was going to visit Lewis, and that the two of them would be bonding over this bike stuff, which I'd never really been interested in . . . Again that sense of displacement swept over me, like somehow I was on the outside of my own family. I'd hoped that speaking to Mum and Dad would make me feel better, but if I'm being really honest, I felt worse.

I hung out solo in the flat for most of the morning, until Sai came back from his brunch date with Lily. I wandered out into the kitchen to find him singing at the top of his voice as he made a cup of tea.

'Someone's in a good mood,' I said. 'Good night?'

Sai stopped in the middle of stirring his tea. 'Oh, mate, Lily is SO amazing. I think I might be in love.'

'Already?' I said with a smile. 'That's fast.'

'She's just so great and she gets me, you know?' Sai said. 'She loved Oblix last night – the restaurant in the Shard. It cost me an arm and a leg, but the view is incredible. Romantic and all that.'

'I'm really happy for you, mate,' I said, meaning it. It was great to see Sai so loved up. I had to steel myself for what was coming next. 'Look, Sai, have you heard from Austin today? He didn't sleep in the flat last night. Do you know where he stayed?'

Sai took a sip of his tea and nodded. 'Yeah, he messaged me earlier. He stayed at Ethan's. I think he's still round there now, actually.'

'At Ethan's?'

'Apparently. Ethan's parents have got a big flat somewhere trendy and expensive in east London.'

'Oh, right,' I said, taken aback. I'm not going to lie: I felt terrible hearing that my best mate was hanging out with my nemesis. Gutted.

'Is that so bad? They get on well, I think,' Sai said, clocking my reaction. 'Jack, spit it out, man. What's up?'

And then I was spilling my guts, telling Sai about the events of the night before and Austin's conviction that I'd told Ethan something I definitely hadn't. I daren't go into detail over Austin's anxiety, because having Austin think I'd been disloyal twice was only going to make the situation worse; I just left it that he was really broken up about his split with Jess, and that he'd told me in confidence just how low he was feeling.

'. . . so basically he thinks I betrayed him and nothing I say can make him believe that I didn't.'

'God, I knew there was something going on,' Sai said. 'He hasn't seemed himself lately, but I hadn't realised the break-up was affecting him this much.'

'Please don't make a thing of it, Sai,' I said. 'I only told you because I think he's going to need your help now. I can't help him; he's too angry with me for that. He didn't really want anyone else to know how bad he was feeling. Only me.'

'And now Ethan knows,' Sai added disapprovingly.

'Yeah, but—'

'Look, I don't want to take sides, Jack, but I can see why Austin would be annoyed. I mean, that's really private stuff.'

'Are you not hearing me, Sai?' I said, irritated. 'I didn't say anything. I don't even like Ethan!'

'And that's what I don't understand,' Sai said. 'Ethan seems like a decent bloke. You should at least give him a chance; it would make everything a lot easier. We can all sense that you don't like him, and it's making it difficult for the rest of us.'

'Is it?'

Sai nodded. 'Of course! Look, Ethan's helped put us in a great position and most of the time he's singing your praises, banging on about what a great presenter you are. What more do you want? He's a good bloke, Jack, you just won't see it.'

'He's not a good bloke, Sai. He's—'

'What exactly has he done that's so frickin' bad? Tell me that, because I don't get it,' Sai said, raising his voice slightly. 'Do you know what I think the problem is? I think maybe you and Ethan are too similar. You're both, like, leading-man types, and that's what's causing such a competitive element. It's not healthy.'

'Leading-man types?'

'Yes. You're both competing for the limelight. The alpha-male position. You're both outgoing and confident and—'

'But that's my point, Sai. When we met Ethan, he wasn't like that. He's completely metamorphosed. Don't you find that weird?'

'No, I don't,' Sai said. 'He's just got to know us, that's all. Look, I don't think we should talk about this any more. I don't like bad-mouthing someone behind their back.'

'OK, Sai, I hear you,' I said. He finished his tea in silence while I headed back to my computer.

Well, that went well. If Sai didn't believe me either, then what were the chances that anyone else was going to?

THE LAST STRAW

A whirlwind week of non-stop filming later, I still hadn't made any progress with Austin. He was giving me the silent treatment, refusing to speak to me either at the studio or at the flat, which, of course, made things awkward for everyone else. Ella and Ava kept asking me what had gone down between us, but I couldn't find a way to answer truthfully without giving too much away about Austin's anxiety issues. Sai was doing his best to be diplomatic, acting as a go-between whenever Austin and I needed to communicate on set, but at times I was very tempted to call Austin out over his behaviour, which seemed pretty childish to me. I knew Austin, though, and I knew that he was so hurt over what he thought had happened that he just couldn't bring himself to talk to me. Flat-out ignoring me was the only option for him. It didn't give me much chance to stand up for myself, though, and whenever I tried to plead my case it just reignited his fury and he stormed off.

It didn't help that Ethan had stepped efficiently into the role of best mate, hanging out with Austin in the lounge area whenever we had a (rare) break, and even sitting with him hunched over a MacBook, spouting his wisdom on the GenNext promo for *Emerge*, which had me seething because the five of us had agreed that we wouldn't let anyone else get involved with anything to do with the GenNext website. Ethan was too clever to lord his victory over me in front of the others, but when we found ourselves alone at the coffee machine one morning, he just couldn't stop himself.

'Mate, such a shame about you and Austin falling out,' he said from behind me as I hit the button for a cappuccino.

I spun around to face him. 'Are you kidding me?!'

He shrugged. 'You're such good friends; I'm sure you'll sort it all out soon. Once he's got over the trust issue, of course.'

I saw red. 'There IS no trust issue. He's only refusing to speak to me because of the lies YOU told him!'

'Whoa, Jack.' Ethan was smiling pleasantly, and he took a step back with his hands held up in front of him. 'I'd watch yourself. Chucking around accusations isn't going to help the situation. Especially when we've got to pull together to wrap up on filming. Be a team player, mate.'

Before I could respond, he'd sauntered off, leaving me so angry I could barely speak. There was no point talking to the others about it, though. The conversation I'd had with Sai had proven that, and Ella already thought I had a bee in my bonnet about Ethan. Saying anything more might come off as jealousy, and I was way too proud to risk that.

At least I didn't have too much time to dwell on things, because as filming went on and we got closer to the end, the pace became more and more manic. I guess none of us had realised quite how tough this kind of schedule was going to be: filming and editing five full episodes in three weeks. It wasn't just the stuff in the studio either. On top of that, there was the last of the documentary location material to shoot with each artist in turn (with Ethan carefully planning the schedule so that Ella and I were always in a different location, of course). Of all the things GenNext had done, this was without doubt the toughest, and we were all working insanely hard, aware of just how much there was yet to achieve. Olympia, meanwhile, tried to keep us buoyant, constantly reminding us how amazing the rewards were going to be at the end of it all.

One bright spot was that in amongst all the madness, Ella and I managed to grab a quick dinner together one evening away from the studio, even though we had to get straight back to work afterwards. I didn't feel like it was the best time to go deep on all the things that were worrying me – Ethan, Austin, the weirdness of the Lewis situation (Dad had sent me several photos of him and Lewis at the bike rally at the weekend, holding pints and grinning at the camera) – but at least we had a good chat about how *Emerge* was going, and how excited the GenNext audience seemed to be for our TV debut. It was just like old times. In fact, I could feel some of the tension that had been there ever since Total melting away, just a bit.

'It feels nice being here, just the two of us, doesn't it?' I said, pushing my empty plate away.

'I know! It's like, we've been in the same two buildings but we've hardly seen one another,' Ella smiled, and I fought the urge to mention Ethan's complete monopolisation of her. 'Still,' she went on, 'from what Ethan's been saying, we'll be flying off to America together soon. He's pretty confident the American network are going to pick up the show.'

'That's amazing,' I said. 'And there's you who doesn't even want to go to America.'

Ella elbowed me in the side playfully. 'I said I didn't want to live there; I can work there for a couple of months, can't I?'

'I guess so,' I said, really pleased that we seemed to be on the same page about the possibility of *Emerge* doing a stint in America. Then Ella did that very cute nose-wrinkling thing that I loved, and I bent down towards her, and we kissed. God, I needed this right now. This renewed closeness. I don't know what had brought it on, but whatever it was, after all the weirdness with Austin and Sai and Mum and Dad, I *really* needed it.

In a haze of coffee, adrenalin, late nights, and headaches from sitting in front of monitors or Macs for way too long, finally the Owl and GenNext teams wrapped up the filming on the first five episodes of *Emerge*. The live episode, featuring the winner's showcase gig, would all be shot on the night.

When Glen finally called 'It's a wrap!' it was a pretty proud moment for the team, I have to say. We congregated in the middle of the studio, laughing and high-fiving, knackered but triumphant. The only fly in the ointment was that Austin was still deliberately avoiding me, but overall the mood was upbeat. Not even Ethan's presence could bother me at that moment. Now it was time for all of us to blow off some steam – and Olympia had invited everyone who'd worked on *Emerge* to a swanky cocktail party at a mansion in Mayfair that evening. AJ and Lily were going to be joining us too. All the bigwigs from Owl TV and Channel 4 were going to be there, and Olympia promised us that it was going to be awesome.

'Jack, what are you wearing tonight?' Sai shouted the minute I got through the door that evening. I'd stayed on after the others had left to work on some GenNext social media content, and now I was running late. 'Should I wear a short-sleeved shirt, or can I get away with a muscle-fit T-shirt?' he went on.

'Just a suit and a blue shirt,' I said. 'Erm . . . as impressive as your muscles are, Sai, I'm not entirely sure if a muscle-fit T-shirt is quite the right look . . . Tonight sounds like it's going to be a pretty classy affair.'

'Oi! I'm class personified,' he said, offended.

'Of course you are, mate. But . . . you know . . . maybe the short-sleeved shirt, just to be on the safe side?'

At that moment, the front door swung open behind me and Ella and Ava bundled in, dressed in their evening finery. Ava had scrubbed up nicely in a black and red printed dress; it looked awesome with her bright red hair, which she'd tousled into curls, and vampy red lipstick. And Ella looked totally amazing – she was wearing a dress I'd never seen before, a long silk ivory number with a slit up one thigh that stopped just short of being outrageous and instead looked incredibly sexy. As always, I felt a swell of pride that she was my girlfriend.

'Sorry, I'm having an outfit crisis,' she said, before I had a chance to tell her how fantastic she looked. 'Nightmare! Can I use your bathroom for a minute?'

She thrust her beaded handbag at me and dashed past

into the bathroom. Ava shrugged and followed me into the living room.

'You'd better get a move on, Jack. The cars are coming soon,' she said.

'Seriously? I've literally just got in. Haven't I even got time for a bloody shower?'

'Just wash the important bits and throw on something dazzling,' Ava laughed. 'And make it snappy.'

There was a semi-desperate cry from Ella from my bathroom. 'Ava, can you come here a sec? Have you got any safety pins?'

'You'd better use Austin's bathroom,' Ava said to me, heading for the door. 'Sounds like Ella and I could be some time.'

'Why not? He's not using it,' I muttered to myself. Austin had barely been at the flat during the week; he'd stayed over at Ethan's quite a few times.

I put Ella's bag down on the coffee table, but I hadn't realised it wasn't zipped up, and everything shot out and fell onto the floor. I bent down to pick up the make-up, the tissues and her iPhone – which pinged with a WhatsApp as I scooped it up.

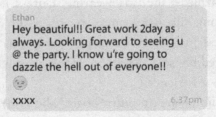

Ethan
Hey beautiful!! Great work 2day as always. Looking forward to seeing u @ the party. I know u're going to dazzle the hell out of everyone!!
😉
xxxx   6.37pm

For a moment, I felt like my head was actually going to explode. My face was burning and my mouth went dry. Ethan was messaging my girlfriend – what the hell? I knew it. I *knew* he'd been trying to move in on Ella. Sure, he was stealthy about it, but I'd clocked it even if nobody else had. And Ella – had she been messaging him back? When had she even given him her number? I trusted her, of course I did, but Ethan had already managed to turn my best friend against me – was he trying to do the same thing with my girlfriend?

For a while I just stood there, looking at Ella's phone in my hand, the message still lit up on the screen, and wondering what on earth to do.

'Almost ready,' Ava suddenly called from the bathroom. 'Crisis averted with safety pins. Sai? Jack? Are you all suited and booted?'

The cars were due any minute. Shaking myself out of my trance, I dropped the phone back into Ella's bag and went to get showered and dressed as quickly as humanly possible. The euphoria I'd felt after Glen had called a wrap on filming was draining away fast, and all the fatigue and uneasiness of the last week or so, since I'd fallen out with Austin, was coming back with a vengeance. Suddenly a party was the last thing I felt like . . . and I knew I was going to have to tackle Ella about the message at some point. There was no way I could let that one lie.

Fifteen minutes later, I'd hastily thrown on a suit and squirted on some Armani and we were in the car en route to Mayfair. Sai sat up front next to the driver, and Ava, Ella and I were in the back. The others were all excited, laughing and chattering about the party. I tried to join in but I couldn't concentrate, the words from Ethan's WhatsApp message running on a loop through my mind, so I turned and looked out of the window instead. London was whizzing past, wet and grey, and as we drove through Piccadilly Circus and around the statue of Eros, I looked up at the massive moving ads flashing above Barclays Bank and Boots. Suddenly something caught my eye . . . something familiar.

'Oh my God, look at that!' I shouted.

Sai, Ava and Ella all turned at once, leaning over to get a good look out of the windows on my side of the car.

Ava made a shrill squeaking sound. 'Is that . . . ? Oh my God, it is.'

There we all were: flashing one by one and larger than life on the giant billboard: Ella, Austin, Sai, Ava, me . . . and Ethan. The words 'GENNEXT: *EMERGE*. COMING SOON TO CHANNEL 4' rolled at the end of the sequence.

'Whoa!' Sai said. 'Look at my triceps.'

We'd had a fairly low-key photo shoot on set during the first week of filming, with Olympia telling us that the shots would be used for press and online advertising plus a few TV teasers, but none of us had expected anything like this. This was huge.

'Incredible,' Ava said in hushed tones, visibly awed.

Ella was shaking her head. 'Ethan said we could expect to see the ads soon and that it would be a bit of a surprise, but . . . oh my God, I never thought they'd be up in Piccadilly bloody Circus!'

'Ethan and Olympia are the bomb,' Sai agreed.

I gritted my teeth.

THE WRAP PARTY

The car drove towards a wide metal door, which slid open onto a massive cobbled courtyard with several garages. The house itself was huge – four floors – and as we approached we could hear the music and loud chatter of the party, already well under way, emanating from the open windows on the first floor.

'This is a bit of all right,' Ava said, as the four of us headed through the enormous entrance and up the grand stairs. 'I could see myself being quite comfortable living here.'

The stairs swept upwards to an enormous living room with shiny wooden floors and ridiculously high ceilings adorned with the most elaborate crystal chandeliers I'd ever laid eyes on. The house itself was old, but the furniture and fittings were all very chic and modern, and this room looked like it was the hub of the party, packed with people dressed to the nines.

A waiter was moving through the crowd, holding a platter of champagne flutes aloft. Sai and Ava headed in his direction and Ella went to follow them, but I grabbed her hand.

'Ella, could we have a quick word?' I asked. I knew the party wasn't the best time for this conversation, but I also knew there was no way I could make it through the next few hours with Ethan's WhatsApp preying on my mind. I needed to confront this head on.

Ella looked a bit surprised. 'Sure,' she said. 'What's up?'

I guided her over to a slightly quieter corner of the room, near the window.

'Did you see that message on your phone?' I said. 'The one from Ethan?'

Ella frowned. 'Yes, I did. Why?'

'I saw it too,' I said. 'When it flashed up on your screen earlier.'

'And?'

'*And* I think it's really weird that Ethan's messaging you like that. He's making a move on you – it's obvious.'

'Oh, that's ridiculous, babe,' Ella said. 'No way.'

'He's kept us apart for pretty much the entire duration of filming,' I said. 'Don't you think that's odd?'

'Come on, Jack, you're overreacting,' Ella said firmly. 'Ethan's been doing what's best for the show, that's all. He's just a mate and he's been good to me . . . to us, I mean.'

'Yeah, well, maybe he's got an ulterior motive.'

'What, you mean like supporting and encouraging me in my career?' Ella said, her temper clearly fraying.

I was dumbfounded. 'You mean like I don't?'

She shrugged. 'It's not that you don't, as such . . . I know that you've been trying, babe. But Ethan . . . he just gets it.'

It was like a red rag to a bull. 'I know we have a few different ambitions and goals, and that we're still figuring it all out, but . . . Don't you see, Ethan's obviously using all this to make you believe I'm a crap boyfriend who's not supportive.'

'Oh God! Why are you so against him, Jack? I just don't get it!' Ella sounded like she was on the verge of tears, and that was the last thing I wanted. 'He's a lovely guy who's only ever helped us!'

'It's just that—'

I was interrupted by Ava, who appeared brandishing two glasses at us.

'I bring you champagne!' she said, and then she clocked Ella's distraught face. 'Hey, are you guys OK?'

'We're fine, babe,' Ella said, taking a glass. She gave me a look. 'Let's just park all this till later, Jack. Tonight's meant to be fun.'

'Of course it is,' I said, frustrated.

'I'll see you later, then. We should probably mingle.' And she headed off into the crowd, pulling Ava along with her. Ava turned to give me a WTF? look, before being swallowed up by a group of very elegantly dressed partygoers.

I stayed on the fringes of the crowd for a while, feeling pretty crap, it has to be said. Ella's implied accusation stuck with me. Sure, I'd been gutted when I'd realised that we wanted different things . . . but of course I supported her. Didn't I? I loved her. Jeez, maybe I hadn't made that clear enough. Maybe I'd let everything that had happened since Total get in the way of us, and now Ethan was swooping in, ready to take advantage.

I tried to chase away my dark thoughts, sipping champagne and people-watching as the crowd buzzed around me. A lot of them looked a fair bit older than us, but there was a younger crowd too, who were hanging out together near the enormous fireplace on one side of the room. This lot looked a bit *Made in Chelsea* to me – or at least they didn't look as if they'd have any trouble scraping the money together for a decent pub lunch. Lots of big hair and posh accents. A few minutes later, two guys walked into the room and wandered over to join them. My stomach turned over. It was Austin . . . and Ethan.

This was my cue to go and get a refill, so I left the room by its other entrance – yep, it was grand enough to have two entrances. I kept my head down so that I didn't have to witness Austin noticing me and then pretending he hadn't. After grabbing another glass of champagne and wandering around the ridiculously extravagant rooms for a bit, I eventually found Sai and Ava, leaning against a massive balcony that looked down over yet another huge foyer. Ella had disappeared.

'Jack, my man,' Sai said. 'Having fun?'

'The time of my life,' I muttered.

Sai was looking at his watch. 'Lily should be here soon,' he said. 'I can't wait to see her. Now *she* would have appreciated a muscle-fit top.'

'I'm sure she would, Sai,' Ava said with a smile.

I recognised a burst of laughter ringing out from the next room. Looking in, I noticed Olympia, surrounded by a group of people on a huge turquoise couch. She was holding court, gesturing wildly with a half-full cocktail glass.

'Hey, there's Olympia,' I said. 'Shall we go over and say hello?'

We'd only walked a few steps when Ava froze. 'Oh crap!'

'What's wrong, Aves?' I said.

'Suki. Suki's over there with Olympia.'

'Didn't she tell you she was coming?' I asked, surprised.

Ava shook her head, looking like she was torn between excitement and horror.

I glanced over to see Suki standing behind the couch Olympia was sitting on, laughing and joking with the people surrounding them, all of whom seemed to know her pretty well. As usual she looked amazing, in a black halterneck, pinstripe skirt and purple belt, heels and lipstick, that edgy style of hers standing out amidst all the cocktail dresses and suits.

I nudged Ava and nodded encouragingly. 'Let's go say hi, shall we?'

'OK,' Ava said, sounding unsure. 'I just didn't expect her to be here, Jack. We haven't seen each other since Total, although we've been messaging loads, and—'

'Come on,' I said, grabbing her hand and pulling her along behind me. 'It's time the two of you sorted this out properly.'

Olympia stood up as we got close, but Suki was engrossed in conversation so didn't notice us at first.

'Ah! Here they are – my stars!' Olympia trilled. 'Come over here and meet some of my friends, guys.'

'This is all really cool, Olympia,' I said, joining the group of people surrounding her.

'And so was the enormous ad for *Emerge* flashing all over Piccadilly Circus,' Sai added.

Olympia hugged and kissed the three of us in turn. 'Oh, I know! I'd intended to do a big announcement tonight, but it all went live this afternoon. Did you love it?'

'It was a brilliant surprise,' Ava said. 'Olympia, this party is amazing. Is this your house?'

'Oh my God, no! I mean, I wish,' Olympia laughed. 'It belongs to one of the main owners of Owl TV, who also owns half the commercial radio stations in the country. It's actually his party, which I've semi-hijacked for us. Isn't it gorgeous?'

An army of waiters and waitresses swept around us, serving drinks and canapés, while Olympia introduced us to one person after another, none of whose names I remembered thirty seconds later. Suki eventually noticed us and broke away from her admirers, greeting Sai and me excitedly. When she got to Ava, there was a moment of tangible awkwardness, and it was clear that neither of them quite knew how to behave.

'I didn't know you were coming,' Ava said softly, giving Suki the briefest of hugs. 'You didn't say.'

'I figured you'd be mad busy wrapping up the show . . . and I was only invited last-minute, by Limpy,' Suki replied.

'Oh . . . by Limpy?' Ava said.

'Yeah. I thought . . . I thought you might be pleased to see me.'

Just at that moment, Olympia draped her arm around Suki, pulling her away from Ava.

'Isn't it wonderful that Suki could make it?' she asked, leaning her head on Suki's shoulder. 'How lovely that the entire GenNext team is here. Are you all having a nice time?'

'Amazing thanks, Olympia,' Sai said appreciatively, grabbing a mini burger from a passing tray and stuffing it into his mouth, happily oblivious to any tension. 'This party is fierce!'

Suki looked like she was about to say something else to Ava, but Olympia tugged on her arm and drew her into conversation with a tall, glamorous woman who looked vaguely familiar – one of the Owl big cheeses, I guessed. A flash of frustration passed over Suki's face, and I could see that her gaze was still on Ava even as she chatted to the woman.

Beside me, I heard Ava sigh. She turned to walk away, but I grabbed her arm. 'Where are you going, Aves?'

'I'm not sure I can do this, Jack,' she said, looking at Suki and Olympia over my shoulder. 'It's just too hard.'

'You haven't got to do anything,' I said. 'Just be yourself. Talk to Suki.'

'It's just . . . Suki's like this beacon of light. She knows everyone and she just seems to naturally attract people, and . . . It's always been the same with us. She's this ultra-cool successful career woman and I always feel like some geeky little kid running around after her. It's fine when we're on our own, but in situations like this, it all becomes glaringly apparent.'

'That's insane,' I said. 'You're just as amazing as Suki. Not everyone has to be larger than life, you know.'

'I know you mean well, Jack, but . . . I'm just so worried that people like Olympia fit in with her in a way that I never will.'

'That's rubbish,' I said, but Ava was already fighting back tears.

'Look, I'm just going to get some water,' she said, and headed over to the bar before I could console her any further.

I stuck with Sai, who was scoffing all the canapés he could get his hands on, making small talk with Olympia's group. Eventually Suki broke away and came over to us, looking around for Ava.

'She's gone to get a glass of water,' I supplied helpfully. 'That was, erm . . . about fifteen minutes ago.'

Suki sighed. 'What is *with* Ava tonight, Jack? I've been really looking forward to seeing her and then she goes all weird on me. It's like she doesn't want me here at all.'

'Maybe you should tell her how much you've been looking forward to seeing her,' I said. 'I think that would be a good start.'

'OK. Anything else you think I should know?' Suki said, her eyes narrowing.

'Just talk to her. Let her know what's going on with the two of you.'

'I only wish I knew myself,' Suki said, looking somewhat defeated.

Before I could say anything else, I felt myself being pulled by the elbow away from Suki and across the room. Oh God, it was Ethan. His smart blue shirt was a similar colour to mine. In fact, with his new haircut, we looked way too alike for comfort.

'There you are, Jack. I've been looking for you.' That perpetual smarmy smile was on his face. 'Enjoying yourself?'

'What do you want, Ethan?' I said, yanking my arm away

from his grip. I thought about the text he'd sent to Ella and I had to resist the urge to deck him then and there.

'I just want you to meet Simon Smyth, one of the directors of Owl,' Ethan said, steering me towards a middle-aged man with slicked-back grey hair and a bad suit. 'He's a big fan of yours; wants to hear all about the show. He's a real VIP in the world of TV, so keep him sweet, won't you?'

Less than five minutes later, I was locked in conversation with a man who had to be the most boring person in the room, if not on the planet. I wish I could tell you what we were talking about, but I really didn't have much of an idea myself. As far as I could make out, it was something to do with advertising revenue and projected viewing percentages and God knows what else. It turned out that Simon was indeed a director of Owl TV – a *financial* director, one with a nasal, monotonous voice and who sprayed saliva in my face as he talked. Ethan, meanwhile, had melted away, leaving me on my own with this charmer. Of course, he was bound to have an ulterior motive for landing me with Simon, and it didn't take long for me to work out what it was. Across the room, Ella had reappeared and straight away Ethan commandeered her, taking her over to meet a tall dude in a tux and a Melissa McCarthy doppelgänger, who looked a hell of a lot more fun than Simon Smyth. Taking a second glance, I realised that she was Lucy Wilson, an acting agent who worked for one of London's biggest agencies. I recognised her from her Twitter profile picture; Ella and I had looked her up earlier that day, because Ella was so excited about meeting her. Out of the corner of my eye I could see Ethan moving closer and closer to Ella as they talked. My blood was boiling, but there was nothing I could do. While Simon droned on at me, Ella's group seemed to explode into gales of laughter every five seconds. At one point, I caught Ethan's eye and he gave me a smug smile, moving his hand up to rest possessively against the small of Ella's back.

I'd had enough. As soon as I could, I excused myself from the conversation with Simon, saying that I needed to go the bathroom. It was tempting to go over to Ethan and tell him to keep his hands off my girlfriend, but I knew that it would only make things worse with Ella if I caused a scene, especially when she was in the middle of speaking to someone who could potentially influence her acting career. Instead, I headed down the enormous staircase and onto the terrace outside. On the way I passed Austin, who looked my way just long enough for me to catch the now customary flicker of hurt on his face.

This was getting ridiculous. I needed fresh air, and I needed to get away from Ethan.

I found a stone bench on the far side of the terrace and sat down, breathing deeply. It took a while for the temptation to storm back inside and have it out with Ethan to subside, but eventually I started to calm down a little. I really should have been inside socialising: networking with all the TV bigwigs and chasing opportunities for GenNext – plus I hadn't even seen AJ or Lily yet. But right now I was too upset, and the weird feeling of being on the outside that I'd felt with Mum, Dad and Lewis was now slipping into GenNext, too. It was as if Ethan was slowly separating me from my friends, and no one could see what was happening.

I sat outside for what seemed like forever, still in a bit of a daze. Then I heard footsteps and looked up to see Ava.

'Is this seat taken?' she asked, pointing at the bench.

'There's room for a small one,' I said, scooting over so she could sit down.

'What are you doing lurking out here by yourself, Penman?'

For a split second I considered spilling my guts about Ethan, but I knew Ava would insist that his WhatsApp to Ella was no big deal. Plus, she thought the sun shone out of Ethan's behind, too – even more so since he'd recently told her that he'd watched her coming-out video on YouTube and it was one of the most powerful things he'd ever seen. Such a creep.

'Just having a bit of time out – it was pretty hectic in there. You OK, Aves? Did you speak to Suki?'

She looked down at her feet. 'No. Not yet.'

'She told me that she'd been really looking forward to seeing you, you know.'

Ava looked up. 'Really?'

'Yes, you doughnut. PLEASE will you talk to her?'

Ava was silent for a few moments. Then she stood up. 'Right, I'm going to do it. I'm going to find Suki and talk to her.'

'Good for you,' I said.

She reached a hand down to me. 'But you're coming with me.'

It didn't take us long to find Suki. She was sitting on a fancy chaise longue in one of the smaller, slightly quieter rooms, with Olympia's arm around her. My heart sank when I saw that

Olympia was gently stroking her hair, her mouth close to her ear as she talked. Oh God, this was not going to end well.

They looked up as we approached, Suki immediately shaking Olympia's arm off when she saw Ava.

'Jack! Ava! Hi,' Olympia said. 'Is everything OK?'

Ava had frozen, horrified. 'I'm not sure,' she said slowly. 'You tell me.'

'Ava, hang on . . .' Suki stood up, but Ava had spun around and was halfway down the stairs in a matter of seconds. I followed, calling after her, but she ignored me and kept going: past the room where the party was in full swing and down yet more stairs that led to God only knew where.

'Ava, where are you going?' I shouted. 'That's not the way out. Ava!'

When I finally caught up with her, she'd made her way into an enormous room housing a full-size indoor swimming pool, with several lockers and changing rooms on one side and some poolside furniture and a jacuzzi on the other.

'Bloody hell,' I said, as I emerged into the room behind her.

'I know. Who the hell is rich enough to have a frickin' swimming pool in the cellar?' she said angrily.

Suki came down the stairs after us, her insanely high heels clattering on the wooden slats. She didn't look like she was feeling guilty, though. She looked angry.

'Ava, what's going on? Why are you behaving like this?'

'How exactly would you like me to behave, seeing you like that with Olympia?' Ava snapped.

'Like what?' Suki said, folding her arms. 'What do you think was happening there?'

'Well, it looked like a pretty compromising position to me,' Ava said, fighting tears. 'Wouldn't you say, Jack?'

'Don't look at me,' I said, stepping back. 'This is between you two.'

'Well, I know what I saw,' Ava said. She turned to push past Suki back up the stairs, but Suki grabbed her arm and spun her around so that they were facing one another.

'I was upset, that's all, and Olympia was comforting me. I was upset because all I've wanted to do, all evening, is speak to you. *You*, Ava! But every single time I've tried, you've given me the brush-off, like you don't care . . .'

'But—'

'But nothing,' Suki said, her voice bouncing around the pool area. 'Just remember, Ava, you were the one that broke up with me, not the other way around. You're not the only one with feelings and an ego, you know. I was hurt. It wasn't what I wanted. Remember that.'

'So what *do* you want then?' Ava said.

'I want to be with you, of course, but not like this,' Suki said. 'If we're ever going to be together again, you need to sort yourself out and accept me – and my job and my life-style – for what I am. You need to shake off that insecurity and accept that I love you whatever. If you can't do that . . . well, there's really no point, is there?'

Ava closed her eyes, saying nothing. Suki sighed and turned away. 'Right. I guess I'll see you later, then.' Her heels echoed once again as she started back up the stairs.

'Ava. Call her back!' I said, but Ava shook her head.

'I'm too tired to argue, Jack. I just need to think. And to sit down for a minute.'

She sat on the edge of the pool, took off her shoes and plunged her feet into the water, swishing them back and forth.

'What are you doing, you nutter?' I said, looking around to make sure no one else was watching.

'I'm paddling,' she said. 'I'm paddling and "sorting myself out", and I think you should do the same.'

So I sat down next to her, took off my shoes and socks and slid my feet into the water next to hers.

The feel and sound of the water gently splashing against my legs was quite soothing. It was a good couple of minutes before either of us spoke again.

'OK,' Ava said. 'What now?'

I thought for a moment. 'Well, now we go home and regroup,' I said, thinking about my own situation as well as Ava's. 'But first . . . we dry our feet.'

THE FIRST EPISODE

On the Monday night that the first episode of *Emerge* was
due to air on Channel 4, Ava and Ella rounded up the troops
and organised a get-together at their apartment so that we
could all watch the show. Even though I was still on shaky
ground with Ella after our argument about Ethan's message,
and Austin and I still weren't talking, *Emerge* was a massive
leap forward for us, and it was too big a night for GenNext
not to be together when the first episode aired. Plus, Ethan
wasn't going to be there because he was watching the show
with the Owl TV bosses at their offices, and I was very
happy about that.

'Come on in, boys!' Ava greeted Sai and me warmly at
the door of the girls' apartment. 'We've got drinks and nibbles
aplenty.'

'That's an understatement,' Ella said, giving me a quick
kiss as I walked through to the living room. 'There was
nothing but tumbleweed left in the Waitrose party food aisle
by the time she'd finished.'

AJ and Lily were already in attendance, perched on the

large L-shaped couch, while Austin was hunched awkwardly in the very cool 1960s leather chair in the corner. He seemed twitchy and uncomfortable, like he didn't want to be there.

'All right?' he said, nodding vaguely in my direction.

I smiled back nervously. 'Hey, Austin.'

OK, it wasn't much, but it was the most he'd spoken to me in almost three weeks, so I was grateful for small mercies.

'Right! Who's for a drink?' Ella said. 'We've got ten minutes before the show starts, so that should give everyone enough time to eat their own weight in mini onion bhajis and duck spring rolls.'

Sai draped his arm around Lily. 'Sounds good to me; I'm starving,' he said.

'So is anyone nervous at all?' Ava asked.

'I am a bit,' I laughed. 'It's like we're about to be judged by the nation or something.'

'I definitely am,' Ella said, on her way to the kitchen area. 'HD can be merciless, close-up on a large screen.'

'I don't think you've got any worries there,' Ava said, winking. 'Not so sure about Jack, though.'

Sai had already shown us all his rough cuts of the show, so we kind of knew what to expect, but it was one thing watching it on a MacBook and another thing entirely knowing that it was going out to the whole country on primetime telly.

'Don't sweat it, guys, it's going to be amazing,' AJ smiled. 'I've got complete faith in all of you.'

'Absolutely,' Lily chimed in, before planting a massive kiss on Sai's cheek. 'Especially you.'

I clocked Austin biting his lip and looking away from the loved-up pair and I suddenly felt really bad for him. Whatever was going on with him, it didn't seem to be getting any better, despite finding a new BFF in Ethan. I only wished I could somehow get through to him, but . . .

'Here you go, Jack.' Ella handed me a beer and sat down next to me while Ava grabbed the remote and flicked on the TV. It was almost time.

Although we'd all seen the *Emerge* opening titles half a dozen times already, tonight, flashing in front of us on a fifty-inch Samsung, they looked extra shiny. Extra exciting. Extra impressive. You could feel the excitement in the room as we all put down our plates of food and leaned forward to take in everything that was about to come. And there I was: first on screen with the opening intro to the show and, I'm happy to report, looking pretty decent. Ava and Ella both screamed with excitement as Ella appeared next, explaining the concept of the show along with Ethan. It was weird how we were all reacting to it. We'd seen ourselves on screen a thousand times, but somehow this was very different: slick and polished. Real TV, as Ella might say.

As the show got going, however, I started to realise that something wasn't quite right, though I couldn't quite . . . Hang on . . . wasn't I supposed to be doing an introduction piece before this band? Yes, I was; I remembered it from the rough cut. So where the hell had it gone? I mean, where had *I* gone? Maybe my bit had been moved to after the performance. But no. Straight to the post-performance interview with Ella and Ethan, who, I grudgingly had to admit, were pretty good together. Then on to the next band and another of my intros . . . but no shot of me. Just my voice-over documentary footage of Ace Love, and then straight to her performance. It was the same with the next performance, and by this time I was flabbergasted, not to mention furious. Seconds before the first commercial break, I finally appeared onscreen again, cheerfully informing the viewers that we'd back in a couple of minutes . . . and that was it! I looked around the room, speechless, and I could see from the rest of the gang's expressions that they were as dumbfounded as I was – even Austin.

Sai was the first to speak. 'Er . . . it's quite different from the rough cut, isn't it?'

'Did you see this version at all?' AJ said, frowning. 'It's a bit Jack-light, isn't it? Did we approve this edit?'

'I wasn't in on the final edit,' Sai said. 'We were told it would just be a properly colour-graded version of what we'd already seen.'

'It's a joke,' I said bluntly. 'An absolute joke.'

'Look, I expect you'll feature more in the second half,' Ava said, but I had a sinking feeling that I wouldn't.

I looked over at Ella and she shrugged, her expression confused, just as the commercials ended and the second part of the show started. Far from Ava's prediction, this section was even worse. After a quick 'welcome back' from me, I as good as vanished until the end of the show: the intros and links I'd filmed occasionally audible over footage of the bands, but never visual. In short, I'd become a voice-over.

Nobody said very much at all once it was over. Everyone

shifted uncomfortably in their seats, trying their best not to make eye contact with me. It was clear that they'd all been surprised by my lack of screen time but didn't know what to say about it, and to be honest, I was pretty much speechless, too. The worst part about it was that the show itself was fantastic and everything we wanted it to be. It was fast, exciting, professional, and the GenNext vibe was totally there throughout – apart from my conspicuous absence, that is. I knew only too well why and how this had happened. It was Ethan's doing, without a doubt.

'So what did everyone think?' Austin said, finally breaking the awkward silence.

'Well, it was amazing, but there wasn't really enough of Jack,' Ella said.

'You think?' I said, but felt immediately bad. I mean, I wasn't angry at Ella, or arrogant enough to think that I should have been the star of the show. I was perfectly happy for her to have more airtime – she was brilliant. No, the anger was because I knew what Ethan had done, essentially cutting me out of *our* show.

I swiftly excused myself from the gathering, telling the gang I had to pop back to our apartment for something and would be back in ten. I needed a few minutes to process what had happened, and work out what I could do about it. If indeed there was anything I *could* do about it. As soon as I got back to our apartment and into my bedroom, I opened my Mac and instinctively headed straight to Twitter to check out the reaction to the show. Just glancing at a few of the comments told me that it was confused, to say the least.

@AliciaFord12
Loved #Emerge can't wait for tomorrow's ep. Great stuff @GenNextOnline!

@Littlepuffdragon
Bit weird that @JackGenNext has been replaced but great show guys. #Emerge

@JennaRoper777
Loving #Emerge and the new look @GenNextOnline!!
@EllaGenNext and @TheEthanHarper are so cute together.

@BabycakesLouxx
Missing my dose of @JackGenNext but loved loved loved the first show
@GenNextOnline #Emerge

My heart sank like a stone. I loved GenNext and all our fans, and looking at the Tweets and comments it was obvious that the first show had gone down an absolute storm, which was great. Only . . . after everything that had happened and all the hard work I'd put in, was that it? Was I that easily replaced? Were people ready to accept somebody else stepping into my shoes just like that? Suddenly, my head was all over the place. OK, so things hadn't exactly been going my way over the last few weeks, but up till now I'd felt like I at least had some kind of a grip on it all. No matter how much I loathed Ethan and the havoc he was trying to wreak between Ella and me, I'd naively seen the end of filming as the cut-off point. The show would be done, at least for the time being, and I'd have time to pull GenNext back together before we moved forward. Time to get back on track with Ella, and regain Austin's trust. But after tonight, it was obvious that the tricks Ethan had pulled up till now had been a mere warm-up. My virtual disappearance from *Emerge* felt like the next stage of whatever he had planned . . . and a much more dangerous one.

A knock on my bedroom door shook me out of my thoughts.

'Jack, can I come in?' It was AJ. 'Are you coming back to the girls' place?'

'Yeah, in a while,' I shouted through the door.

'It's just that Ella asked me to come and find you to make sure you're OK, and Ethan is on his way over. He's got some good news apparently. You coming?'

I hopped off my bed and opened the door, about to politely decline, when AJ cut in again.

'I think you should. I didn't want to say too much in front of the others, but I think we need to tackle him about your lack of airtime on the show tonight.'

'Really?'

'Yes, I found it a little odd,' AJ said. 'Let's make sure it's not a regular thing, shall we?'

I smiled and nodded. Finally, somebody was on my side.

'Absolutely, AJ,' I said. 'I'll be right there!'

THE POST-SHOW SHOWDOWN

Ethan was already there by the time I got back to the girls' apartment, beer in hand and firmly in the midst of everyone's enthusiastic babbling about the show: how great it had all looked and how brilliant the reaction had been so far. OK, so it wasn't exactly the ideal time to tackle him, what with everyone still buzzing, but AJ wasted no time in pulling him over to the kitchen area for a private word before he delivered whatever earth-shattering news he'd come to tell us. I followed them over, certain that the others would know exactly what we were talking about, but not really caring. This was something that had to be sorted. Now.

'I think I know what this is all about,' Ethan said, looking down at the floor guiltily.

Of course he bloody well knew!

'I'd just like to know why Jack's role in the show was so diminished,' AJ said. 'It wasn't what we saw in the earlier edits and it certainly wasn't how the show was originally set out. What's going on?'

I looked at Ethan, waiting to hear what he had to say. AJ

had suggested that I let him do the talking – he was our manager after all – so I was keeping my mouth shut, with difficulty.

Ethan looked sorrowful and convincingly genuine. 'You have to know it wasn't my doing, Jack. It was Glen's call. I mean, he is the director after all. And then Olympia got involved, and . . .'

'And what?' AJ said calmly.

'And you know how she thinks Ella and me presenting together is a good fit, so I think that played a part in how things panned out,' Ethan went on. 'I really don't have a say in the final edit, trust me.'

Ethan uttering the words 'trust me' sounded like the most ridiculous thing that had been said in the history of the universe – ever! Of course he was lying. For a start, Glen was the director only in name, and anyone with a pair of eyes in their head could see that the poor guy was only there to make the show what Ethan wanted it to be. On top of that, Glen liked me and was as wary of Ethan as I was, so there was no way he'd have hacked all my shots out of the first episode if he hadn't been leaned on.

'In that case, Ethan, I'll have to tackle Olympia about this,' AJ said. 'GenNext, on screen, really is both Jack and Ella.'

'The thing is, it's all down to artistic integrity at the end of the day,' Ethan said. 'Olympia would simply have done her best for the programme and all the artists involved, taking the best footage and turning it into a top-notch show. That's what she does.'

I couldn't stay silent any longer. 'So what you're saying

is that my parts weren't as good, therefore they didn't make the cut. Is that it?'

'It's not personal, Jack,' Ethan said reasonably. 'It's just the way Olympia is. She's got this instinct for what works and what doesn't.'

I opened my mouth to speak again, but AJ held up his hand, signalling me not to. 'I think this is something I need to discuss with Olympia, Jack. It's clearly not in Ethan's remit, so let's leave it until tomorrow, shall we?'

I looked across to the living room, where the others were gathered, muttering nervously amongst themselves while our quiet confrontation was happening a few feet away.

'So what's this news, Ethan?' Sai called over. 'Come on, we're all waiting.'

'Yeah, and get out of my kitchen, you lot; I want to put some more samosas in the oven,' Ava laughed.

Ethan glanced at me, a smile creeping across his mouth, then he crossed the room towards the others. AJ and I followed him over.

'Well, I actually come bearing gifts tonight,' he said. Grabbing his bag off the couch, he pulled out a wad of papers, waving them around in front of him and grinning. 'Contracts from the American partner channel. They had them drawn up as soon as they saw the first rushes of the show, and they absolutely flipped out over the first three episodes when we sent them over a couple of days ago.'

'Are you serious?' Austin said, his mouth falling open. 'Contracts already?'

'Oh my God,' Ella said, grabbing my hand. 'This is amazing.'

'Yeah, well, they didn't want to waste any time,' Ethan said, handing out contracts to each of us in turn. 'They're positive that they're on to a really hot thing and they knew that as soon as the show aired there'd be a ton of other channels trying to get their mitts on it. Didn't I tell you this was going to happen?'

Ella grabbed me and kissed me and there was another mad burst of excitement, with the gang all jumping up and down and shouting like crazy. Meanwhile, I wasn't sure whether to laugh or cry. I was only just getting my head around the disappointment of the first UK airing of the show, and now we were expected to start planning an American one. I looked over at AJ, who was busy scanning the contract, his brow knitted.

'Hang on a minute, is this right?' he said.

Everyone stopped and Ethan looked up. 'Something wrong, AJ?'

'Jack's role in the show is what's wrong,' AJ said, holding the contract out. 'I mean, the way this reads, *Emerge USA* is to be presented by Ethan Harper and Ella Foster, and Jack Penman is . . . well, it's difficult to see what his role is at all, to be honest.'

'What? No way,' Ella said. 'That's got to be wrong.'

'It's a bit weird,' Ava added.

'It's not weird at all,' I said, almost under my breath. I could feel a tightness in my throat and beads of sweat on my forehead. *Hold it together, Jack. Don't lose your temper.*

Ethan looked at his copy of the contract and shook his head slowly. 'Well, the channel will have made their decision on presenters based on the episodes they've seen.'

'So you mean Jack doesn't feature in the other episodes either?' Ella said, her brow wrinkling.

'I haven't actually seen the rest of the episodes, Ella,' Ethan said.

Yeah, right. He'd probably gone through them all personally, deleting any footage of me.

'As I said to AJ, this is Glen and Olympia's call,' Ethan went on. 'You know what the Americans are like; they'll have their own take on who's hot property as far as TV personalities go.'

'Yeah, but this *is* a GenNext show, after all,' Sai said. 'AJ, is there something we can do about this?'

'Look, it'll be fine. I'm going to call Olympia now and get to the bottom of it,' AJ said, pulling his phone from his pocket. 'I'll just tell her that without Jack there is no show.'

Ethan put his hand on AJ's arm. 'Let me talk to Olympia,' he said smoothly. 'We have to play this very carefully with the American partners. They're putting a lot into this and we need to look like we're all on the same page. I'll sort it out.'

I felt like I was in a daze. How the hell could all this have happened in the space of a couple of hours? It was like everything was crumbling around me, too fast to stop it. I looked over at Austin. He appeared just as baffled as everyone else, but he hadn't said a word . . . my best mate hadn't even spoken up in my defence . . . and that was when I cracked.

'OK, this needs to stop,' I heard myself say. 'This ridiculous sham needs to stop right now.'

Ella touched my arm gently. 'It's OK, Jack. Ethan is going to make this right.'

'No, Ella, he's not,' I said angrily. 'That's the last thing he's going to do.' I turned to Ethan. 'You've been out to screw me over from day one, haven't you?'

Ethan gave a surprised laugh. 'Jack, I—'

'You've done your utmost to sabotage all the GenNext stuff. You've made moves on my girlfriend and tried to make me look bad while you're at it, and you've stuck the boot in between me and Austin. I'm still not sure how you did that, but you did, didn't you? And now I'm being pushed out of my own TV show – is that what's happening next?'

'Sorry, *your* show?' Ethan stepped back with a look of phoney indignation. 'Jack, *Emerge* is *everyone's* show. It is and always has been a team effort and I'm going to do my best to make it work, I really am. And as for all that other stuff . . . mate, I really don't know where it's coming from. You know how much I think of you, Jack, and I've only ever wanted to support you—'

'Oh, drop the act, Ethan, it's getting really dull.' I was on the verge of totally losing it with this guy.

'Jack, just calm down a bit,' Ella said softly. 'This isn't helping.'

'Ella, can't you see what's going on?' I said, my voice cracking. 'Can't any of you?'

'Look, what happened between us wasn't Ethan's doing,' Austin said, finally speaking up. 'I think you're upset about the way the show panned out and you're taking it out on him.'

I shook my head in disbelief, my whole body trembling. 'Taking it out on him? I've kept my mouth shut for weeks. Guys, this is all wrong. Ethan is . . . he's—'

'Look, I'm going to go,' Ethan cut in. 'Jack, I'm sorry you feel like this, I really am. I've only ever looked up to you, so this is all a bit shocking to me.' He grabbed his bag and coat from the couch, that sorrowful yet understanding expression back on his face. 'AJ, I'll speak to Olympia as soon as I can, I promise.'

'Jack, you're shooting the messenger here; this is *not* Ethan's fault,' Ava said, as Ethan headed for the door.

'Yeah, let's not turn the whole situation on him,' Sai added. 'That's just bad vibes.'

'If you guys think this is all perfectly reasonable, then I give up,' I snapped.

'Jack, I really think you need to go back to your apartment and calm down.' This was AJ, and by the look on his face I'd lost him as well. 'I think all this is making you stressed and you're just lashing out without thinking about what you're saying.'

I took a few deep breaths and looked around the room as Ethan closed the door behind him. 'I know what I'm saying, AJ. Trust me. I know.'

'Come on, I'll go back to yours with you,' Ella said gently.

'I think I need to be on my own for a while,' I said. I felt as if someone had turned the gas down underneath me all of a sudden, my heart rate slowing.

'OK. I'll come down in a while and make sure you're all right,' she said.

'Thanks,' I managed. I looked around again at the others, Austin, Sai, Lily and Ava, who were all staring at me with mixed expressions of annoyance and concern.

'Are you OK, Jack? Can I get you anything?' Lily said.

I shook my head, turned round and left the apartment without looking back.

Outside the girls' place, I felt so rattled that for a moment I couldn't even remember which way my own apartment was. Eventually I headed up the corridor, my mind a mess of divergent thoughts and uncertainties. As I passed the lift, a voice spoke behind me. 'Hey, Jack!' I stopped in my tracks and looked over. Ethan was standing there, smiling like butter wouldn't melt. My first instinct was to walk over and punch the dude, but all the anger had drained out of me, leaving me feeling tired and confused.

'Why?' I asked simply. 'Why are you so determined to mess with me, Ethan?'

The smile never left his face. 'I tried to be your friend, Jack, I really did.'

'You have never tried to be my friend,' I said through gritted teeth. 'Not once.'

'Oh but I did,' he said. 'I knew you wouldn't remember our first meeting, and it was only, what, just over a year ago.' He shook his head. 'So arrogant.'

'What first meeting?' I asked, mystified.

'I came to interview you for my college news website last September. Ring any bells?'

I shrugged, my mind a blank.

'I came all the way from Brighton that day and you didn't have time to talk to me,' he said. 'Too busy getting ready to film your mate Cooper whatshisname's show that night. Really nice.'

The smile had finally slipped and his face was just blank, his eyes cold. Somehow it was even creepier.

'I remember that day; it was crazy,' I said, scrambling to recall the details. 'I'm sure I would have tried to rearrange—'

'That's beside the point, Jack. You dismissed me. Just like you did when I sent the audition tape in.'

'Are you serious?' I said, stunned.

'What gives you the right to treat me like that, Jack? What makes you think you deserve everything you've got?'

'Deserve what? What have I got?' I could hardly believe what I was hearing.

Ethan's expression had changed again; now his face was tight and angry. 'GenNext, with all the fans and followers. Your friends. A beautiful girlfriend. Why should you have all that when you couldn't even be bothered to give me the time of day?'

It suddenly occurred to me that he was even more of a nut-job than I'd first thought. And a dangerous one.

'Look, Ethan, I think there's been some kind of misunderstanding—'

'There's no misunderstanding.' He cut across me. 'What goes around comes around, Jack, and it's time for me to get what *I* deserve. What I've worked so hard for.'

I looked at him, not knowing how to respond to this new Ethan: this calculating, sinister Ethan finally showing his true colours.

'So let me get this straight,' I said, slowly. 'You think you deserve my life, is that what you're telling me?'

Now the smile was back. 'You said it, Jack, not me.' He

pressed the button for the lift. 'And don't think I'm finished yet, either.'

I felt a surge of anger. 'Do your worst! Those are my friends. I'm part of GenNext, and you will never be.'

Ethan snorted a laugh. 'Yeah, good luck with that,' he said. 'It's not looking too good for you at the moment, is it? And there's more to come, just you wait. We'll see who your friends – and the fans – prefer in the end.'

The lift pinged as it arrived, and Ethan stepped into it. 'Sweet dreams, Jack,' he said, disappearing behind the closing doors.

And then I was alone in the corridor. Freaked out, and wondering what the hell I was going to do next.

THE STING IN THE TAIL

You know what it's like when you have an argument or confrontation? When you just keep turning it all over and over in your head, torturing yourself about how the outcome could have been different: I wish I'd said this, or why didn't I do that? Well, that's what I was doing all the next day. I kept thinking about the scene with the GenNext team, and then the disturbing conversation with Ethan afterwards. The one thing I couldn't forget was the look on his face as he'd stepped into the lift. The sinister, triumphant look that said that he'd won, at a game I hadn't even realised I was playing.

I kept telling myself that I should get out and about to try and clear my head, but I ended up just sitting in the apartment, alternating between looking at the online reaction to *Emerge* and checking my phone, which stayed silent. I couldn't get hold of anyone, not even AJ, and that took me even closer to the edge. Where was everyone? Why was Ella ignoring my WhatsApps? And where was Sai? I hadn't clapped eyes on him all day, and we were living in the same apartment. Surely I hadn't been such a nightmare yesterday that nobody even wanted to face me . . . had I?

So that was my morning: full of questions and uncertainty. While I should have been looking forward to the rest of the week's episodes, instead I was dreading them; imagining my part getting smaller and smaller as each show went on until, by Friday, I was completely non-existent. And then there was Ethan's ominous parting shot last night to consider. What the hell had he meant when he said he wasn't finished yet? The only thing I knew for sure was that I had to get my friends back on side – especially Ella and Austin. I had to make them understand what was really going on; tell them in a calm, collected way so they'd realise I was deadly serious that Ethan had this spectacularly mad agenda that included – no, *depended* on – my downfall. Then, once I had my team back on side, we could all move forward without Ethan Harper, and if that meant losing the American show, so be it. Anything was better than having that snake in our lives. It all sounded OK in my head. In fact, after a couple of hours, I'd actually managed to turn my mood from despair to hopeful determination. It wasn't to last, though. There was more to come, and it was even worse than I could have imagined . . .

Around midday, there was a loud bang on the door that almost shook me out of my skin.

'JACK! Jack, are you in there?'

If I wasn't very much mistaken, this was AJ's 'officially angry' voice, and it was accompanied by him pounding on the door like there was a fire. What on earth was going on?

Then I heard Sai speak. 'Hang on, AJ, I've got a key here.'

There was a rustling noise, followed by Ava saying, 'Would you just open the flipping door, Sai!' Her tone was more than a little panicky.

Not wanting to face everyone in my Diesel pants, I dived into my bedroom and practically leapt into a pair of joggers, just as Sai opened the front door and I heard the clatter of feet heading up the hall towards my bedroom.

Then I heard another voice: 'Jack, it's Ella. Are you home?'

Hang on! Ella was here, too? 'Yeah, I'm in the bedroom,' I called out. I pulled on a T-shirt and threw open the bedroom door, half smiling, half bemused. 'What's going on, guys?'

They all stood in front of me like a police line-up, with their expressions ranging from serious to distraught to furious: Sai, Austin, Ava, Ella and AJ. That was when I knew for sure. Something bad was going down.

'How could you do it, Jack? How *could* you?' Ava's eyes were filled with tears. My mind exploded, firing every which way. What the hell was she talking about?

'Do what?' I said.

For a few seconds everyone talked at me at once, too fast for me to make out any of what they were saying, aside from the fact that they were all angry and upset. In the end, Ella calmed everyone down and spoke softly, her voice quavering. 'This is bad, Jack. Owl TV have seen the emails and they know everything.'

'Emails?'

'Between you and Glen,' Austin said furiously. 'Don't pretend you don't know what we're talking about, Jack; this is really bloody ugly.'

'Not to mention hurtful,' Ava said.

There was another blast of group jabbering, even more agitated than the last, while AJ stepped forward and handed me an A4 printout of a short exchange of emails between Glen and me. Confused, I looked through them. The emails had been sent from my address and even had my email signature at the bottom – the one with my Twitter username and link to GenNext. Only . . . I'd never sent an email to Glen. God, I'd never even sent the guy so much as a text, and as far as I could remember I'd never received one from him either.

'I can't actually believe this is happening, Jack,' Ella said, as I scanned the words on the page as quickly as I could.

'What do you have to say for yourself?' Austin demanded.

'Hang on! Just let me just read this,' I said sharply, but the more I read, the more horrific it became, and the sicker I felt. The gist of the emails was that Glen and I were running some kind of scam together to rig *Emerge* so that one of the acts – Ace Love – would ultimately win the showcase and the record deal. Whoever had faked them had done a very nifty job too, because the language was just subtle enough that I had to read them twice before I could work out the hidden meaning behind the words. But there was no mistaking the fact that this fabricated scam had a massive financial pay-off, although the exact source of the money was never specified. Whatever the case, the information on this single A4 sheet was enough to convince anyone that Glen and I were being paid a large sum of money to screw over our employers, our colleagues, our friends . . . and the British public.

For a few moments, I actually thought I might throw up. Then I started pacing up and down, still staring at the words and trying to take them in. 'No, no, no. This is some kind of joke; it's got to be. Tell me you guys aren't swallowing this. This has got Ethan Harper written all over it . . .'

'How did I know this was coming?' Sai muttered, shaking his head.

'Oh come on, Jack,' AJ said. 'I think we've all heard enough of the Ethan conspiracy to last us a lifetime. Why on earth would he want to sabotage his own show? If this gets out in the press, *Emerge* will be dead in the water and so will Ethan's chances of presenting a US TV show.'

'There's no way Ethan would do that,' Ella said firmly.

I felt like I'd been sucker-punched. Ella thought that Ethan wouldn't . . . but that *I* would? That was what she was saying. It was crystal.

'What were you thinking?' Ava said, the tears spilling down her cheeks. 'You've betrayed us in the worst possible way, Jack.'

'What happened, J?' Austin said. 'Did you just hate the fact that you weren't able to run the show like you always do, so you decided to make a big fat profit out of it instead?' There was such a biting edge to his voice it took me aback. 'Is that what this is all about? Your bruised ego?'

'No! This is Ethan,' I yelled, flabbergasted. 'I have no knowledge of any of this. I've never seen these emails before!'

'Come on, man, it's there on the page,' Sai said. 'How could Ethan possibly have done this? Stitched you and Glen up with computer identity fraud? I don't think so.'

AJ held up a hand. 'Look, everyone, let's just calm down.' Then he looked at me, sighing wearily. 'Jack, I've known

you for a long time, and if you're saying you didn't do it
. . . well, then I'm giving you the benefit of the doubt.'

I was about to fall back against the door with relief, but
then he said: 'There's just one thing that I have to do, and
I'm really sorry, Jack, because I so don't want to . . . I need
to check your phone. Just to be sure.' He held out his hand.

'My phone?'

I looked around at my friends. Ava turned her head away,
not meeting my eye, and Austin was still glaring at me indig-
nantly. I picked my phone up from the arm of the couch,
entered my passcode and handed it to AJ. I didn't know why
he wanted to look at it, but I knew I had nothing to hide.
He scrolled through it, brow furrowed, for what seemed like
ages, and nobody said a word. For a moment I wondered if
my alarm might go off and I'd wake up, realising that this
was all just a nightmare, but that wasn't about to happen.

'Jack, can you explain this text?' AJ said finally, holding
out the phone to me.

'What is it?'

'Well, it seems to be a text from you updating an unknown
number with details similar to those in the email, and
confirming an amount of money. A very large amount.'

'Show me that!' I snatched the phone from AJ's hand and
looked down at the message, horrified. 'I've never seen that
before. That's just . . . God, I don't even know whose number
that is, OK?'

'I know exactly whose number it is,' he said sadly. 'It's
Glen's.'

Now I was just numb. Words were coming out of my
mouth but I hardly knew what I was saying. 'Look, I don't

know how, but yes, somehow . . . Ethan has . . . he's got into my computer and my phone and . . . Look, he's got this really intricate plot to get rid of me. Right back from Total Festival.'

'Intricate plot?' Ava said. 'Jack, can you hear yourself? You sound insane!'

'You should have heard him last night, after I left your apartment, Ella. The guy was threatening me with all sorts.' I was desperate now, but Ella just looked disappointed; hurt.

'Well, that's weird, Jack, because not long after he left our place, I got a message from him saying how gutted he was about the edit of the show, and the contracts. Saying he was going to get to the bottom of it and try to make it right.'

'Yeah, that's what he wants you to think,' I said. 'God, it's like he's brainwashed you all. Have you completely lost the plot? This isn't me. I . . . He's framed me . . . he's . . .'

I was stuttering and floundering, and the pitch of my voice was getting higher by the second. I knew how bad it sounded and the look on my friends' faces confirmed it.

Then AJ cut in. 'Look, this is getting us nowhere, and in any case we've got to go: Olympia has called us in for an immediate crisis meeting at Owl. In the light of what you're saying, Jack, I think it's best you don't come with us. I don't want this turning into a huge fight between you and Ethan. We need damage limitation now, not more drama. You should stay here and wait for me to call you.'

'Are you serious?'

'Deadly,' AJ said, his eyes angry. 'This is bad, Jack. Very bad. Glen's already been fired.'

'No way! They fired Glen without giving him a chance

to have his say?' I was horrified. 'This is . . . AJ, you have to help me with this. I swear—'

'I'll relay everything you've said to Olympia, but that's all I can do for now,' AJ said.

Everyone turned and left except Ella, and for the first time in forever I had absolutely no idea what to say to her.

'Ella, I—'

'I don't feel like I even know you any more,' she said sadly. 'This is too much, Jack. It's just . . . too much.'

'Ella, wait a minute, please!' I said desperately. 'For God's sake, you can't possibly think—'

She turned her back on me. 'I don't know what I think. Look, I've got to go with the others. Maybe we can talk later.'

'Maybe?' I said, but she'd gone, closing the door quietly behind her. I was left reeling and confused, unable to believe what had just happened. The fact that Ethan had somehow found his way into my computer and gone to such lengths to screw me over was horrendous enough, but the idea that my friends – all of them – would assume that I was guilty of this . . . this crime destroyed me.

The miserable truth was that it all made so much more sense now. Of course Ethan had got into my computer. That was how he'd known about Austin's depression and anxiety. Since we'd got back from Total, I'd emailed back and forth with Austin a few times about his state of mind, and it was clear that Ethan had read them. God, what a bonus that must have been for him: the opportunity to inflict maximum damage. I looked again at the emails on the printout. They'd all been sent within five minutes of one another. *Think,*

Jack, think! I closed my eyes and pictured my MacBook lying open around the studio on any number of occasions . . . sometimes my phone too: while I shot my scenes, while we all went to get lunch, and even when I'd left the studio for some much-needed air, just to get away from the sight of Ethan and Ella filming their increasingly chummy, cosy interview segments together.

I sat down on the sofa, a chill washing over me from head to foot as I suddenly recalled Glen tearing around the studio in a panic one morning shouting, 'Has anyone seen my Samsung? I thought I'd left it on that coffee table but it's literally vanished and I definitely had it earlier. Please look around, my loves, I'm expecting a text message from a very cute Colombian Pilates instructor, so it's pretty much life or death.' Ava and I had both cracked up laughing and helped him look for it, to no avail. It had turned up much later that day, lying underneath the couch in the lounge section of the studio, with Glen insisting that he'd already looked there several times. I hadn't thought it weird at the time – why would I? But now . . .

I left the apartment, stuck my headphones in and just walked, desperate to figure some way out of this horrible situation, and at the same time wanting to block it all out with ear-blisteringly loud music. I had no idea where I was walking to or even in which direction; all I knew was that I had to keep moving. I must have been wandering for over an hour when I found myself at an area called Shad Thames: a stretch of the river overlooked by Tower Bridge, full of smart-looking apartments, restaurants and offices. I sat down on a bench, took my headphones off and looked out over the water. I pulled out my phone, thinking that I should probably call Glen and find out his side of the story. After all, he was as innocent as I was, surely. Or maybe Ella had called me by now. Or AJ. There was a message, but it wasn't from Ella or AJ. It was an email from Olympia, and I opened it full of dread.

Jack. I'm sure you can imagine how devastated I am by this. We all are. You'll be hearing from our lawyers, but in the meantime I don't want you showing your face anywhere near Owl TV, for obvious reasons. I have to extricate all of us and *Emerge* from this mess in the best and most efficient way I can, and your presence here will not help matters. If you choose to ignore this warning, I will have no choice but to contact Ofcom, who deal with this type of fraud within TV and broadcasting, as well as the police, in which case you may be looking at arrest and subsequent legal action. For the future of the show, we have agreed between all of us that your mutually agreed departure from GenNext will be announced on Saturday's live episode, and, moving forward, Ethan will be confirmed as a permanent replacement. There is no room for discussion on this. AJ has persuaded me not to take further action, but these are my conditions and the others are on board with them.

I'm sorry it's come to this, Jack. I thought so much better of you.

Olympia Shaw

So there it was. I'd challenged Ethan to do his worst, and he had. And what an impressive catalogue it had turned out to be. As well as destroying my friendships, my relationship and my career, his crowning achievement was to have me branded a fraudster and a criminal, just for good measure. God, it was all so impressively neat. Nothing forgotten, no loose ends and, as far as I could see, no way back. I read Olympia's email once more, swallowing hard and fighting stubborn tears as I reached the end of it. Saturday. They were going to announce my departure from GenNext on Saturday. That gave my four days. Four days to prove my innocence. Four days to save myself.

THE PHONE CALL

Back at the apartment later that evening, the others still nowhere to be seen, I felt as though I was wandering around in some kind of parallel universe. The initial shock of it all had worn off a bit, but the sheer impossibility of the situation was still too much to take in, and the ball of hurt and anger in my gut was spinning faster and growing bigger by the minute. The worst part of it was that I just felt so alone. More alone than I had ever been in my whole life. At least if I'd been at home I'd have had Mum and Dad to lean on, but here in London, I felt lost and desolate.

I found myself standing in front of the TV, gripping the remote and unable to decide whether I should bite the bullet and watch the second episode of *Emerge*, which was due to start in the next ten minutes. There wasn't much point, to be honest: I'd seen the rough edits, I knew what the vibe of the episode was, and by now I knew well enough that I wouldn't be making much of an appearance – if any. I hadn't heard a single word from AJ or any of my friends, so it was official: everyone hated me.

In the end, I tossed the remote, sat down on the couch and flipped open my MacBook. I couldn't face the GenNext forum or Twitter, so I headed to my Facebook page, where something caught my eye almost immediately – Lewis was online. My half-brother Lewis, who insisted he barely ever touched a computer, let alone perused Facebook. I was intrigued but conflicted. Should I ping him over a friendly greeting? Or was engaging in a conversation with him the last thing I needed right now? I'd already had several updates from Dad telling me what an amazing time he'd had in Cornwall, and how Lewis was thinking about coming to Hertfordshire to spend Christmas with us. Did I really need to hear it all over again from Lewis? In the end, perhaps in a semi-masochistic moment, I fired him over a message. What the hell, I thought. It's not like I could feel much worse.

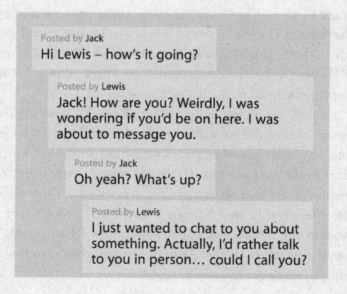

Posted by **Jack**
Hi Lewis – how's it going?

Posted by **Lewis**
Jack! How are you? Weirdly, I was wondering if you'd be on here. I was about to message you.

Posted by **Jack**
Oh yeah? What's up?

Posted by **Lewis**
I just wanted to chat to you about something. Actually, I'd rather talk to you in person... could I call you?

> Posted by **Jack**
> **Sure. Now?**

> Posted by **Lewis**
> **Is it convenient now? Isn't your show about to come on?**

> Posted by **Jack**
> **It's fine. Go for it.**

I sat staring at my phone, wondering why on earth Lewis might be looking for me online and what he might want to chat about. Obviously this was something to do with Dad. God, maybe I should have just kept my head down. Didn't I have enough going on without adding to it? I wasn't actually sure my brain could cope with even one more tiny morsel of data without crashing completely. Still, when my phone rang I dutifully grabbed it, and when Lewis spoke, his tone, I was happy to hear, was friendly and upbeat.

'It's good to hear your voice, man,' he said.

'You too,' I said, actually meaning it.

After the usual pleasantries – How's it going? What's happening? Have you spoken to Dad? etc. – Lewis got right to the point. 'Look, Jack, the reason I wanted to speak in person was to kind of . . . apologise, I suppose.'

'Oh?'

'Yeah! I hold my hands up, man: I was a bit of a douche during my visit, I know that. All that dissing technology and social media on my part was not cool when I knew how into it you were. I was actually really impressed by all your techy knowledge, especially being so into it myself once upon a time.'

'Really?' I said, surprised. 'Cheers, Lewis, that's—'

'Actually,' he went on, 'since we met up, I've been making a bit of an effort to get back into it again – hence me being in front of a computer tonight and not hanging out on the beach with my surfing buddies.'

'Oh, right! Wow, that's—'

But he was in full flow. 'Oh, and I watched your first show on TV last night – amazing! Then I checked out the footage of the Total Festival. It was awesome. Man, that must have been a blast! You guys make a great team, too.'

'Yeah, it seems like a million miles away now,' I said sadly.

'You know, when I think about it, I was trying so hard to impress Paul that day . . . Dad, I mean . . . that I didn't stop to think about how you must be feeling about it all,' he admitted. 'Selfish, really.'

'Well, maybe I was as much to blame,' I said, steeling myself. I respected his honesty and now it was time to be honest in turn. 'I genuinely did try to put myself in your shoes, Lewis, but then this weird jealousy vibe started to take over. I just couldn't control it. Yeah, I was happy for you and Dad, but at the same time I was scared that him having another son meant that he was somehow going to be less of a dad to me. It sounds pretty stupid saying it out loud.'

'It doesn't sound stupid at all, man. I totally get that,' Lewis said. 'I'd been so fixated on finding my real dad once I found out about him, I never really factored a brother into the equation, even after I knew you existed. It was totally my bad, but you know what? After spending time with Dad in Cornwall and hearing how he talks about you, I started to realise that maybe having a brother as well as an old man is even more of a bonus, do you know what I mean?'

'Yeah, I think so,' I said, my voice cracking slightly. 'So Dad talked about me to you, did he?'

'Man, he didn't stop. It was sickening.' Lewis laughed. 'Telling me how proud of you he was, and what a strong, honest person you were, and—'

'Stop. Don't say any more,' I said, finally breaking. I took in a long, shuddering breath and felt a rogue tear splash onto my arm. 'I'm really sorry, mate, I just . . .'

'Jack, are you OK? What's wrong?' God, practically breaking down on the blower to my long-lost brother wasn't something I'd planned. I took another breath, pulling myself together. 'Actually, Lewis, I'm far from all right,' I admitted. 'I couldn't be less all right, to be honest.'

By the time I'd filled Lewis in on every minute detail of the utter nightmare I'd found myself in, taking him right from the moment we arrived at Total up to that very second, it was after midnight. He had been so quiet for the last ten minutes of my diatribe that I had to check he was still on the line and hadn't fallen asleep.

'Could you take all of that in, Lewis, or was I babbling?'

'Yeah, I took it all in,' he said. 'I just can't get my head around what you're telling me.'

'I know. It's pretty bad at the moment,' I said. 'I'm at a bit of a loss as to what to do next.'

'I'm not just saying this, but you can tell that guy Ethan is a bit of a snake,' Lewis said. 'I thought that when I watched the Total Youth footage. Even the way he is on TV – he's too nice, man, too smarmy. I mean, all that fake-geeky stuff is so obviously an act.'

'Yeah, well, I wish everyone else could see it, but it's as if they're blind to what he's really like,' I told him.

'And you seriously think that he has this crazy vendetta against you just because you sacked off some interview with him over a year ago?'

'That's part of it,' I said, thinking again of Ethan's cold gaze as he told me that he deserved everything I had. 'But it goes deeper than that somehow. Like he really, really hates me. He seriously thinks I've taken something from him.'

'Hmm,' Lewis considered. 'That's weird, man. And none of the others have clocked on to any of this?'

'Ethan's clever – really clever. He's brainwashed everyone into thinking that he can do no wrong, and he's done it right under my nose. Naively I thought I could keep a grip on it all, but it's gone too far now . . .'

'No!' Lewis said firmly. 'You can't just sit back and let this happen, Jack. You're not the villain here. Look, I know just from the way Dad talks about you that you're a good and totally honest bloke. We don't know each other all that well yet, but I know that you'd *never* do what they're accusing you of. This is wrong, and you've got to make it right.'

'Easier said than done,' I said. 'The guy seems to catch me out every way I turn.'

'So we catch *him* out. Look . . . how would you feel about me coming up to London? Maybe I can help. I could come tomorrow; just get on my bike and bomb straight up. I'd be there sometime in the evening.'

'Wow!' I said, taken aback. 'That's really good of you, mate, but—'

'I hear you were a bit of a hacker in a former life, right?' Lewis really had done his homework. 'Well, so was I before I binned all the technology stuff. In fact, I was brilliant, if I do say so myself.'

'Were you?' I couldn't help but crack a smile at the thought of surfer-dude Lewis as a world-class hacker.

'Why don't we put our heads together?' he said, excitement leaping into his voice. 'Maybe Ethan's blind desperation to bring you down could be his downfall. There's got to be a way to expose this dude. Let me help you do it, Jack.'

My mind raced for a moment. He was right, of course – I needed to fight, and fast. How weird, though, that of all people, Lewis was the one to offer to stand in my corner with me. This guy I hardly knew, and whom I'd felt such resentment for not all that long ago. My brother.

'You know what, Lewis, you're on,' I said resolutely. 'Yeah, Ethan might be on top right now, but he's seriously under-estimated me if he thinks I'm going to sit back and let him take everything I've worked so hard for. Screw that!'

Lewis whooped down the phone. 'Yeah! That's more like it, dude!'

'I think I've known it all along,' I said, smiling. 'I just needed to say it out loud to somebody.'

'I hear you, Jack,' Lewis said. 'OK, message me your address, and I'll see you tomorrow.'

I ended the call. The agony of the last couple of days was still there, but now it had met its match in the form of a rising and determined adrenalin. God, it felt good that someone was on my side at last; that in the midst of all this mess, Lewis actually believed in me and was prepared to stand up for me.

I headed to the kitchen area to make myself a coffee, my throat dry because of all the talking I'd done. After the long phone call with Lewis, I knew I wasn't going to be able to close my eyes. I was too tightly wound up for sleep; but that was fine by me. After all, I had a lot to think about. And even more to plan before Saturday.

THE DISCOVERY

Despite a new and much-needed burst of positivity, the next day dragged by like an eternity. I'd heard nothing from any of the gang, and even after leaving what seemed like a million messages for Ella, there was still nothing. Tumbleweed. I had no idea where Sai had stayed last night, but he certainly hadn't made an appearance at the apartment. That morning, I bluffed my way through a tricky phone call with Mum and Dad, who'd instinctively known that something wasn't right with *Emerge* as soon as it had hit the TV screen. They were confused, not to mention upset, by my very conspicuous absence from it; I told them that I'd been upset by it too, but it was something that AJ was dealing with and would definitely be rectified asap. I tried to sound as upbeat and vibey as possible, but I'm not sure how convincing I was. I was just relieved that it had only been a phone call and that we weren't chatting on FaceTime. One look at me and they would have known instantly that things were far, far worse than I was letting on. And what would have been the point of telling them? It's not like they could have done much, if anything, to help me. No. I'd decided to keep shtum about all of it – even Lewis's impending visit to help me bring Ethan down. Yeah, especially that.

Eventually AJ messaged me late that afternoon to suggest a meeting to discuss the terms and conditions of my departure from GenNext the following week. In the meantime, I should think about packing my stuff up and moving into a hotel or back to Hertfordshire as soon as possible. His text was pretty straight to the point, but reading between the lines, it was clear that he was deeply disappointed in me. Grim, right? Then, at about 6 p.m., Ella sent me a WhatsApp.

> Ella
>
> Jack. I got your messages. I've been told by the legal people at Owl that I should have no contact with you at the moment, and for the sake of everyone else and the show, that's how it has to be for now. I'm sorry. Ella
>
> 6.04pm

It was clear and concise and each stark word of it felt like a tiny dagger in my heart. At the end of the day, whatever was happening to me – being expelled from GenNext, being accused of cheating, losing my friends and my reputation – *this* was the worst thing of all. Losing Ella. That was what I was facing, and I could hardly stand to think about it.

Lewis's arrival was just the shot in the arm I needed. In fact, I felt a surge of reassurance wash over me the minute he stepped through the door. He looked kind of different from how I remembered: was his hair a tad shorter? His once scruffy stubble a bit neater? His tan definitely wasn't as deep as I recalled. So he really had swapped sun and surf for a bit more time in front of the old computer!

'How are you doing, Jack?' he smiled, dropping his rucksack on the floor.

'Oh, you know . . . been better.'

He put his arm around my shoulder. 'Don't sweat it, man, we're going to sort this. Trust me.'

It was a stark contrast to the awkwardness of our first meeting; this time I was very happy to see him, and as we headed into the living room, Lewis looked around in awe.

'Wow! This is a pretty nice place you've got here.'

'Yeah, it's a pretty nice place that I'm being thrown out of tomorrow,' I said.

'You're kidding!'

'It's fine. I've booked a couple of rooms in a hotel,' I said. 'AJ knows I'm going to be here until then, so we won't be disturbed. Do you want a drink before we get started? I must warn you, I haven't got any herbal tea or any of that non-polluted gear you like to sip.'

Lewis laughed as he sat down on the couch. 'OK, I guess I deserve that one.'

'You do,' I said. 'And as for all this stuff about you turning from beach bum to technical genius overnight . . . I'm not quite sure I'm buying that, surfer boy!'

'Oh no?' he said, and I shook my head.

'Pass me your phone, dude, and tell me . . . which games are you into at the moment?'

I opened one of my newer game apps and handed him my iPhone, sitting down on the couch next to him.

'Level sixteen – pathetic,' he mocked.

'Oi!' I laughed. 'Have you tried getting past that level? It's bloody impossible.'

'Yeah, there's a trick to it. Watch this,' he said, tapping and swiping so fast I could hardly see what he was doing. In about ten seconds the screen refreshed, revealing a set of tasks and characters I'd never set eyes on before.

He handed the phone back. 'There you go. Level twenty.'

I looked at the screen in awe. 'Whoa! Dude, how did you do that?'

Lewis winked at me. 'Are you still doubting my technical prowess?'

'Absolutely not. That was amazing,' I said. 'Right. Let's see if you can put those skills to use investigating our friend Ethan Harper!'

Within half an hour we'd shoved the coffee table in the living room out of the way and covered the rug with laptops, phones, notebooks, pens and Post-it notes. The two of us sat there, cross-legged, beavering away to uncover as much as we could about Ethan.

'Now, we have to get to his private files. That's a given, right?' Lewis said. He was sipping the coffee I'd made him to help him stay awake after travelling most of the day. Clearly, his no-caffeine rule had also gone out the window.

I grinned. 'I think between the two of us we can do that.'

Twenty minutes later, I was still struggling to find a way into Ethan's accounts. Lewis, busy making notes on his laptop, looked up and over at me.

'How's it going?'

'Yeah, it's been a while,' I said, my brow knitted. 'Since I went legit, I haven't had cause to do much of this kind of stuff.'

Lewis smiled and dragged my MacBook across the floor towards him. 'Let me have a look.' He peered at the screen, tilting his head to one side like that might somehow help him figure things out. 'I feel like I'm trying to break into the vaults of some evil criminal mastermind,' he said, narrowing his eyes.

'I don't suppose that's too far from the truth,' I said.

'Hang on. Let me try something,' he said.

I watched in awe as he started banging away at the keyboard, concentrating hard. It took a while, but . . .

'There you go,' he said finally, smiling. 'We're in.'

'Dude, that was slick,' I laughed.

'I guess it's like riding a bike,' he said. 'Now, what have we got?'

It didn't take much poking around to uncover some stuff that made my jaw drop.

'Lewis, take a look at this! It's really, really weird.' In a folder simply marked 'G', there was file upon file upon file of information about GenNext: documents, schedules, screenshots and footage. The more I searched, the more I found. 'God, it looks like he's been collecting information on us from the moment we started; like he's been studying us.' My mouth went dry. 'Why the hell would he have all this stuff?'

'I don't know,' Lewis said, frowning as we clicked through the files together. 'It's freaky.'

I carried on clicking open PDFs, JPEGs, and tons of movie files. 'Look, this is Ava's coming-out vlog. And here's footage Sai put up of a kung fu tournament he competed in. And here are photos of Ava and Suki together. It's like we were being watched all this time without knowing.'

We continued to unearth more and more files until a folder marked 'F&P' made it alarmingly clear what Ethan's main obsession was. The F and P obviously stood for Foster and Penman, and in the folder there were dozens of photographs of Ella and me, taken from various social media: shots of us at events, screen grabs from our online shows, even intimate pictures of us holding hands or kissing. This was twisted even by Ethan's standards, and as I took it all in, a shiver ran up my spine. It was like one of those movies where the police finally break into the creepy apartment of the prime suspect in a string of murders only to find a wall covered in pictures of the victims and newspaper articles about his crimes.

'Anything else we can use?' Lewis said, peering over my shoulder.

'Just a few shots of Ethan and Ella on stage together at Total, which are making me feel sick,' I said. 'Hang on, what's this?'

I opened a movie file called 'Ethan GenNext' and there he was, beaming that annoying smile, being filmed outside a venue where punters were just starting to pour out of a gig.

'Hi, I'm Ethan Harper, outside the Charlie Puth gig in Camden, and I'm here to get some reactions from the crowd about what they thought of tonight's show . . . exclusively for GenNext . . .'

I shut the clip down as fast as I'd opened it. 'Exclusively

for GenNext? What? That gig was months ago, and we were there ourselves, getting the crowd's reaction.'

'Well, so was he by the looks of it,' Lewis said. 'Didn't you see him?'

I shook my head slowly, the thought of Ethan being there right under our noses, passing himself off as a member of GenNext making me go cold all over again. Then something else caught my eye – another photograph – and my heart felt like it had jumped up into my throat. I enlarged the image and stared at it in total disbelief.

'No . . . no, surely not . . .'

Lewis caught my expression. 'What is it, Jack? Do you know those two guys with him?'

I nodded slowly. It was the two guys from the fight on the first night of Total Festival, standing with Ethan. The guys who'd hassled Ella and then attacked me. They were all grinning and holding up bottles of Budweiser.

'We got into a scrap in the hospitality enclosure at Total, but Ethan stepped in to save the day,' I told Lewis, still staring at the photo, just to make doubly sure I wasn't imagining this.

'What, and he knows them?' Lewis said.

'This photo was taken outside a London bar, so obviously he does,' I said. 'God, do you think he arranged for them to beat me up just so he could look good? I mean, he did seem to appear from nowhere like bloody Spiderman.'

'Man, after all we've seen here, nothing would surprise me,' Lewis said, shaking his head. 'It's obvious that this guy is completely obsessed with you and GenNext. I mean, it's all here, isn't it?'

I knew Lewis was right, but it was still a huge amount for me to get my head around. This vendetta went deep. We weren't dealing with a mentally stable person here. This was dangerous, for Ella and my friends as well as for me.

'The thing is . . . what do we do with all this stuff now?' I said.

'Let's just show it to the others,' Lewis said.

'Yeah, we need to do that, of course,' I said. 'But we need something more airtight than that. At the moment, this is just me hacking into Ethan's online drive and it leaves me open to all kinds of accusations. For all anyone else knows I could have just planted this stuff to get me out of a hole.'

Lewis thought for a moment. 'Well, one idea I had was that I try to somehow get some time with Ethan. I mean, he doesn't know me, right? None of your friends do.'

'True . . .'

'Tell me if this sounds mad, but what if I pretend to be some kind of journalist . . . and say that I want to interview him or something. . .'

'Go on . . .' I said, intrigued.

'Well, I haven't completely thought it through . . .' Lewis said with a smile.

'No, but it's a good start,' I said. 'If you can appeal to his vanity: ingratiate yourself with him and then try to trip him up somehow, he might take his eye off the ball for a moment. That's all we need. A moment.' I could feel my heart pounding as we spoke, searching every corner of my mind for a spark . . . an idea . . .

Lewis nodded. 'OK, but we need a plausible story. It has

to be totally credible, and then you'll have to point me in the direction of who I need to contact to get to the dude.'

'OK, let's get on it,' I said. 'Let's make a plan.'

We spent the rest of that night searching and scheming, trying to figure out the best way to make use of everything we'd seen and everything we knew about Ethan. The following day, with a certain amount of sadness, I packed up my stuff. I still hadn't seen Austin or Sai since the showdown, and although I knew they didn't want to see me, I felt pretty low leaving the place that we'd all arrived at with such excitement for *Emerge*. Still, having Lewis around helped – it helped a lot.

We moved to the Hoxton Hotel in Shoreditch, which would be both a comfortable home and a headquarters for us to continue planning, and once we'd unpacked and got settled in our rooms, we wasted no time in diving straight back into it. Finally, later that evening, we closed our laptops and lay back on my already trashed hotel room floor – two fried heads – thinking that we just might have cracked a pretty decent plan to topple Ethan. And while it didn't sound like the easiest thing in the world to execute, it was the only plan we had.

'OK, man, I really need to eat before I pass out,' Lewis said, looking at his watch. 'Shall we get some room service?'

It was then that it dawned on me that we'd barely stopped for a drink all day, let alone any food.

'No, let's go out and grab something,' I suggested. 'I could do with getting some air anyway. I feel like I've done a hundred squats, kneeling down here on the floor for hours.'

'Sounds good,' Lewis said, jumping up.

'I suppose we'll have to find some organic, eco-friendly vegetarian café for you, right?' I laughed, holding out my arm towards him.

Lewis gripped my hand and pulled me up off the floor, grinning widely. 'Screw that, bro. Let's go to Five Guys.'

THE TRUTH

It was just after midnight when my phone rang. At first the noise sounded like it was part of the disturbing dream I was having: Ethan's leering face dancing round in my head as he whispered, 'Don't think I'm finished yet, Jack.' But as the ringing carried on, I slowly came out of the deep sleep I'd fallen into an hour or so before. I grabbed the phone from the bedside table just as it went silent, and stared at it groggily. Seconds later it started up again; the call was from a London landline, but not one of my contacts and not one I recognised.

I picked up. 'This had better be good,' I croaked out.

'Jack. It's me.' I sat bolt upright in bed. 'It's Ella.'

'Ella! What—'

'Just listen, please.' She sounded weird: panicky, and on the verge of tears. 'I'm at a Texaco petrol station somewhere near Old Street.'

'What's going on? Are you OK?'

'No, I'm not. I haven't got my phone or any money or cards with me, and . . . Look, would you please jump in an

Uber and come pick me up, as soon as you can? I'll tell you everything then.'

'God, of course. I'm getting dressed and coming right now,' I told her, jumping out of bed. I could hear her speaking to someone else in the background, asking for the address. 'Jack, it's 241 City Road. Did you get that?'

'I did. I'll be there as fast as I can. Be careful, OK? Stay inside the petrol station.'

I was up, dressed, out of the hotel and into an Uber in about six minutes, fuelled by a rush of pure adrenalin. It didn't take me long to get to the petrol station, my heart racing at a hundred miles an hour as I urged the driver to go as fast as he could. When we pulled up on the forecourt, Ella ran out of the shop and got into the back of the car. For a split second we just stared at each other – then she threw herself into my arms.

'I'm so, so sorry, Jack,' she said, breathing hard. 'I'm so sorry about everything.'

As good as it felt to hold her and to hear those words, I had to find out what was going on; I'd never seen her this rattled.

'Ella, what's happened? Are you all right? What are you doing on your own this late, with no phone and no money?'

'Not yet. Wait until we get to the hotel,' she said. 'Just hold me for a minute, will you?'

Ten minutes later we were sitting side by side in a quiet red leather booth in the hotel bar, which was still open. By then Ella, shaken and angry, was ready to tell me what had happened.

'It was after tonight's episode of *Emerge*,' she said,

brushing a tear away with the back of her hand. 'We all went out for a quick bite and then Ethan invited me round to his.' I felt my whole body stiffen at her words, at the thought of Ella being alone with that psycho. 'I only went because I was so upset about the situation with you, and I needed the company of a friend. Honestly, Jack, I would have just hung out with Ava, but she was off seeing Suki to try and sort things out between the two of them, and Ethan was being so kind about the whole thing . . .'

'It's OK, you don't have to explain,' I said softly, dreading what was coming next. 'Go on.'

'Anyway, when I got there, we were just talking about GenNext and *Emerge* and the US show for ages . . . and then I started talking about you, and how hard it was for me to accept all the stuff with Glen and that I didn't know what to do next . . . And Ethan was all nice and understanding at first. But then he started saying stuff that made me feel a bit weird . . .'

'What kind of stuff?' I asked.

'Stuff like how I needed to forget you and move on. He said that any association with you would jeopardise the show moving forward and that I needed to accept that you weren't the person I thought you were . . .'

'That's rich coming from him,' I said, thinking of all the creepy stuff that Lewis and I had found on Ethan's online drive.

'He just kept saying that he knew how hurt I must be, but that in time I'd be able to get over it,' Ella said, looking down. 'And then he . . . Oh God, it makes me so angry thinking about it.'

I noticed that she was shaking, but with fury rather than fear. 'What, Ella? What did he do?' Anger was rising inside me like mercury in a thermometer.

'He tried to kiss me,' Ella said. 'I mean, it wasn't that bad at first; we'd been sitting together on the sofa and he'd made it all very cosy and intimate, and I thought he'd just misjudged the situation – thinking it was something it wasn't – so I politely set him straight.'

'OK . . .' I said, trying to clamp down on the horror I felt at the thought of Ethan trying to get cosy and intimate with Ella.

'But then he did it again. He kept trying to kiss me, and he wasn't taking no for an answer. I don't know if he thought I was just being coy or something; every time I said no, he just dismissed it with a laugh, saying that I didn't mean it. I saw a side to him I hadn't seen before . . . and I didn't like it one bit.'

'God, Ella, what a creep,' I said, taking her hand. 'That must have been really scary.'

'I was more angry than scared at that point,' she said. 'I mean, how dare he? How dare he treat me with such a lack of respect? Anyway, when I told him categorically to back off, he got really worked up and then started saying some totally weird things.'

'Like what?'

'Things like I was just as bad as you and Glen,' Ella said. 'Like, why couldn't I see that he and I would make an amazing team, that together we could take GenNext to the very top, and why was I so blind. That he would be a much better match for me than you ever were. He was shouting and his

face was bright red and I've never seen anyone so furious
. . . He just lost it, Jack. It was like a switch flipped. Then
he started going on about how I was trying to ruin everything.
Well, then I did feel scared, so I got out of there as fast as
I could. I stupidly left my bag behind with everything in it,
but by the time I realised that, there was no way in hell that
I was going back.'

'Jesus, Ella, I'm going to kill him,' I said, jumping to my
feet, but Ella grabbed my hand and pulled me down again.

'Calm down, Batman,' she smiled, wiping a final tear
from the corner of her eye. 'I'm fine, honestly, just a bit
shell-shocked. It was all so horrible, and so completely unexpected; I never saw it coming. The worst part of all this is
that I didn't listen to you, and I feel terrible and really stupid.
It's obvious that Ethan concocted all this fraud stuff, and I
can't believe I ever thought otherwise. I am truly so, so sorry.'

'Look, I'm just glad you're OK,' I said, squeezing her
hand. 'And you can't imagine how happy I am to have you
next to me again.'

'Can you forgive me?' she said.

'God, of course,' I said, and I meant it. Ethan had spun
such a clever web of lies; I couldn't blame Ella for getting
caught up in it. I was just so relieved to have her back again,
to know that she knew I was innocent.

I pulled her in for a hug, and then we kissed, gently and
for a long time.

'I've missed you, Ella Foster,' I said.

'It's only been a few days,' she smiled. 'And you've missed
me that much?'

'Not really just a few days,' I said. 'I feel like we lost each other sometime during Total Festival. As soon as Ethan appeared, actually. I feel like he's been out to destroy us from the get-go.'

'God, how did none of us see it?' Ella said.

'Look, I've seen how manipulative he can be,' I said. 'Somehow he managed to wind everyone round his little finger, and by the time everything went down there was so much at stake, what with *Emerge* and the American deal. He never showed any of you the side of him that he showed to me. The nasty side. He was very smart about that.'

'I'd call it downright evil,' Ella said sadly.

'The one thing I want you to know is that I *am* really supportive of your career. I couldn't bear that Ethan had made you think I wasn't. This whole mess has made me realise that, yes, GenNext is important, and it'll always be something amazing that the five of us created together, but what's even more important is that we use it as a springboard to grow, and to follow our dreams and ambitions – even if those dreams are different. Part of being in love with someone is making it work together, and supporting the other person no matter what, you know?'

Ella smiled, the anger and sadness in her eyes finally evaporating. 'Wow! Jack Penman, inspirational speaker,' she said, touching my cheek.

'Are you taking the mick?' I laughed.

'Absolutely not,' Ella said, her eyes crinkling. 'I knew deep down you would always support whatever I wanted to do. I just had my head turned by all Ethan's grand promises, and somehow I let him convince me that he was the supportive one, not you. I'm truly sorry for that.'

We kissed again, but this time it was cut short by a voice from behind me.

'Man, how did I know I'd find you in a bar with a beautiful woman?' I looked up to find Lewis grinning down at the two of us. 'Ella, I presume,' he said, holding out his hand. She looked momentarily confused as the unshaven, tattooed figure in a yellow vest and multicoloured jogging pants sat down on the bench opposite. 'I'm assuming you guys have kissed and made up.'

'Ella, this is Lewis,' I said. 'My brother.'

'Oh my God!' Ella squealed. 'How . . . ? But I don't . . .'

'Your boy here was in trouble, so I came to London to save him,' Lewis grinned.

'Yeah, whatever, dude!' I scoffed.

'It's really good to meet you, Ella, but I feel like I know you already with this guy gushing about you every five seconds,' Lewis said.

Ella's eyes were shining. 'Well, I'm really happy to meet you too, Lewis. And I'm even happier to see that you and Jack are friends. This is . . . it's amazing. Are you staying here, too?'

'I am,' he said. 'I couldn't sleep and I had a few fresh thoughts about our plan, Jack, so I went to your room to see if you were still awake. Then when you didn't answer I figured you were either dead to the world, down here in the bar, or that you'd just decided to give it all up and throw yourself out of a fourth-floor window.'

'I like your style of humour, Lewis,' Ella said, giggling. Then her face turned serious. 'Now, what's this about a plan?'

Lewis looked at me and then back at Ella. 'OK, do you want to tell her, Jack . . . or shall I?'

THE PHONE CALL

Lewis: Hello! Am I speaking with Ethan Harper?

Ethan: You are. Who's calling?

Lewis: My name's Mark Knowles; I'm a journalist with Savage Online. You know it?

Ethan: Doesn't everyone? How can I help you, Mr Knowles?

Lewis: Well, we'd very much like to do a piece about you to coincide with the live final of *Emerge* tomorrow.

Ethan: What sort of piece? About the show?

Lewis: It's a profile of you, Mr Harper, charting your rapid rise to popularity since the show started.

(Silence for a few moments)

Ethan: Go on . . .

Lewis: The focus of the piece is how you're emerging – no pun – as the new star of GenNext now that Jack Penman appears to be off the scene. We're very keen to get an exclusive before everyone else starts clamouring to interview you.

Ethan: I see. And when were you thinking of conducting this interview?

Lewis: I'd like to do it this afternoon. I'll be down at the venue, watching the live showcase. It would be fantastic to interview you shortly before the show kicks off, to capture the atmosphere and excitement beforehand. Would that be convenient for you?

Ethan: Today? It's going to be very busy; there'll be a lot of preparation before the show . . .

Lewis: I just need five minutes with you, Ethan. It's the perfect time to do it, and it'd be really great if we can get the piece up online right after the show airs. It'll be the lead article on the website this week, and I'm sure I don't need to tell you that our site receives more traffic worldwide than any other. This would be VERY high-profile.

Ethan: The lead article, you say?

Lewis: Correct.

Ethan: I'm certainly very interested, Mr Knowles. Can I come back to you on this number? I'll need to check your credentials online, as I'm sure you can understand.

Lewis: Of course. I'll be on this number all day. Do let me know what you decide.

THE DAY OF . . .

Lewis was pacing around his hotel room like a caged tiger, muttering to himself every now and again in an attempt to get into character ahead of his important mission. It was a mission that we both knew relied on perfect execution, precision timing . . . and luck. We were on the cusp of something major, and for this to work, we couldn't afford any screw-ups. While he paced, I sat in the corner of the room in an armchair sipping coffee and feeling eerily calm. It was Saturday. The day of the *Emerge* live final at the Camden Electric, when the ultimate winner of the competition was to play a showcase gig in front of an audience of millions. The day I was due to be disgraced and replaced by Ethan Harper. The day we put our plan into action.

'Aren't I supposed to be the one who's bricking it?' I said as Lewis strode past me for the twentieth time. 'I'm the one whose career and reputation is hanging on a twig, dude. Sit down, will you? You're making me dizzy.'

'Shut up and drink your Starbucks, man. I always walk when I'm thinking: usually on a beach, but we're a bit short of those in London, so this will have to do,' Lewis said. He checked his watch. 'We still haven't heard back from him. It's been an hour since we spoke. Do you think he really bought the whole journalist thing? I mean, the guy's no idiot. What if he's seen straight through the fake profile we set up?'

'No way. We put so much detail into it; it was foolproof,' I told him. 'He will call, I'm sure of it. However smart he is, he's too bloody conceited to ignore the chance of that sort of online glory – I know him.'

Fifteen minutes later, the sign we were waiting for finally came. A text to Lewis's phone . . . from Ethan.

> Hi Mark.
> Yes, I can give you ten
> minutes today around 6.15pm.
> Call me when you're at
> the venue.
> EH.

We'd gone over the plan about a thousand times in the last two days – or at least that was the way it felt – but now that it was actually on, it felt scarily real. At times, I was certain that we really had a chance and that everything was going to come good, but in moments of doubt it felt like a ridiculous long shot that was never going to work, and I swung violently between the two trains of thought on an hourly basis. The truth was, if this went wrong and it all blew up in my face, I was going to be in even worse trouble than I already was. I'd be done for. Finished.

One of the things I was most unhappy about was the fact that Ella was going to have to spend the day with Ethan after everything he'd done. We didn't really have a choice. For our plan to work, he had to believe that she was on side and totally committed to the show. The prospect of that was the hardest part of the plan for Ella, and I could hardly blame her.

I thought back to Thursday night, the night she had run out of Ethan's flat. She'd been pretty freaked out, especially after Lewis and I filled her in on all the private pictures and GenNext files on Ethan's online drive. She'd been even more horrified at my discovery that Ethan was involved with the two idiots who'd started the fight at Total. When we got back to the hotel room that night, her instinct had been to tell AJ and the rest of the GenNext team everything we knew straight away.

'Who cares if it's the middle of the night? Let's just call them,' she'd said urgently. 'Let's put a stop to this now, Jack. I never want to have to look at that creep again.'

'Look, Ella, I get where you're coming from, and it does seem like the obvious thing to do,' I said, putting my arm around her. 'But even if we convince the rest of the crew that it's all true, Ethan could still release his fabricated evidence about Glen and me trying to rig the competition, and that could ruin both of us. Plus, it would trash GenNext's name forever and sink *Emerge* totally, and we've worked way too hard for that to happen. Trust me, the fewer people who know what we know, the better. That way, it'll be harder for Ethan to slither out of it once we finally show him for what he really is.'

Ella's expression of anger changed into one of weary realisation. 'Oh God, I never thought of that. You're right, he's likely to get desperate, and he might do anything if you try to alert the others.'

'Exactly,' Lewis agreed. 'I don't think we're dealing with a rational bloke here. Who knows what he'd be capable of if he feels like he's backed into a corner?'

'The only way we're going to expose him is to let him think he's winning,' I said. 'And that means you're going to have to bite the bullet, babe, and play along like nothing happened the other night. It's hard I know, but it's the only way. Obviously we'll make sure that you're never, ever alone with him.'

Ella had set her jaw determinedly. 'It won't be easy, but I'm willing to do whatever it takes, Jack.'

I'd gone to sleep that night feeling pretty confident about our plan, particularly having Ella both on my side and by my side. But when we woke up yesterday morning, it was to some heavy online speculation that all was not as it should be in the GenNext camp: various websites, including E! Online, Huff Post and BuzzFeed were speculating that I was being axed from GenNext for some serious but unspecified wrongdoing, to be replaced by Ethan. It didn't exactly take a world-class detective to work out that this was the work of Ethan himself, drip-feeding his poison to the online press and laying the groundwork for the announcement of my departure in Saturday's live show. It was hardly a surprise that he'd agreed to the interview with Lewis aka Mark Knowles; he probably had half the tabloid journalists in the country on speed dial. In fact, all the time we'd been gathering ourselves and formulating a plan, he'd been busy inflicting carnage, and if we didn't act fast, it would be too late. The damage would be irreparable. My morning didn't improve after that: while Ella, Lewis and I ate breakfast at the hotel, a courier delivered an official letter from GenNext's management company, Metronome. It was a stiffly worded document, signed by AJ, informing me that I was being let go from GenNext and from Metronome itself. Seeing it down on paper like that, with Metronome's familiar logo at the top, was gutting.

Ella, noticing the desolate look on my face, took the letter from me and read it once I'd finished.

'Oh Jack, this is so, so awful,' she said sadly. 'How could it have happened?'

Lewis put his hand on my shoulder across the table. 'Don't worry, man, this is all going to be over tomorrow. We're going to expose this guy, trust me.'

I nodded slowly, hoping that he was right and that our plan would work. And if it didn't? Well, even if I was able to convince my friends that I was innocent, there was no telling what Ethan might do; he'd sooner ruin GenNext entirely than hand the reins back to me, I just knew it.

Last night, I'd finally persuaded Ella to call Ethan. He'd left her a voicemail earlier on in the day asking her where she was and if she could call him back, and the way he was talking it was as if absolutely nothing had happened between them. It was creepy.

'Just be as natural as possible with him,' I said as Ella stood looking down at her iPhone and biting her lip. 'We need him to believe that you're back on side. Why don't you put it on speakerphone so Lewis and I can hear, too?'

Ella nodded, her mouth drawing tight in a grim line. 'I'll do my best, Jack, but it's not going to be easy knowing what I now know about him.'

She dialled Ethan's number and then put her phone on speaker.

He picked up almost straight away. 'Ella! You never called me back earlier.' There was an edge to his voice.

'Yeah, sorry about that, Ethan,' Ella said. 'It's been a bit of a crazy afternoon.'

'Sure.' There was a pause. 'I just want to make sure that we're cool after last night. You know it was just a laugh, right? I was playing around.'

'Playing around?' Ella said incredulously.

'Of course; it's just my sense of humour. You took me too seriously, that's all. God, I thought we were supposed to be friends. I was a bit hurt by your overreaction, to be honest.'

'Of course we're friends, Ethan,' Ella said gently, although the expression on her face was murderous. 'And I'm really sorry if I hurt your feelings.'

Lewis rolled his eyes and made a hand gesture to show what he thought of the conversation.

'Good. That's really important, because the fans love seeing us together. We can't let them down, can we? I *have* to know I can still rely on you, Ella.' His tone had switched in a flash from petulant to demanding. 'Can I trust you to get past this so that we can work together? GenNext is relying on us. *Emerge* is relying on us.'

'Of course you can,' Ella said. She looked at me and mouthed a swear word. Lewis stuck two fingers down his throat and pretended to gag, silently.

'Good girl,' Ethan said, oozing satisfaction. 'I just need to ask, though. You haven't said anything to Jack about our little misunderstanding, have you? The guy's in big trouble

– like it or not – and if he comes anywhere near *Emerge*, it's only going to get worse for him, trust me. And you know that anyone associated with him is at risk, too – it'll look like they were involved in the scam. Do you understand what I'm saying?'

I could see Ella mentally biting her tongue as she thought about how to respond to his thinly veiled threat. Meanwhile, I was ready to grab the phone and throw it out of the window.

'No, I haven't even spoken to Jack. I know you're right; I can't trust him any more.' Her voice had softened for effect. 'I'm glad it's going to be you and me up there tomorrow night, Ethan. The truth is, we make a much better team than Jack and I ever did.' She looked like she'd just uttered the most disgusting sentence of her life, but to me it sounded like a stroke of genius.

'I knew that was how you really felt,' Ethan said arrogantly. 'I knew you'd get there in the end, Ella, once you realised what a lowlife Jack Penman is. He doesn't deserve to be part of GenNext, but I – *we* – do. I'm looking forward to being up there together with you, too. I can't wait, actually.'

'Great,' Ella choked out. 'I'll see you tomorrow.'

'You most certainly will,' Ethan said. 'Bring your A game, babe.'

Once she'd hung up, Ella threw her phone on the bed.

'That was officially the most hideous thing I have ever, EVER had to do,' she said, looking traumatised.

I put my arms around her. 'I know, I know. He is just such a complete and utter snake. You were seriously amazing, though. I think you said exactly what he wanted to hear.'

'The more I know about this guy, the more he totally

freaks me out,' Lewis said with a shudder. 'He really is one deluded nut-job.'

Ella sighed. 'Well, at least I've got him back on side. Now it's just tomorrow to get through . . . and then hopefully none of us will even have to look at Ethan Harper ever again.'

That had been last night. Now here we were on the day of the show. Ella was with the rest of GenNext preparing for *Emerge* to go live, and Lewis was still pacing the floor of the hotel room. He'd now been at it for almost an hour.

'What if Ethan sees through me?' he said.

'He won't,' I replied. 'He's got no reason not to trust you. You'll be fine, Lewis, I know you will. And at the risk of sounding excessively mushy, I can't tell you how much I appreciate you doing this for me. I don't know what I would have done without your help.'

He smiled. 'You know what I was thinking?' he said. 'Can you imagine if Dad and your mum knew about everything that's happened in the last few days? If they knew what we were doing today . . . the two of us . . . together?'

He had a point. Dad wouldn't have imagined in a million years that his two sons would be hanging out in London together, let alone teaming up against an enemy force. Still, he'd know soon enough . . . once all this was over.

Just then, my phone pinged with a message from Glen. Yes, I'd roped him into helping us enact our insane plan. Glen knew everyone on the *Emerge* production team, and had an encyclopedic knowledge of the Camden Electric. He needed to clear his name as much as I did mine; his reputation and career were on the line, too. Aside from that, there was also the threat of both of us being arrested if it all went the wrong way. The best thing about Glen's involvement was that he'd got plenty of friends on the *Emerge* team who knew without question that he would never have committed the attempted fraud he'd been accused of. A fraud that, thankfully, Olympia had managed to keep out of the press so that the show could go on. Glancing down at Glen's text, it looked as though everything was going smoothly so far.

> Everything sorted, babes. Luckily, my friend Shania's stage-managing the whole show today, and is completely up to speed with the plan. She's sorted an AAA pass for your brother so he can get backstage and she's going to smuggle the two of us in a back entrance so we won't be spotted and turfed out onto the street like common criminals!!! There's a Pret A Manger right near the venue – meet there at 5pm? Glen x

I looked at my watch: 3 p.m. Lewis was reading Glen's message over my shoulder.

'Two hours till showtime,' he said.

While we waited, I logged on to the GenNext forums and Twitter account to see what the online chat was like about the live broadcast.

OK, not such a good idea. Seeing all the fans tweeting and commenting about how excited they were just made me feel worse. The fact was, after a week of *Emerge* episodes there seemed to be a growing fan base for Ethan. He was obviously killing it and I'd had no way of combating that, being totally out of the loop. God, was I too late? Were the fans getting used to GenNext without me? Was GenNext *better* without me? It was a grim thought, and I chewed on it for a few minutes before eventually pulling myself together and reminding myself that even if Ethan *was* amassing all this love online, those fans didn't have a clue what he was really like.

Still, as the minutes ticked by, my anxiety mounted. There were just too many ways that the plan could go wrong, and I couldn't stop each and every bad scenario running through my head, one after the other. It wasn't just my career and reputation at stake either; it was my friendships with Ava, Sai, AJ and Austin. It was everything.

3.30 p.m. I'd texted Ella twice but hadn't heard back, and now I was worrying. Maybe the signal wasn't good in the venue. Maybe they were doing a camera rehearsal. God, maybe Ethan had sussed out what was going on and had Ella tied up in a cupboard somewhere. *No, now you're being ridiculous, Penman.*

By four o'clock, I'd had enough of waiting around. 'I think we should go; I need to get out of here, Lewis.'

He was standing by the wardrobe. 'Yeah, OK. I just need to decide what I'm going to wear to look convincing.'

'Perhaps something smart, dude. The yellow vest isn't going to cut it today,' I said with a straight face. 'Right, I'm going back to my room to grab my stuff. I'll meet you downstairs when you're dressed and ready, OK?'

Lewis nodded solemnly. 'Let's do this.'

THE VENUE

We met Glen at 5 p.m. as planned. I could tell immediately that the last week had taken its toll on him: he looked thinner and greyer than when I'd last seen him, and he had dark circles under his eyes. Still, he gave both of us massive hugs when he saw us, and was clearly as hopeful – and as nervous – as we were about the prospect of taking Ethan down.

When we reached the venue, the queue outside was a massive, excited snake of fans, all ready for the show. I hung back with a baseball cap pulled down over my face and Aviators on, just in case anyone from Owl TV was knocking around outside the venue, or in case any of the fans recognised me, which would be a disaster.

Glen took out his phone. 'Right, we'll scoot past the queue and head round to the back of the building,' he said. 'Shania should be there by now; I'll text her.'

I looked at Lewis, who was pale. 'Are you OK?'

He swallowed hard. 'This isn't exactly what I'm used to in Cornwall, man. My life's normally a bit more chilled than this, you know?'

'You'll be fine,' I said, trying to be reassuring but not quite believing it myself. 'I've got every faith in you, Lewis.'

'Right!' He took a deep breath, then stood up straight, squaring his shoulders. He looked pretty impressive, it must be said. The tattoos were hidden by a crisp long-sleeved shirt, the earrings had gone and he'd combed his hair into a neat and professional side parting. It was a million miles away from his usual scruffy surfer vibe.

When we reached the allocated entrance at the back of the building, Shania, an athletic-looking young black woman with close-cropped hair, was waiting with the door slightly ajar.

'Hey, Glen, how's it going?'

'OK so far, babes,' Glen said. 'Thanks for doing this, Shania. You're an absolute doll.'

'No sweat!' She smiled at us, handing Lewis an AAA laminate. 'This is for you. You need to go back around to the front entrance and get checked in. I've added your name to the press list, so if Ethan should happen to check on you, it'll all look kosher. Mark Knowles, right?'

'That's it. Mark Knowles from Savage Online,' Lewis confirmed.

'OK,' she said. 'I'll meet you in the foyer in fifteen minutes, Mr Knowles. There's a little props room behind the stage; I'll take you there, then go and fetch Ethan to meet you. I'll make sure he knows that you're a VIP.'

'Great,' I said. 'Remember, they're due to meet at six fifteen. No earlier, and no later; it has to be bang-on.'

'OK, Jack.' Shania saluted.

Lewis nervously waved goodbye and headed off towards

the building's foyer, with his access-all-areas laminate swinging around his neck. His press pass – obtained after he called in a favour from one of his old hacker friends based in London – was clipped to his front pocket. We'd even created a fake Savage Online ID card for him to flash for extra authenticity, plus we'd set up a news portal featuring some impressive online interviews that 'Mark Knowles' had done in the past with the likes of Zayn Malik, Alexa Chung and Selena Gomez. A skilled hacker might recognise that it was fake, but I was counting on the fact that Ethan – despite his ability to meddle with other people's computers and forge emails – would think it was legit.

Once Glen and I were inside the venue, we followed Shania stealthily up some stairs and along a warren of corridors. She walked several steps in front of us the whole way, making sure the coast was clear. At every new corner and each new set of stairs, I pictured us running into one of the GenNext gang or Olympia or even Ethan himself, until my stomach had turned over so many times, I felt sick. Finally we reached the props room, which was very close to the stage. So close that we could literally be caught at any second.

'Quick, get inside,' Shania said, swinging the door open. 'Olympia and the others are in the dressing rooms just over there, so whatever you do, don't stick your head out of the door.'

Inside, there was a shortish ginger-haired guy leaning against a desk. He grinned widely when he saw us.

'All right, Glen?' he said. 'How's it going?'

'Been better, babes.' Glen rolled his eyes. 'Looking forward to getting all this espionage out of the way.'

'Jack, this is Pete,' Shania said, her voice low. 'He's going to wire you for sound.'

'Good to meet you, mate,' I said. Pete grinned again and shook my hand, then got busy pinning a tiny mic on my collar, while Shania kept watch to make sure nobody was heading our way.

'Here's your mic pack and an in-ear monitor,' Pete said, handing me a small grey box. 'I've put new batteries in, so it should all be cushty. I'm going out to the sound desk now, but you'll be able to hear me and talk to me if you need to, OK?'

'Got it,' I said.

Pete gave my mic a final tweak and then adjusted my shirt so that it was hidden. 'Right. There's a little cupboard over there. You can just about squeeze in, can't you?'

'Squeeze in?'

'Yeah, that's where you have to wait,' he said. 'If anyone comes near, keep quiet.'

'So I'm hiding in a cupboard?' I said.

Pete smiled. 'That's right, I'm afraid. He pointed up to a corner of the room. 'Ella has already been in and set up your camera, and we should be able to record Ethan's voice on your mic as well as Lewis's.'

'And then what?' Glen said. 'What happens once we've got something on him on film? *If* we get something on film?'

'Ella's linked the live feed to her iPad,' I said. 'As soon as anything happens, she'll make sure Olympia and the rest of the gang see it.'

Everyone looked at me like it was the longest shot in the world, and it was. But if we could just surprise Ethan, put him on the spot and get him to reveal his true colours . . . maybe this would work.

At that moment my phone pinged with a text from Ella.

It was short and sweet, but at least I knew she was OK, and that everything was set to go.

'Look, I have to head out now, Jack,' Shania said. 'I've got to make sure your brother has been cleared by security and then bring him back here.'

'I'll be fine, Shania,' I said. 'Tell Ethan that you recognise Mark Knowles as the hotshot reporter who interviewed Selena Gomez recently, just for extra believability.'

If that didn't prick up Ethan's ears and lure him into our trap, nothing would.

Pete assured me that he'd be on the other end of a radio headset the whole time should I need him, and then he and Shania wished us good luck and headed out of the room. That left Glen and me.

'Right, darling!' he said. 'I'd better make myself scarce. I'm going to hang out at the back of the auditorium and pray nobody from the TV company sees me. The very best of luck.'

I shook his hand. 'Thanks for all this, mate. I don't know how you managed to get so much help on the inside, but I really appreciate it.'

'Don't mention it, babes,' he smiled. 'Shania is like family to me, and Pete and I have worked on tons of shows together; he's a good guy. I knew they'd help. Anyway, it's as much for me as it is for you, right?'

'Of course it is,' I said.

'OK, now get in that bloody cupboard, put your phone on silent and keep your gob shut. And Jack? *Please* look after yourself. Remember that Ethan isn't . . . he isn't *normal*. You're dealing with someone who's prepared to do absolutely anything to get what he wants.'

After Glen had delivered those unsettling words and left the props room, I climbed into the cupboard and pulled the door shut behind me, hearing only the sound of my own breathing and feeling the steady thump of my heart. I took out my copy of the show's running order, shining my phone torch on it so that I could quickly scan through it a final time. Ella and Ethan were due on stage ten minutes before the live broadcast for a camera check, so everything had to be in place at least thirty minutes before that – timing was everything. I shoved the paper back in my pocket and leaned back as far as I could in the cramped space I was set to occupy for the next fifteen minutes or so. Now all I had to do was wait . . . and hope.

THE SET-UP

From my not-so-comfortable position in the cupboard, I could hear the audience packing into the auditorium, chanting and cheering for the start of the show. I looked at my phone — it was just forty-five minutes until the live broadcast, when Ethan and Ella were expected on stage to introduce the three acts that had made the final, before the audience voted for an ultimate champion at the climax of the show. It could all have been so exciting if everything hadn't gone so horribly wrong, and that made me sad. I pictured Ava getting busy and bossing the camera crew around; Sai switching endlessly between screens and devices to make sure that GenNext got the maximum amount of social media while the broadcast was happening . . . and then I thought of Austin, and wondered how he was doing in the midst of all this and whether he'd got his confidence back.

My thoughts were cut short by the creak of an opening door and the sound of Shania's voice. 'Here you go, guys; you shouldn't be disturbed in here. Sorry it's a bit small, but it's close enough for me to come grab you if you're suddenly needed on stage, Ethan.'

'Thank you, Shania,' I heard Lewis say.

'Got it, Shania, thanks.' That was Ethan's voice.

My heart was thundering away like crazy, the noise of the crowd in the background making me feel even more anxious.

'So, Mr Knowles. It's very good to meet you.' That was Ethan again.

'Please, call me Mark,' Lewis said.

'OK, Mark. I was very impressed with some of the interview you've done in the past, I have to say.'

I heard the sound of chairs being pulled out from under the table. We were on; the interview was getting under way. Out in the auditorium, the crowd were getting more boisterous, so I pushed my ear to the door of the cupboard, straining to hear what Lewis and Ethan were saying, and waiting for just the right moment . . . and hoping Ella's clandestine camera would pick up the conversation clearly enough over all the noise.

'So where would you like to start, Mark?' Ethan asked.

'Actually, I'd be really interested to hear how you managed to land such a prestigious gig in the first place, Ethan – I'm hugely impressed,' Lewis said, and I found myself grinning at just how convincing a journalist he sounded. 'I mean, you must be highly thought of by the heads of the production company because GenNext was Jack Penman's thing, right?'

'It was, yes, but—'

'And he's a tough act to follow, wouldn't you say?' Lewis said, goading him.

'You think so, do you?' Ethan's voice sounded thin and clipped.

'Well, everyone loves the guy.'

'Loved,' Ethan snapped. 'Past tense, Mark.'

'So what on earth happened?' Lewis said. 'Was there a clash of personalities between the two of you? Infighting? Why has Jack Penman decided to step down when everything was going so well?'

'He didn't have a choice,' Ethan cut in vehemently, and then I heard a chair scrape against the floor. 'Look, Mark, I didn't come here to talk about Jack Penman. This isn't the interview we agreed to at all, so I suggest we leave it there . . .'

'Just one more thing,' I heard Lewis say. 'What do you have to say about this collection of files? I'd venture that they show an extraordinary . . . no, an *alarming* interest in GenNext over the last year. Wouldn't you agree?'

There was silence, during which I knew Lewis was scrolling through screenshots of the incriminating GenNext files on Ethan's hard drive. Then:

'What the *hell*?!' Ethan snapped. 'What is this? I've never seen those before in my life.'

'I'm not really buying that, Ethan. They were found on your computer. Pretty incriminating, wouldn't you say?'

'Listen, I don't know what you're playing at,' Ethan said viciously, 'but it will take me less than two minutes to have you arrested and thrown out of here. Who the hell are you; are you even a journalist?'

'Well, I'm not a reporter from Savage Online, if that's what you mean,' Lewis said. That was my cue to exit my hiding place. Heart hammering away at a million miles an hour, I burst out of the cupboard.

'Hey, Ethan. How's it going?'

Ethan's eyes almost fell out of his head when he saw me, and he took a step back, his gaze flicking between Lewis and me. 'Is this some kind of joke?'

I stepped forward, the mere sight of him igniting a ball of fury inside me, but I knew I had to stay calm for this to work. It was vital I didn't lose it. 'No joke, Ethan. I'm glad you're already acquainted with Lewis here; he's my older brother, by the way.'

'Your brother?' Ethan's expression was slowly changing from irritation to cold fury.

'That's right,' I said, advancing on him. 'And it's time for some home truths. You're a liar, Ethan. I know you got into my computer, and that's how you framed Glen and me *and* how you found out about Austin's depression. I know everything, and this stops now.'

Ethan's mouth curled into a mocking smile. 'Oh wow! You really are deluded, aren't you? How did you even get in here? Your tiny brain has grasped the important fact that you could be arrested for even showing up, hasn't it, Jack?' He shook his head, and laughed. 'Just wait until I let Olympia know that you've sneaked in. You won't be allowed within a ten-mile radius of GenNext again, ever. You're finished.'

He turned to go, grabbing the door handle. But as per the plan, it had been locked from the outside.

'OK, enough! Let me out of here right now,' he said, turning to face us, his voice low and dangerous. 'Don't make this any worse for yourselves than it already is.'

'Didn't you hear me, Ethan?' I said, ignoring him. 'We know. We know all about you. We've seen your files. I even know that you hired those two guys to beat me up at the festival. And I know what you did to Ella, too. You're the one who's finished, mate.'

Ethan recovered his arrogant grin, but by now he was fraying around the edges; struggling to keep his cool.

'Ella? You don't know what you're talking about. You must be having a breakdown, Jack, just like your mate Austin. And do you know what? Whatever you think you've seen online, you found it illegally – and given that you already stand accused of a major fraud, that isn't going to look too good. There's absolutely no evidence of any wrongdoing on my part. So I followed GenNext. So I had ambition. That's not a crime. Unlike what you did, trying to fool the British public.'

I looked over at Lewis, who shook his head slightly, looking worried. This wasn't quite going the way we'd planned. Ethan was just dismissing everything I threw at him, denying it all. We needed something concrete, some real evidence.

'But that's not the case, is it?' I said. '*I'm* not the dirty cheat here, am I, Ethan?'

Ethan's neck had turned red, his eyes narrowed. 'The evidence against you is irrefutable. You're a spoilt little boy throwing your toys out of the pram because you happened to get caught out.' A manic light flashed in his eyes. 'You really can't handle the fact that GenNext is so much better without you in it, can you? That the fans love me more, that your friends – and your girlfriend – are much happier with me around. Well, get used to it, Jack.'

'You're deluded,' I said. 'Do you really think the others

are going to stick with you when they hear what I've got to say?'

Ethan shrugged. 'They aren't going to care. Olympia wants me at the helm when *Emerge* transfers to America, and the rest of GenNext think the sun shines out of my backside. As for Ella, she'll get over this week's silly tantrum; she's far too ambitious to throw all this away. The thing is, Ella understands what you're too stupid to see: that she and I *are* GenNext. Face it, you were only ever a pointless accessory.' He turned towards the door again. 'Now, I'm really sorry, but I've got a show to do. It was lovely to meet you' – he sneered at Lewis – 'but all this is getting boring. Time to open this door, and for the two of you to be escorted off the premises by security.'

At that moment we heard the sound of a key turning in the lock on the other side of the door.

'Ella?' Ethan looked horrified as she stepped through, shutting the door firmly behind her.

I shot a wide-eyed glance at Lewis; we were both as surprised as Ethan to see her. This wasn't part of the plan.

'So I'm too ambitious to throw it all away, am I, Ethan?' Ella said, and it was clear she meant business. 'Listen to me, you creep. You're the one who should be in prison. You're lucky I haven't reported you for trying to molest me in your apartment. Everything you've ever said to me has been a lie, Ethan . . . EVERYTHING!'

Ethan's jaw dropped and he started breathing hard, his neck now a weird puce colour. 'God, you treacherous little bitch. After everything I've done for you . . .'

'Remind me exactly what that is again,' Ella said. 'Do

you mean trying to split Jack and me up, or attempting to ruin everything we've worked for over the last two years? Do tell!'

I could see a muscle twitching in Ethan's jaw as he looked from me to Ella to Lewis, the ugly flush spreading from his neck to his face.

And then he exploded.

'OH GOD, YOU ARE ALL SUCH IDIOTS!' His eyes were bulging from his head, the veins in his neck a purple road map of fury. 'Do you really think for one minute that I actually need you, Ella? You're as lame as your boyfriend.' He was spitting now, losing control, and Ella, Lewis and I all instinctively took a step back. It was just like Ella had said the other night: a switch had been flipped. 'Face it. GenNext is mine now – as it should be. I deserve it; I was destined to be part of something like this, to *own* something like this. I'm the one who's worked so hard – how can any of you even grasp that when it all just fell into your laps?'

'*You* worked hard?!' Lewis said, dumbfounded. 'What the hell have you done to make you think you have a right to something Jack and his friends created?'

'I've worked for years. Years!' Ethan hissed, his saliva spraying my face. 'Do you know how long I've been trying to get a gig like this; how many audition tapes I've produced, how many companies I've gone to, letters I've sent? No one recognised my talent for what it was, so I ended up fetching and carrying for Olympia Shaw, working on bloody production of all things. It was so glaringly obvious that GenNext was the perfect vehicle for me. Only trouble was, it was already fronted by some pathetic nonentity who was dead set on hogging every last scrap of limelight. So I just had to get a little bit more creative, didn't I? I had to make your friends and fans see what I always saw – that GenNext would be better with me at the helm. Anyway, the public reaction says it all, doesn't it? Do you hear that crowd out there, Jack? Do you think they give a damn that you're not here? Do you think they care that you were barely visible on the show this week? No, they don't. They liked what they saw because it worked and it was brilliant. *I* was brilliant. So much better than you ever were. And Ella, if you're too stupid and insipid to get on board, then so be it. I'll do it myself. I don't need any of you.'

The three of us stood, shocked, open-mouthed and hardly daring to move; just staring at Ethan while he panted like an animal. It was a weird, disconcerting moment, because it dawned on me that in answer to Ethan's ranted question – 'Do you hear that crowd out there?' – the answer was no . . . I *couldn't* hear the crowd any more. The cheering and chanting had stopped; it was as if the entire audience had been beamed up into space or something. What was going on?

Ethan suddenly whirled around and pushed past Ella, heading for the door. But it had been locked again from the outside and wouldn't budge.

The next ten seconds were a blur. Ethan strode across the room, swearing at us through gritted teeth. Before I could stop him, he picked up the chair he'd been sitting on and hurled it at the door, just as I grabbed Ella and pulled her out of harm's way.

'GET THIS DOOR OPEN, YOU SENSELESS, PATHETIC LOSERS!' The dude had completely and utterly lost it; he was apoplectic with rage. Way, way more unhinged than I'd ever dreamed. 'OPEN THE DOOR! OPEN IT!'

And that was when I heard the crowd again, but now they were booing instead of cheering. Just a few of them at first, but then the sound grew and grew until the entire place was in uproar.

Ethan froze and looked at us, his eyes wide with shock. 'What *is* that? What's going on?'

Then the booing morphed into something else; another chant: 'Jack! Jack! Jack!'

Before any of us could react, the door to the props room swung open to reveal Olympia, Ava, Sai, AJ and Austin on the other side, with matching thunderstruck expressions. Behind them stood Shania, with a key in her hand and a smile on her face. None of us had a clue what was going on, and for a moment we all just stared at one another. Then Ava threw herself inside, tears streaming down her face, hugging first Ella and then me. I caught Austin's eye, just for a second. He looked completely stunned. Ethan remained a seething, dishevelled figure in the middle of the room, frozen in horror as he took in the members of GenNext facing him.

Olympia stepped towards him, her face a grim mask of anger. 'Ethan, I'm going to make it my mission in life to make sure you never, ever work in television again, do you understand me?'

'Olympia – no, you need to listen to me,' Ethan spluttered. 'You . . . you need to understand that I've been set up here by these . . . these *freaks*.' He spat the last word. 'I mean, they're amateurs compared to us, they just don't get it . . .'

From the auditorium we could hear the cries of 'Get Ethan

out!' ringing around the building, but he seemed to be oblivious, his gaze focused on Olympia, who was shaking her head in quiet disgust.

'Can somebody please explain to me what's happening?' I asked, which was when Sai stepped in.

'We don't really know what happened, Jack. One minute we were waiting to do a final camera check; the next minute the screen at the back of the stage flashed up with a picture, and the whole audience could see and hear everything that was happening in this room. Didn't *you* set this up?'

I shook my head dumbly. Sure, Lewis, Ella and I had been planning to transmit the conversation to Olympia and the GenNext crew, but not to an audience of thousands.

'No . . . that would have been us.' Pete appeared, joining us in the room with Glen close behind. 'I must have accidentally turned up the wrong faders or something.' He grinned, making it clear that it had been no mistake, and for a moment I wasn't sure whether to be horrified or delighted that our entire showdown with Ethan had just been broadcast to the assembled masses outside.

'Oh my God. Pete, you're a wonderful man,' Ella said.

Glen, meanwhile, was waving an iPad around in front of him. 'Well, you know me; I couldn't bear to see an Oscar-winning performance like that go unnoticed. I just felt it had to be shared with a wider audience.'

Without warning, Ethan erupted into rage again, launching himself at me, cursing and baring his teeth. 'I am going to *destroy* you, Penman.'

Shania was in there fast before he could reach me, grabbing him by the collar and restraining him, pulling one hand behind his back like a pro wrestler. Ethan struggled briefly, but then, realising there was no point, fell still. As he looked at all the shocked faces staring back at him, the rage just seemed to drain out of him as suddenly as it had appeared, and he slumped like a rag doll.

'I trusted you,' Austin said coldly. 'I trusted you and you betrayed me.'

Ethan didn't respond; he didn't even look up, his face unnervingly blank.

'Get him out of here, and please call the police,' Olympia said. 'I'm too disgusted to look at him any more.'

The room went quiet, aside from the clapping and cheering of the audience a few hundred yards away. Shania took Ethan's arm and led him out of the room. Silent. Defeated.

I looked up at Ella, whose eyes were full of tears, and put my arms around her, squeezing her as tight as I could. I felt like I should be yelling and shouting and jumping up and down, but the potent mix of shock and utter relief rushing through my body just wouldn't allow it.

Olympia put her hand on my shoulder. 'I'm so, so sorry, Jack. I don't know what to say.'

'That goes for me, too.' AJ sounded completely distraught. 'I just hope we can get past this and that you might be able to forgive us.'

'We're all really sorry,' Ava said. 'Oh God, Jack, I can't imagine what you must have been going through.'

I looked up and caught Austin's gaze. He was blinking back tears; then he nodded and smiled at me. I smiled and nodded back; it was all we needed right then.

THE LIVE SHOW

The crowd was still raging in the auditorium: whooping and cheering with chants of 'GenNext!' and 'Ella!' and 'Jack!' cutting through sporadically. Inside the props room we were all feeling pretty shaken, trying to digest the events of the last twenty minutes – especially the sight of Ethan looking blank-faced and hollow, the violent anger switched off as suddenly as it had appeared. Ava was wiping away the last of her tears, whilst Austin leaned against Sai for support, his brain clearly whirring away as he tried to process everything he'd just seen and heard. Olympia and AJ deliberated in low voices in the corner of the room, presumably trying to figure out what the correct etiquette was when one of your show's main presenters had just been revealed as a complete psychopath, right in front of your audience, while Pete and Glen looked on from the doorway. I put my arm around Ella and glanced up at Lewis, who looked like he couldn't believe what just happened.

'So . . . I guess our plan worked then?' he said with a wry smile.

I nodded. 'I think we can safely say that it worked to an unforeseen level, thanks to the appearance of Ella here.'

Ella squeezed my waist. 'Hey, once I heard my name mentioned, there was no way I wasn't going to say my piece,' she said.

I kissed the top of her head. 'You were amazing. Seeing you was what tipped him over the edge; if you hadn't come in, he might have just bluffed his way out.'

'Yeah,' Lewis said with a grin. 'You were definitely our secret weapon, Ella.'

'OK everyone, let's get out of this room, shall we?' Olympia said, suddenly springing into action. 'We need to get out there and make some sort of official announcement; although quite what that's going to be, I'm not sure.'

Pete and Glen parted as Shania reappeared at the door. 'Security are taking care of Ethan and the police are on their way. Meanwhile, I think we'd better let the audience know what's happening.'

'Absolutely,' said Olympia. 'I was just thinking about that. Let me take everyone down to the green room and I'll be right with you, Shania. How long have we got until showtime?'

'About twenty-five minutes,' Shania said.

'Right. Well then, we need to move!' Olympia said.

She led us all like bewildered sheep out of the props room and down the corridor to a large, carpeted dressing room, which had been set up with chairs and tables and a make-shift bar.

'There's no one using this room until after the show,' she said, ushering us in. 'I'll be two minutes and then I'll join you. Pete, can you make sure we're all reset, sound-wise, and Glen, sweetie, would you mind coming with me, please? I think I'm going to need all the help I can get explaining to the rest of the production crew just what the hell's been going on.'

'Sure thing, doll,' Glen said, following her out of the room and along the corridor towards the stage.

Lewis, Ella and I sat down, while Ava grabbed some bottles of water for us. None of us said much at first; it was like we were trying to let everything that had happened sink in. Of course, I was massively relieved that the nightmare was over, but I was still shaking; the adrenalin that had flooded through me during the showdown not yet dispersed. AJ, Sai and Austin stayed standing, nervously talking over one another and trying to decide on a strategy of damage limitation, working out what Ethan's sudden departure meant for a show that was due to go live at any moment. In the end, they decided it was going to have to be Olympia's call, and AJ sat down next to me, shaking his head.

'Jack, I really am so very sorry. I can't believe it came to this. I just—'

'We all are,' Austin said. 'Me more than anyone. I let Ethan fool me completely. He caught me when I was at a low ebb, and I stupidly fell for all his crap. It seems ridiculous now, but at the time he just wormed his way into my head: telling me how smart I was and how I should be the one taking the reins at GenNext. Then when he lied and said you'd been mouthing off about my depression, Jack, I just . . .' He looked down at the floor.

'You're not the only one he fooled, Austin,' Ella said. 'Trust me.'

'It's OK, Austin,' I said.

'It's not, though,' he said. 'I should have known; I should have believed you. I'm so, so sorry, Jack.'

I got up and put my hand on his shoulder. 'Look, this is all I ever wanted. This. All of us back together again. At the end of the day, Austin, you and I are always going to be friends. We all are. I'm just happy this is over.'

Austin nodded. 'Me too, J.'

'Did he really plan the fight at Total?' Sai said. 'It actually went that far back?'

'Right from the start,' Lewis said, standing up. 'He'd been hatching this plan for months.'

'Yeah, it seems like his popping up and being all helpful on the first day of the festival was no coincidence,' I said.

'Man, that's just too weird.' Sai shook his head.

'Yeah, all that learning our set list off by heart and throwing himself into the frame when I got ill. It was just a ploy to ingratiate himself with all of you and then gradually isolate me,' I said.

'He did a bloody good job of it, too,' Sai said.

'God, I just feel numb,' Ava said. 'All that time we've spent together, and we never knew.'

'And wait till you see the files we found on his online drive,' Lewis added. 'He was completely fixated by you all from the start – it's pretty scary stuff.'

I thought about Ethan for a moment and found myself feeling strangely sorry for him – yes, even after all that. The guy was obviously completely messed up; eaten up by this insane jealousy that had somehow got his mind tied up in knots. All those things he did to me . . . they weren't the actions of a sane or happy person. It was actually quite tragic.

Ava was staring at Lewis, momentarily confused. 'Sorry, I'm not being funny – Lewis, is it? Who exactly are you again?'

'Oh, sorry, yeah,' I said casually. 'Lewis, meet everyone, and everyone . . . this is Lewis. My brother.'

'Your what?' Sai said, his jaw dropping, and I suddenly remembered that I'd only ever told Ella about Lewis, and then sworn her to secrecy.

'That was a joke, right, Penman?' Ava said.

'God, we all thought he was some private detective you'd hired or something,' AJ said, jumping to his feet.

'No joke,' Lewis smiled.

'But it's *definitely* a bit of a long story,' I said. 'I'd rather fill you all in later, if you don't mind.'

At that moment, Olympia swept back into the green room with Pete, Glen and Shania tailing her. 'OK, listen up, everyone! We have exactly fourteen minutes before the *Emerge* final is broadcast live to the nation. One of our main hosts is currently being questioned by two of the Metropolitan Police's finest in a room along the corridor, our audience are going loopy after being treated to a full fly-on-the-wall exposé of everything that just happened in the props room, and I'm about to have a very serious nervous breakdown. Any suggestions? Jack, what say you?'

'Are you asking me to step in and host the show, Olympia?' I said, grinning.

'I think that's exactly what she's asking,' AJ said.

'Well, let's put it this way,' Olympia said. 'If you can find it in your heart to forgive my utter blind stupidity in thinking you'd be capable of doing any of those things we accused you of, I'd be honoured to have you host the show with Ella, yes.'

'Of course I'll bloody do it,' I laughed.

'What, in that outfit?' Ava said, looking disdainfully at my baseball cap, sweatshirt and burgundy ASOS joggers ensemble.

'Oh God, yeah. What am I going to wear?'

'I've brought clothes for the after-party,' Austin jumped in. 'Come down to the dressing room and you can borrow them.'

'Perfect,' Olympia said. 'Now, I've reinstated dear Glen here, and he's about to go out and make the announcement to our audience – if he can calm them down – that due to today's unfortunate events, Ethan Harper will no longer be involved in tonight's live show, and that Ella Foster will now be presenting along with Jack Penman. Is everyone in agreement? This is *your* show as much as mine.'

'It sounds perfect, Olympia. We can deal with the press and everyone else after the show,' AJ said.

'I'm afraid the opening titles still feature Ethan; unfortunately it's too late to change that now,' Olympia said.

'That's cool,' Sai said. 'I'll put the word out on GenNext and Twitter that Jack's back so the fans know what's going on.'

'Jack's back,' Ella said, smiling. 'That has a rather nice ring to it.'

'Jeez, it's going to go OFF when all this gets out,' Austin said.

'Don't worry about that,' Sai laughed. 'You know me; I'll find a way to turn it to our advantage. You know what they say about all publicity being good publicity.'

I turned to Pete, who was about to head back out to the sound desk, ready for the show. 'Pete, Shania, thank you *so* much for all your help: getting us into the building, and the mics, and making sure Ethan was where we needed him to be . . . everything. And Glen, we couldn't have done this without you, mate.'

Glen did a quick twirl. 'Don't mention it, babes. As I said, it was as much my career at stake as it was yours, and I thank you, too. I just can't believe how far down the line Ethan got with it all.'

Olympia stepped forward, clearly back in control again. 'Look, this is all very lovely, but I really need you to get out and speak to the audience, Glen. And Jack, you need to go and get ready. We've got less than ten minutes, people.'

'Look at him, he's dying to get back up there,' Glen said, waving his arm around my head. 'Go on! Go and get your party frock on, Cinderella.'

'Yeah, quick march, Penman, we've got a show to do,' Ella said.

'This is brilliant,' Austin said, smiling. 'Just as it should be.'

It was the first time I'd seen him smile like that in ages – just like his old self, in fact.

As soon as Glen had made the announcement about the dramatic change in line-up, the audience's excitement shot up another few notches, if that was even possible. It was as if they'd been watching some reality TV show or soap opera up on the screen, witnessing Ethan at his worst, and now they were all gagging for the happy ending. They weren't the only ones. The other members of the GenNext team dashed to their various posts in the sound and vision galleries in the huge broadcast trucks outside the building, where they'd be controlling and directing the broadcast along with the camera director. Meanwhile, Ella and I waited in the wings for the show to kick off. The chants of 'JACK AND ELLA!' accompanied by a thousand people stamping their feet reverberated around the building until it felt like the very foundations were shaking. It was completely insane, and I could feel the nerves kicking in as each second ticked by. Behind us, the three final acts, Ace Love, The Makers and The Getaway, were all geared up and ready to hit the stage. It struck me that once all the Ethan stuff got out, *Emerge* was going to be the most talked-about TV show of the month. Well, as Sai said, all publicity is good publicity . . . and hopefully it would be an amazing platform for whichever act ultimately won.

'Are you OK?' Ella said, snapping me out of my thoughts.

'Yeah, I'm OK. I'm great, actually,' I said, realising that it was true. 'What about you?'

'I think I'm just about coming back down to earth at last,' she said.

'You really were brilliant, you know,' I said. 'I'm just so glad it's all over.'

'And I'm glad we got through it together,' Ella said, grabbing my hand. 'We make a pretty good team, you and me.'

'And Lewis,' I laughed.

'Yeah, and Lewis.'

Suddenly Shania appeared beside us. 'OK, guys, sixty seconds.'

Emerge was about to go live, and yet my head was still spinning. How did I even get here? How did I get from that messy hotel room a couple of hours ago, feeling like I'd lost everything, to this moment and this stage? It was mad, but there was no time to process it now . . . we were on any second.

'I haven't even looked at a bloody script,' I said, turning to Ella.

'Just follow my lead,' she said. 'And for the rest of it, you can fly by the seat of your Calvin Kleins. You've always been good at that.'

'Maybe,' I said. 'But Ethan did quite a number on my confidence, you know. I hope I haven't lost it.'

'You haven't lost it,' Ella smiled. 'No way.'

This was live TV, though. There was no retake if you got it wrong, no second chance. Once that sixty-second count-down finished, there was no going back. From then on, the show would be a blur of intros, performances, lightning-speed set changes – and at the centre of it would be Ella and me, holding it all together in front of an audience of millions. So exciting. So utterly terrifying.

Without warning, there was a voice in my earpiece.

'OK, here we go. Five, four, three, two, one . . .'

An explosion of sound signalled the opening titles, and Ella and I stepped out onto the stage, hand in hand, with the audience taking the roof off. As I headed to my marked position, clutching my mic, I spotted Suki and Lily, standing up in the front row of the audience, yelling and cheering with the rest of the screaming crowd. I thought about Mum and Dad, proudly watching at home on the sofa, and suddenly, it was OK. I was home. I was about to do what I loved doing, what I did best, on a massive scale . . . and at that moment, the spectre of Ethan Harper evaporated. He'd left the building. Gone.

'Ladies and gentlemen! Welcome to the live final of *Emerge* 2017! I'm Ella Foster . . .'

'. . . and I'm Jack Penman . . .'

'And we are . . . GenNext!'

THE WINNER

'And now, finally, people . . . give it up for the winner of *Emerge* 2017, the incredible . . . ACE LOVE!'

Ella and I tore off the stage amidst an explosion of pyrotechnics as Ace arrived with her three-piece band, all set to kick off her three-song showcase performance to the venue's thousand-strong audience, who were going nuts, plus the millions of viewers watching live on GenNext and Channel 4. It was over. We'd done it!

'Oh my God, that was just unbelievable,' Ella said, as we fell breathlessly into the wings.

'It seemed like the whole show lasted about two minutes rather than ninety,' I laughed. 'Did I even say everything I was supposed to say?'

Olympia was waiting for us as we stepped out into the corridor. 'Trust me, Jack, you were one hundred per cent professional up there. You both were.'

'Really?'

'Really,' she said, with a huge smile. 'Your delivery and energy was spot on. And if the frenzied text messages AJ was getting from Sai are anything to go by, the viewers agreed. We won't know the official viewing figures until tomorrow, but social media has gone ballistic; it's exactly what we all wanted it to be. Well done, guys!'

As we headed down the corridor to watch Ace's performance on the big screen set up in the green room, AJ appeared from one of the dressing rooms, brandishing a glass of something fizzy.

'Ella! Jack! Just brilliant!' he beamed. 'I'm so, so proud. The two of you were fantastic up there.' I couldn't remember ever seeing AJ this excited; he was usually the epitome of cool while we were all jumping up and down, going crazy.

'Cheers, AJ,' Ella said. She was still grinning from ear to ear – both of us were on a major high.

The green room looked smaller now it was so much busier: full of wardrobe and make-up people, their jobs done for the night, plus assorted members of the production team and various Owl TV and Channel 4 bigwigs. As Ella and I squeezed inside, the crowd whooped and clapped, congratulating us on how well the show had gone. I put my arm around Ella's waist and we both smiled and nodded at everyone, while I scanned the room for Ava, Sai and Austin. They weren't there, so I figured they were still outside in the broadcast trucks, making sure everything went smoothly during Ace's set, which was now launching into its second song.

'Jack! Ella!' A young guy wearing a bad tank top suddenly shoved a recording device in my face. 'I'm Jake from Radar Online. Can you tell us what happened between you and Ethan Harper today? Is it true that he was trying to push you out of GenNext? Ella, is it true you were at the centre of the animosity between Jack and Ethan?'

'Sorry, buddy,' I said, gently pushing the recorder sideways and out of my face. 'We really aren't talking to anyone about this right now.'

'Yeah, tonight's all about the show and Ace Love,' Ella said.

'But there's so much speculation about Ethan out there already,' Jake carried on, following us as we headed to the table where drinks were being served. Jeez, this guy was persistent. 'Don't you want to set the record straight? Don't you owe it to your audience?'

'Right now, I just want to drink something cold,' I said. 'Later, dude!' Ella and I left Jake standing in the middle of the room, mouth opening and shutting like a fish.

Once we'd grabbed a drink each, Ella and I quickly located Lewis and dragged him over to the least-populated corner of the room, from where we could watch the rest of Ace's performance on the screen. I for one was extremely happy she'd won the competition. For a girl who'd once found herself homeless, to get to where she was now was nothing short of brilliant.

Lewis turned to me and gave my arm a gentle punch. 'Dude, this is perfect!' he said. 'This girl is so good! I'm happy that I'm here to see this, man.'

'And I'm really glad to have you here,' I said, returning the friendly punch.

As the last rattle of drums and guitars subsided and the audience erupted once more, the rest of the GenNext crew bounded into the green room. Sai's hands were raised above his head in a triumphant double fist-pump, and Ava and Austin were beaming, looking knackered but happy. After they'd all grabbed drinks they came over to join us, dancing through the throng in a makeshift conga line and waving their hands in the air in celebration.

'So, how was it for you guys?' Ava asked, clinking her glass against mine. 'It looked like you were having a pretty amazing time up there.'

'Oh yeah,' Ella laughed. 'We most definitely were . . . at least, what I can remember of it. With the lights and the adrenalin and trying to remember where I was supposed to be every second, it was all a bit of a blur.'

'Yep. We're definitely going to have to watch it back later, just to figure out what the hell was actually going on,' I said.

'I'm so impressed,' Lewis said, putting his hand on my shoulder. 'I might be able to ride a ten-foot beach break, but in a million years I couldn't do what you just did out there, bro. You've got some pretty decent TV presenting skills going on.'

'Hey, don't forget that I wouldn't have been doing it at all if it wasn't for you,' I said. 'You did so much for us today, Lewis, and for that I will forever be grateful.'

'Don't mention it, dude,' he said with a grin.

'You guys were sick up there,' Sai said. 'I've never felt a buzz like it.'

'You're not kidding; it was incredible,' Austin said. He looked thoughtful for a moment. 'I think I might even be ready to try a bit of on-camera presenting myself sometime soon.'

Our mouths fell open in unison. 'A-man! You, presenting?'

I said. 'Now that *would* be phenomenal – and I think we need to make it happen as soon as humanly possible.'

'Jack! Ella! Guys!' Olympia arrived at our spot in the corner, along with AJ and Glen. 'Guess what – *Emerge* has gone down an absolute storm in the broadcasting world. Channel 4 are over the moon and the American channel were on the blower before the first commercial break, gagging to set up a meeting, and they didn't seem to have a problem when I explained the sudden departure of Ethan, either.'

'Music to my ears, Olympia,' AJ said, raising his glass.

'That's brilliant!' Ella smiled. 'As long as we can have the lovely Glen as our director, of course.'

'Well, remember that I'm hot property, Ella darling,' Glen said, winking. 'Now I'm free and clear of all criminal charges, I'll be able to accept the offer I had to work on a big historical drama for the BBC, with bonnets and everything. Rest assured, though, I'll always make time for GenNext . . . and especially for this one.'

He nodded in my direction and Sai whispered to me and Ava, 'He still wants you, Jack. You know that, don't you?'

Ava burst out laughing at Sai's comment, but then stopped suddenly, her eyes widening. I followed her gaze across the room until it landed on Suki, heading toward us with Lily in tow. Sai opened his arms and Lily gave him a huge squeeze.

'Hello, beautiful,' he said.

Lily looked up him. 'I'm so proud of you, Sai.'

For a moment, Ava and Suki just stood looking at each other, smiling shyly.

'I'm so proud of you, too, Ava,' Suki said. 'I'm so proud of all of you.'

To my surprise, Ava leaned forward and planted a tender kiss on Suki's cheek, her eyes shining.

Suki looked bemused for a moment, then broke into a smile. 'So what did I do to deserve that?'

'Well, you've put up with me being a paranoid nutter for the last few months, so I'd say that was enough,' Ava said.

Suki's expression was suddenly serious. 'So . . . so, what are you saying, Ava?'

'What I'm saying is I've realised that although you have this super-cool lifestyle and you know absolutely everyone, it's not something I need to feel threatened by,' Ava said, her cheeks turning pink. 'And that I'm so, so sorry for letting my insecurities get in the way of this amazing thing we have, and I'm ready to just get over myself and . . . and start again.'

'Really?' Suki's face lit up.

'Really,' Ava nodded. 'All this stuff with Ethan has opened my eyes to what's really important, and *who's* really important. So . . . if you're not involved with anyone else . . .' Her eyes flicked across to Olympia, who was chatting with AJ and Lewis, oblivious to the whole conversation, 'then I'd really like to give us another try. If you'll have me.'

'You *do* know that Olympia and I are just friends, don't you?' Suki said.

I couldn't help butting in. 'See, I told you!'

Ava threw me a dirty look. 'Mind your own business, Penman. And yes, I do know that, Suki. I'm so sorry that I jumped to conclusions before.'

'Well then . . . luckily I *am* still willing to have you, as you so beautifully put it,' Suki said, grinning. 'And if you're willing to make this work, then I am, too.'

I was about to throw my arms around both of them and congratulate them for finally coming to their senses, but before I could, Ava stepped forward and embraced Suki tenderly. When she pulled away again, I could see that both of them had happy tears in their eyes.

Sai, Ella, Austin and I all looked at one another and then backed away slowly, giving them their moment.

As the party swirled around us, getting noisier and more exuberant by the second, my phone pinged with a WhatsApp.

> **Mum & Dad**
> Loved the show, Jack. We're so proud of you. Can't wait to congratulate you properly when you get home. xx

Just as I put my phone away, smiling to myself, Ace Love finally stepped into the green room to a rousing, heartfelt cheer, and I watched as all the press people dived across the room to catch the first post-show interview with the new star. She looked amazingly happy and proud – and so she should. Ace had come out on top. She was the winner. She had every right to be on top of the world . . . and she wasn't the only one. As I looked around at all my friends, seeing just how incredibly happy everyone seemed, I realised how amazing it was to have come through the nightmare of the last week, and for GenNext – for all of us – to have done something so monumental. It felt utterly brilliant.

THE BEGINNING

The doorbell rang just as I stepped out of my bedroom door: showered, shaved and smelling up the hall with the ridiculously expensive cologne that Olympia had very kindly sent me that week by way of a thank you. Yes! It was good to be back home at Mum and Dad's after everything that had happened, but weirdly, it felt like a lifetime since I'd last been there rather than just a few weeks – everything had changed so much. Or maybe it hadn't. Maybe it was just me that had changed.

'I'll get it, Mum,' I yelled, coming down the stairs. 'I think it's Ella.'

Swinging the front door open, I was faced not just with Ella, but AJ, Ava, Suki, Sai, Lily and Austin too, armed with a myriad of bottles, bags and plastic containers.

'Oh, you came en masse,' I said, ushering them in. 'Mother's going to freak because the food's not ready yet.'

'Don't worry, I've brought Nando's,' Sai smiled, waving a bag as he walked past me.

'You brought Nando's to one of Mum's legendary

celebratory buffet suppers?' I laughed. 'You really are in need of some serious help, Sai.'

Sai flexed his guns in my face. 'Shut up, dude. I have to keep up my protein intake and I got hungry on the way.'

Lily smiled and shrugged as she passed me. 'Don't ask me how I put up with him, Jack. I just do,' she said.

I kissed Ella and we all wandered down the hall and into the kitchen, where Mum and Dad were in a food-preparation frenzy, aided by Lewis, who was comically wearing Mum's girliest apron while he battled with the blender, attempting to make fresh guacamole. He'd been staying with us for the whole week, helping me out with a few new ideas for GenNext during the day and trying out some of his clean-eating recipes on the family in the evening. The recipes were actually really good. It was funny: Dad had always loved to think of himself as the accomplished chef of the household, but now he had some serious competition, and it had been hilarious watching them both try to outdo one another.

'The guys are here,' I announced. 'Let's get this party started.'

There was a burst of warm 'hellos' and 'good to see you agains' between my friends and Lewis and my parents, and then we all headed out to the garden, where dinner was going to be served on the long outdoor table on the patio. It was generously warm for a late-September evening, and after a completely insane couple of months, everything felt . . . just right.

'OK, I've got loads of food here,' Ava said, unloading plastic boxes out of a Greenpeace bag-for-life. 'I thought there would be a ton of meat for all you carnivores, so I've brought some other bits and pieces for the vegetarians amongst us.'

'So it's just you and your bloody falafel and chickpea nonsense then,' I laughed.

Suki threw her arm protectively around Ava. 'Oi, Penman, watch it. That's my girlfriend you're talking about.'

Ten minutes later, while everyone else was lost in a whirl of drinking and chattering, I clocked Austin hanging out by himself by the pear tree. He was holding a beer but not drinking it, just staring up into the clear sky. I headed over, slightly concerned that he might still be feeling adrift after everything that had happened.

'How's it going?' I said, shaking him out of his trance. 'Is everything OK, Austin?'

His mouth widened, turning into an unexpected grin. 'Yeah, J, I'm just thinking. I'm actually feeling really happy.'

'Yeah?'

'God, yeah! Since we made up, and after the success of the show, I just feel so much more confident about everything. It's like the fog is lifting, do you know what I mean?'

I nodded. 'I think so, yeah.'

'I've even called Jess and made up with her,' he said.

'What, so you're back together?'

Austin shook his head categorically. 'Jess wasn't right for me and I let it go on way too long. In the end, I was blaming myself for a break-up that was always on the cards. The problem was, I let her prey on all my insecurities. She was forever criticising me and I should have told her where to go, but instead I just took it all on board and then felt crap about myself.'

'Well, it's good that you know that,' I said. 'You've got no reason to feel crap about anything, mate.'

'I'm starting to realise that now. I actually had my first couple of therapy sessions this week.' He was reddening slightly but I could tell that he was happy he'd told me.

'And? How were they?'

'I think they might be a life-saver,' he laughed. 'I wish I'd reached out for help earlier, J. If I could have been more honest about my weird state of mind, Ethan would never have been able to drive a wedge between us in the first place.' He took a slug of his beer, looking thoughtful. 'Actually, if it's cool with everyone else, I'd like to do a really open, honest vlog for GenNext about what I've been going through.'

'That sounds a very cool idea,' I smiled.

'It does, right?' Austin said. 'I mean, there must be loads of other young guys like me who suffer in silence, so maybe I can help people like that . . . I don't know . . .'

'You're just dying to get in front of a camera now, aren't you?' I said, grinning.

'Yeah, that too,' he laughed. 'Watch your back, Penman, I'm coming for you.'

'Chicken and hot dogs are done!' Dad shouted, coming into the garden with two large roasted chickens.

'But my stunningly excellent triple-cooked chips will be another few minutes,' Lewis added competitively.

By the time we sat down at the large wooden table, the temperature had dropped a little, so Dad fired up the patio heaters and we all pulled on sweaters and hoodies so we could hang out in the garden late into the evening. Mum had put a checked tablecloth out and decorated the table with tiny tea lights, and as it got darker, Dad's solar lights, woven into the branches of the pear tree and scattered all around the garden, twinkled into action so the whole place looked cool and sort of magical. It was good to see the gang chattering noisily across the table, laughing and stuffing themselves silly with all the amazing grub, and the fact that Lewis was there with us made it even better. Who'd have bloody well thought it, huh? That annoying surfer dude I'd once been so worried about meeting had turned out to be not just a long-lost brother, but a true friend.

I glanced over at him tucking into a ketchup-drowned hot dog like a hungry caveman. 'Er . . . excuse me, Lewis. Didn't you once tell us, not all that long ago, that you never ate processed food?'

'The occasional sausage, man,' he said, grinning. 'The occasional sausage.'

'OK, I'll let you off,' I said.

Dad scooted Sai out of the way and sat down next to me. 'I'm really chuffed you two are getting on, Jack. You know it means a lot to me.'

'Yeah, well, I'll get back to you after that bike rally I've agreed to go on with the pair of you next week,' I laughed. 'Maybe the novelty will have worn off by then.'

'I doubt it,' Mum said, hovering over us with a plate of chicken breasts. 'I think you and your brother are more alike than you think, Jack.'

Lewis smiled at me. 'Yeah, I think we probably are.'

Ava, who was sitting next to me on the other side, nudged me in the ribs, dropping her food back onto the plate. 'Do you know what? I'd be enjoying this falafel wrap a damned sight more if I wasn't being choked by your insanely over-powering aftershave, Penman. What the hell is that?'

'Is *that* what it is?' Lily giggled. 'For a minute I thought it was some kind of weird spice in the chicken.'

'It was a gift from Olympia, and I like it.' I was slightly offended. 'It actually arrived yesterday with a handwritten note of congratulations on how well the live show went down, and acknowledging her terrible lack of judgement over Ethan.'

'God, she should have bought you a frickin' house for that,' Sai snorted.

'Yeah, well, he had us all fooled,' Austin said, looking down.

'At least it sounds like he'll be getting the help he needs now,' Ella said gently. She was referring to the fact that after Ethan was questioned by the police, he was taken to a nearby psychiatric unit for evaluation. The staff there had been keeping Olympia updated, and seemed confident they could get him the right treatment, even though it might be a long road.

There was a moment of silence before AJ lightened the mood. 'I spoke to Olympia this morning,' he said. 'She is most definitely keen to go ahead with the US deal and wants to be sure, after everything that's happened, that you're all still on board.'

'Well, that's good news,' Suki smiled.

Ella looked nervously around the group. 'Is it, though? I mean . . . what do you all think?'

Ava and Austin both shrugged, turning to me as if I might give them a sign.

'What's to consider?' Sai said, clearly surprised at the lack of excitement. 'I'm happy to start packing when I get home – as long as Lily can come with me.'

Lily laughed, elbowing him in the gut. 'Try and stop me, muscle boy.'

'I just think it's something we really need to think about carefully after the events of the last couple of months,' Ella said.

This time I understood Ella's trepidation about working in America. Before the summer we'd have all leapt at the chance to go and work on a TV show there, but it just seemed like every time GenNext got involved with a new partner, something went horribly wrong. Maybe we were better off staying just as we were and always had been – five friends, doing something we all loved.

'When do we have to decide by, AJ?' Austin said. 'Is it imminent?'

'We can't hang about, let's put it that way,' AJ said. 'I'll have to meet Olympia sometime early next week and start the ball rolling if we want to go ahead.'

I looked around the table at Ella, Austin, Ava and Sai and something struck me. It didn't really matter what we decided to do. Whatever happened, we'd still all be friends, and GenNext would always go on in some form or another. Sure, it might reshape itself along the way, and some of us might have other goals and ambitions we wanted to pursue, but nothing could change the fact that GenNext was something amazing that the five of us had created . . . together.

*

Later in the evening, I found Ella alone in the kitchen, helpfully stacking the dishwasher. As I watched her, a wave of happiness washed over me. I loved this girl so much.

'Do you know how incredibly sexy you look stacking a dishwasher? You definitely need to do that more often,' I said, knowing full well that there was a distinct possibility I was about to get a dinner plate smashed over my head.

Ella whirled around. 'Did you *actually* say that, Jack Penman?'

'Yeah, but I was just kidding,' I laughed. 'I'm well aware that if we ever got married or lived together, I'd be the one stacking the dishwasher and looking half as good doing it.'

'Yes, well, there's no chance of any wedding bells if you keep on making comments like that, sunshine.' She crossed the room, putting her arms around my waist and pulling me in close. 'So what do you think about this American thing? Are you still keen to do it?'

'I think we're all going to have to sleep on it, but whatever happens, it's not going to change anything between us,' I said.

Ella smiled up at me. 'Are you sure about that?'

'Very,' I said, kissing her. 'Even if I decide I want to go, and you decide you want to stay here and go to drama school, we'll make it work, I promise. We're strong enough to get through anything, including a bit of long-distance. If I've learned anything over the past couple of months, it's that we both have to follow our own path. We all do. Destiny and all that stuff . . .'

'Destiny and all that stuff.' Ella nodded in agreement.

'You know, that's extremely profound, Jack Penman . . . and do you know something else?'

'What, Ella Foster?'

She stood on tiptoe and kissed me once more. 'That after-shave really, *really* needs to go.'

ACKNOWLEDGEMENTS

Well, I can't quite believe that *Generation Next: The Takeover* is here! It feels like the first book only came out yesterday. I was pretty nervous at the thought of doing a sequel because I wanted it to be as good as the first, but I can confidently say that I'm extremely happy with how this new book has turned out!

I want to thank Emily, Louise, Naomi and the rest of the team at Hodder for being amazing throughout the whole writing process; I couldn't have done any of this without you.

I want to thank Terry, my co-writer, for once again smashing it and making my vision come true; you've done such an incredible job, mate!

I want to thank Sophie, Molly, Rory and the rest of the James Grant team for believing in me and for always pushing me to do my very best.

I want to thank my amazing mum, my dad and my awesome brother James for supporting my crazy, strange job – although I still don't think they understand what it is that I actually do half of the time. Haha!

And I finally want to thank all of you who are reading this. As I always say, the support you guys give me is overwhelming, and I couldn't wish for a better audience. I certainly wouldn't be having so much fun and enjoying all these unbelievable experiences if it weren't for you. You've made me who I am today and I hope we can continue this epic adventure together.

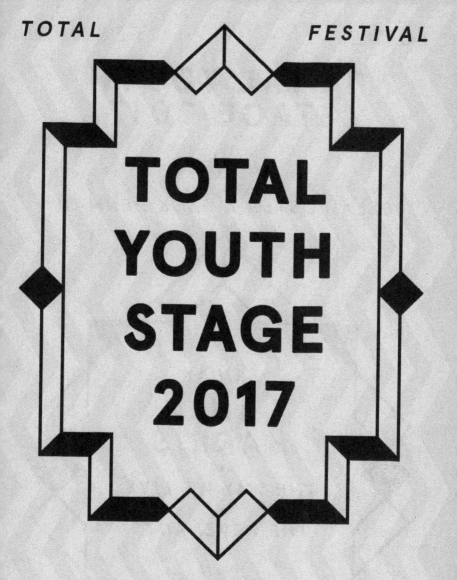

TOTAL   FESTIVAL

TOTAL YOUTH STAGE 2017

HOSTED BY

GENNEXT

STAGE GUIDE   &   TIMETABLE

TOTAL   FESTIVAL

TOTAL YOUTH
STAGE 2017

HOSTED BY
GENNEXT
PRESENTERS
ELLA FOSTER & JACK PENMAN

FRIDAY
LAURA
HARRIS
·
THE WAY WE LIVE
·
THE REVENANTS
·
PAN

TOTAL FESTIVAL

SATURDAY
OUTSIDE GIRLS
·
BEAUTIFUL CREATURES
·
PATRICK SWIFT
·
THE DAUGHTERS

SUNDAY
HARRIET RUSHWORTH
·
NO REMAIN
·
THE AVALANCHE
·
THE BARBARIANS

TOTAL   FESTIVAL

HARRIET RUSHWORTH

Born in 1994 in Nashville, Tennessee, singer-songwriter Rushworth originally debuted on the professional scene as a country and western singer. Since then she's moved over into mainstream pop music, and has quickly established herself as one of the most successful young stars the world has ever seen. Her most recent album, Jeopardy, sold over one million copies in its first week on sale, and smashed records for the highest ever recorded volume of digital downloads in one hour. Rushworth has collaborated with Rihanna, Calvin Harris and Ed Sheeran, amongst others.

LAURA HARRIS

Australian-born Harris is an international DJ and broadcaster. Hailed for her eclectic personal taste and fresh, modern sound, Harris's career kicked off with a bang in 2009, when she was only eighteen, with the compilation album Regress which became an instant global hit. As well as hosting a primetime radio show on Australia's Underground Radio, Harris is in high demand from major stadiums, superclubs and festivals around the world.

OUTSIDE GIRLS

The alias for non-identical twins duo Sasha and Alyssa White, Outside Girls are a progressive rock- and dance-pop act from Calgary, Canada. Both sisters are classically trained pianists and violinists, a talent which they've drawn into their unique musical style to much critical acclaim. In 2013, the duo released their debut studio album Two Beating Hearts, which peaked at number 3 in Canada and went on to sell over 500,000 copies internationally.

A Q&A WITH OLI WHITE

**Was it fun to write about the same characters again in
Generation Next: The Takeover?**

Yeah, it was very fun! It was great to build on their characters and express more of their personalities, and to show
the readers more of who they really are. Plus it was really
interesting to explore more about their lives, and to see
what kind of new situations they ended up in.

***Generation Next* featured a few events from your own
life; does *The Takeover* feature any?**

Yes, it does! It features quite a few different Easter eggs.
Not as many as in *Generation Next*, but there are a lot of
things in there which definitely represent a few different
parts of my life. Particularly the setting of Total Festival
– I've been to Coachella a few times with my friends, so
that's where we got the idea.

Do you have a favourite moment or scene in the book?

I have loads, but I really love the bit where Jack gets into a
bit of a scruff at Total Festival; that's when the reader finds

out that Ethan is a really sly character, even if Jack's friends don't realise it at that point. I also love the big showdown at the end, when Jack, Lewis and Ella challenge Ethan and expose him to everyone.

What's the best part about the writing process?

The best part is seeing your thoughts and things that have only been in your imagination coming to life on paper. These ideas have been going round in your head but getting them written down and developed into a story is incredible; you get to see everything you wanted to happen come true.

Have you got a favourite character and if so, why are they your favourite?

Jack's definitely my favourite – obviously! Some parts of the book do reflect my life, and Jack's definitely the character I can relate to most closely.

Was it a different experience writing the sequel, compared to writing the first book?

Yeah, it was completely different. We already had a structure to work with because we already had those characters, and we knew who they were and how they acted, so it was a lot easier to imagine what they'd do next. It was harder to keep the storyline engaging and exciting because there was so much drama in the first book – but actually I think we did an amazing job, and there's so much action and so many things happen, which I'm really pleased about.

OLI WHITE'S FESTIVAL FAVOURITES

Travel: I've travelled to a couple of festivals in a big car with my friends. That's always really fun because you can get the party started early! I also went to the Isle of Wight festival in a speedboat, which was amazing.

People to go with: Of course, it's got to be the boys!

Outfit: I'll either go very plain and casual, or wear something a bit crazy: a brightly coloured or patterned T-shirt, usually with shorts, a shirt and sunglasses; an outfit with a festival vibe.

Music: I've seen loads of amazing artists: Drake, Justin Bieber, Skepta. In general, hip-hop is my favourite music to listen and dance to.

Festival must-haves: a charger pack for my phone, because I always try and capture everything on Snapchat and Instagram, and my phone just dies within an instant. And a poncho, in case it rains!

Festival top tips: Always check the weather before you go!

Festival don't-dos: Do NOT run off from your friends! Festivals don't always have signal so you might end up getting completely lost and never being able to find them again!

Stay in touch with
OLI WHITE

YouTube
OliWhiteTV

🐦
@OliWhiteTV

@OliWhiteTV